Lethal Remedy

"*Lethal Remedy* boasts a gripping medical plot that only an insider could write so believably. Dr. Mabry takes his knowledge of the medical profession, combines it with a ticking clock, and gives the reader a problem we'd all be terrified to face. What more could the reader of good medical suspense ask for?"
—Susan Sleeman, author of *Behind the Badge* and the Justice Agency series

"*Lethal Remedy* is the perfect cure for boredom: a first-rate medical thriller with humor, engaging characters, and realism that only a seasoned doctor could bring to the story."
—Rick Acker, author of *When the Devil Whistles* and *Blood Brothers*

Other Books in the Prescription for Trouble Series

Code Blue
Medical Error
Diagnosis Death

Lethal Remedy

Prescription for Trouble Series

Richard L. Mabry, M.D.

Medical Suspense with Heart

Abingdon Press fiction
a novel approach to faith

Nashville, Tennessee

Lethal Remedy

ISBN-13: 978-1-4267-3544-8

Published by Abingdon Press, P.O. Box 801, Nashville, TN 37202

www.abingdonpress.com

Published in association with WordServe Literary Group, Ltd.,
10152 S. Knoll Circle, Highlands Ranch, CO 80130

Cover design by Anderson Design Group, Nashville, TN

Library of Congress Cataloging-in-Publication Data

Mabry, Richard L.
  Lethal remedy : medical suspense with heart / Richard L. Mabry.
    p. cm. — (Prescription for trouble series)
  ISBN 978-1-4267-3544-8 (trade pbk. : alk. paper)
  1. Women physicians—Fiction. I. Title.
  PS3613.A2L47 2011
  813'.6—dc22

                                    2011020590

Printed in the United States of America

1 2 3 4 5 6 7 8 9 10 / 16 15 14 13 12 11

This book is dedicated to you, my reader.
On so many occasions, your comments about
my previous books have stoked my creative fires
when they were about to burn out.
And your support of those novels is what
made this one possible.
Many thanks.

Acknowledgments

When I wrote the acknowledgments for my last book, *Diagnosis Death*, both Abingdon and I thought it would be the last in the Prescription for Trouble series. But we were wrong, weren't we? So I'm back, grateful for another opportunity to visit with you again.

My thanks begin, as always, with my fantastic agent, Rachelle Gardner. She's been a friend, encourager, and editor through my journey of development as a writer. Barbara Scott at Abingdon Press saw promise in my fiction, and I'm grateful that as one of her last acts before retiring she made sure that Abingdon would publish this novel. Ramona Richards, who has stepped in to very capably fill Barbara's shoes, is a joy to work with and deserves my thanks. Maegan Roper and Julie Dowd have labored behind the scenes to get the word out about this book and all the others Abingdon publishes. I appreciate them and everyone else at Abingdon Press who has contributed to this project.

So many in the writing community have encouraged me that it's impossible to list them all. One of the truly fun things in switching from medicine to writing has been the opportunity to meet a neat group of people who share the frustrations and triumphs known only to those who labor over a computer—sweating bullets to achieve word counts, meet deadlines, and above all to produce a product that will grab readers and hold them for hundreds of pages. Thanks for what you've taught me and for your friendship.

I believe I'm the only one in my family who continues to be astounded by the success of my books. My children—Allen, Brian, and Ann—have always had unbridled faith that their dad could do anything, and have been forgiving if he couldn't. And, of course, my wife, Kay, deserves a special "Thank you." She eagerly reads every word I write, and her suggestions for revision are always spot-on. She attends the same conferences I do, and apparently pays attention in class, because her touch on my manuscripts is truly golden. People ask how I can write about a female protagonist and make it believable. There's a one-word answer: Kay. Thanks, dear, for teaching me so much, including how to once more enjoy life.

My first tentative steps into writing included a firm conviction that God wanted me to witness for Him through this medium. From my first book to this one, I've tried to do just that. I'm glad He has given me yet another opportunity, and I hope I've succeeded.

1

No one knew the man's name. White male, probably in his late seventies, found unresponsive in an alley about two o'clock in the morning and brought to the emergency room. Just another homeless derelict, another John Doe.

"Pneumonia, late stages," the intern said. He yawned. "Happens all the time. Drank himself into a stupor, vomited, aspirated. Probably been lying in that alley for more than a day. Doesn't look like he'll make it."

"Labs cooking? Got a sputum culture going?"

"Yeah, but it'll take a day or two to get the results of the culture. The smear looks like *Staph*. Guess I'll give him—"

"Wait. I've got access to an experimental drug that might help. Let me start him on that."

The intern shrugged. It was two in the morning. He'd been on duty for more than twenty-four hours straight—why'd Johnson's wife have to go into labor today?—and he was bushed. The bum probably didn't have a snowball's chance of surviving anyway. Why not? "You'll be responsible?"

"I'll take it from here. Even do the paperwork."

"Deal," the intern said and ambled off to see the next patient.

Three hours later, John Doe lay on a gurney in a corner of the ER. An IV ran into one arm; a blood pressure cuff encircled the other. Spittle dripped from his open mouth and dotted his unshaven chin. His eyes were open and staring.

"Acute anaphylaxis, death within minutes. Interesting." He scratched his chin. "Guess I need to make some adjustments in the compound." He picked up the almost-blank chart. "I'll say I gave him ampicillin and sulbactam. That should cover it."

The woman's look pierced Dr. Sara Miles's heart. "Do you know what's wrong with Chelsea?"

Chelsea Ferguson lay still and pale as a mannequin in the hospital bed. An IV carried precious fluids and medications into a vein in her arm. A plastic tube delivered a constant supply of oxygen to her nostrils. Above the girl's head, monitors beeped and flashed. And over it all wafted the faint antiseptic smell of the ICU.

Chelsea's mother sat quietly at the bedside, but her hands were never still: arranging and rearranging her daughter's cover, twisting the hem of her plain brown skirt, shredding a tissue. Sara decided that the gray strands in Mrs. Ferguson's long brunette hair were a recent addition, along with the lines etched in her face.

Sara put her hand on the teenager's head and smoothed the matted brown curls. The girl's hot flesh underscored the urgency of the situation. Since Chelsea's admission to University Hospital three days ago, her fever hadn't responded to any of the treatments Sara ordered. If anything, the girl was worse.

"Let's slip out into the hall," Sara said. She tiptoed from the bedside and waited outside the room while Mrs. Ferguson kissed her sleeping daughter and shuffled through the door.

Sara pointed. "Let's go into the family room for a minute."

"Will she be—?"

"The nurses will check on her, and they'll call me if anything changes." Sara led the way into the room and eased the door closed. This family room resembled so many others Sara had been in over the years: small, dim, and quiet. Six wooden chairs with lightly upholstered seats and backs were arranged along three of the walls. Illumination came from a lamp in the corner. A Bible, several devotional magazines, and a box of tissues stood within reach on a coffee table.

This was a room where families received bad news: the biopsy was positive, the treatment hadn't worked, the doctors weren't able to save their loved one. The cloying scent of flowers in a vase on an end table reminded Sara of a funeral home, and she shivered as memories came unbidden. She shoved her emotions aside and gestured Mrs. Ferguson to a seat. "Would you like something? Water? Coffee? A soft drink?"

The woman shook her head. "No. Just tell me what's going on with my daughter. Do you know what's wrong with her? Can you save her?" Her sob turned into a soft hiccup. "Is she going to die?"

Sara swallowed hard. "Chelsea has what we call sepsis. You might have heard it referred to as blood poisoning. It happens when bacteria get into the body and enter the bloodstream. In Chelsea's case, this probably began when she had her wisdom teeth extracted."

I can't believe the dentist didn't put her on a prophylactic antibiotic before the procedure. Sara brushed those thoughts aside. That wasn't important now. The important thing was saving the girl's life. Sara marshaled her thoughts. "We took samples of Chelsea's blood at the time of her admission, and while we waited for the results of the blood cultures I started treatment with a potent mixture of antibiotics. As you can see, that hasn't helped."

"Why?"

Sara wished the woman wouldn't be so reasonable, so placid. She wished Mrs. Ferguson would scream and cry. If the roles were reversed, she'd do just that. "While we wait for the results of blood cultures, we make a guess at the best antibiotics to use. Most of the time, our initial guess is right. This time, it was wrong—badly wrong."

"But now you know what's causing the infection?" It was a question, not a statement.

"Yes, we know." *And it's not good news.*

Hope tinged Mrs. Ferguson's voice. "You can fix this, can't you?"

I wish I could. "The bacteria causing Chelsea's sepsis is one that . . ." Sara paused and started again. "Have you heard of Mersa?"

"Mersa? No. What's that?"

"It's actually MRSA, but doctors usually pronounce it that way. That's sort of a medical shorthand for methicillin-resistant *Staphylococcus aureus*, a bacteria that's resistant to most of our common antibiotics."

Mrs. Ferguson frowned. "You said most. Do you have something that will work?"

"Yes, we do. Matter of fact, when Chelsea was admitted I started her on two strong antibiotics, a combination that's generally effective against MRSA. But she hasn't responded, because this isn't MRSA. It's worse than MRSA." She started to add "Much worse," but the words died in her throat.

Sara paused and waited for Mrs. Ferguson to ask the next question. Instead, the woman crumpled the tissue she held and dabbed at the corner of her eyes, eyes in which hope seemed to die as Sara watched.

"This is what we call a 'super-bug,'" Sara continued. "It used to be rare, but we're seeing more and more infections with it. Right now, none of the commercially available antibiotics are effective. These bacteria are resistant to everything we can throw at them."

Mrs. Ferguson's voice was so quiet Sara almost missed the words. "What do you call it?"

"It's a long name, and it's not important that you know it." *Matter of fact, we don't use the proper name most of the time. We just call it "The Killer."*

"So that's it?"

"No, there's a doctor doing trials on an experimental drug that might work for Chelsea." *No need to mention that Jack is . . . No, let it go.*

"Can you get some of this? Give it to Chelsea?"

"I can't, but the man who can is an infectious disease specialist on the faculty here at the medical center. Actually, he helped develop it. Notice I said 'experimental,' which means there may be side effects. But if you want me—"

"Do it!" For the first time in days, Sara saw a spark of life in Mrs. Ferguson's eyes, heard hope in her voice. "Call him! Now! Please!"

"You realize that this drug isn't fully tested yet. It may not work. Or the drug may cause problems." *There, she'd said it twice in different words. She'd done her duty.*

"I don't care. My little girl is dying. I'll sign the releases. Anything you need. If this is our only chance, please, let's take it."

Lord, I hope I haven't made a mistake. "I'll make the call."

"I'm going back to be with my baby," Mrs. Ferguson said. She stood and squared her shoulders. "While you call, I'll pray."

"Mr. Wolfe, you can come in now." The secretary opened the doors to Dr. Patel's office as though she were St. Peter ushering a supplicant through the Pearly Gates.

Bob Wolfe bit back the retort he wanted to utter. *It's Doctor Wolfe. Doctor of Pharmacology. I worked six years to earn that Pharm D, not to mention two years of research fellowship. How about some respect?* But this wasn't the time to fight that battle.

He straightened his tie, checked that there were no stains on his fresh white lab coat, and walked into the office of the head of Jandra Pharmaceuticals as though he had been summoned to receive a medal. *Never let them see you sweat.*

Dr. David Patel rose from behind his desk and beamed, gesturing toward the visitor's chair opposite. "Bob, come in. Sit down. I appreciate your coming."

Not much choice, was there? Wolfe studied his boss across the expanse of uncluttered mahogany that separated them. Pharmaceutical companies seemed to be made up of two groups: the geeks and the glad-handers. Patel typified the former group. PhD from Cal Tech, brilliant research mind, but the social skills of a tortoise. Patel had been snatched from the relative obscurity of a research lab at Berkeley by the Board of Directors of Jandra Pharmaceuticals, given the title of President and CEO, and charged with breathing life into the struggling company. How Patel planned to do that remained a mystery to Wolfe and his co-workers.

Patel leaned forward and punched a button on a console that looked like it could launch a space probe. "Cindy, please ask Mr. Lindberg to join us."

Steve Lindberg ran the sales team from an office across the hall. Lindberg could memorize salient scientific material and regurgitate it with the best of them, but Wolfe would bet the man's understanding of most of Jandra's products and those of its major competitors was a mile wide and an inch deep. On the other hand, Lindberg had his own area of expertise: remembering names, paying for food and drinks, arranging golf games at exclusive clubs. No doubt about it, Lindberg was a classic glad-hander, which was why he had ascended to his current position, heading the marketing team at Jandra.

Wolfe hid a smile. *Interesting. The President of the company and the Director of Marketing. This could be big.* The door behind Wolfe opened. He deliberately kept his eyes front. Be cool. Let this play out.

"Hey, Bob. It's good to see you." Wolfe turned just in time to avoid the full force of a hand landing on his shoulder. Even the glancing blow made him wince. Lindberg dragged a chair to the side of Patel's desk, positioning himself halfway between the two men. Clever. Not taking sides, but clearly separating himself from the underling.

Wolfe studied the two men and, not for the first time, marveled at the contrast in their appearance. Patel was swarthy, slim, and sleek, with jet-black hair and coal-black eyes. His blue shirt had a white collar on which was centered the unfashionably large knot of an unfashionably wide gold-and-black tie. Wolfe wondered whether the man was five years behind or one ahead of fashion trends. He spoke with a trace of a British accent, and Wolfe seemed to recall that Patel had received part of his education at Oxford. Maybe he wore an "old school" tie, without regard to current fashion. If so, it would be typical of Patel.

Lindberg was middle-aged but already running to fat— or, more accurately, flab. His florid complexion gave testimony to too many helpings of rare roast beef accompanied by glasses of single malt Scotch, undoubtedly shared with top-drawer doctors and paid for on the Jandra expense account. Lindberg's eyes were the color of burnished steel, and showed a glimmer of naked ambition that the smile pasted on his face couldn't disguise. His thinning blond hair was combed carefully to cover early male pattern baldness. The sleeves of his white dress shirt were rolled halfway to his elbows. His tie was at half-mast and slightly askew.

Patel, the geek. Lindberg, the glad-hander. Different in so many ways. But both men shared one characteristic. Wolfe knew from experience that each man would sell his mother if it might benefit the company, or more specifically, their position in it. The two of them together could mean something very good or very bad for Bob Wolfe. He eased forward in his chair and kicked his senses into high gear.

Patel leaned back and tented his fingers. "Bob, I'm sure you're wondering what this is about. Well, I wanted to congratulate you on the success of EpAm848. I've been looking over the preliminary information, especially the reports from Dr. Ingersoll at Southwestern Medical Center. Very impressive."

"Well, it's sort of Ingersoll's baby. He stumbled onto it when he was doing some research here during his infectious disease fellowship at UC Berkeley. I think he wants it to succeed as much as we do."

"I doubt that." Patel leaned forward with both hands on the desk. "Jandra is on the verge of bankruptcy. I want that drug on the market ASAP!"

"But we're not ready. We need more data," Wolfe said.

"Here's the good news," Patel said. "The FDA is worried about The Killer bacteria outbreak. I've pulled a few strings, called in a bunch of favors, and I can assure you we can get this application fast-tracked."

"How?" Wolfe said. "We're still doing Phase II trials. What about Phase III? Assuming everything goes well, it's going to be another year, maybe two, before we can do a rollout of EpAm848."

"Not to worry," Patel said. "Our inside man at the FDA assures me he can help us massage the data. We can get by with the Phase II trials we've already completed. And he'll arrange things so we can use those plus some of our European studies to fulfill the Phase III requirements."

Lindberg winked at Wolfe. "We may have to be creative in the way we handle our data. You and I need to get our heads together and see how many corners we can cut before the application is ready."

Wolfe shook his head. "You say this drug will save us from bankruptcy. I don't see that. I mean, yes, it looks like we may be in for a full-blown epidemic of *Staph luciferus*, but we won't sell enough—"

Lindberg silenced him with an upraised hand. "Exposure, Bob. Exposure. If we get this drug on the market, if we're the first with a cure, our name recognition will skyrocket. Doctors and patients will pay attention to our other drugs: blood pressure, cholesterol, diabetes. Our market share will go through the roof in all of them."

Wolfe could see the salesman in Lindberg take over as he leaned closer, as though to drive home his point by proximity. "We're preparing a direct-to-consumer push on all those drugs, ready to launch at the same time we release Jandramycin."

The name didn't click with Wolfe for a moment. "I . . . Well, I'll certainly do what I can."

"Do more than that," Lindberg said. "Jandra Pharmaceuticals is hurting. We're staking everything on Jandramycin."

That was the second time Wolfe had heard the term. "What—"

"Stop referring to the drug by its generic name," Patel added. "From now on, the compound is Jandramycin. When people hear the name Jandra Pharmaceuticals, we want them to think of us as the people who developed the antibiotic that saved the world from the worst epidemic since the black plague."

Lindberg eased from his chair and gave Wolfe another slap on the shoulder. "This is your project now. It's on your shoulders. The company's got a lot riding on this."

And so do I. "But what if a problem turns up?"

Patel rose and drew himself up to his full five feet eight inches. His obsidian eyes seemed to burn right through Wolfe. "We're depending on you to make sure that doesn't happen. Are we clear on that?"

Sara leaned over the sink and splashed water on her face. The paper towels in the women's restroom of the clinic were rough, but maybe that would put some color in the face that stared back at her from the mirror. Her brown eyes were red-rimmed from another sleepless night. Raven hair was pulled into a ponytail because she could never find time or energy for a haircut or a perm. *Get it together, Sara.* She took a deep breath and headed for the doctor's dictation room, where she slumped into a chair.

"Something wrong, Dr. Miles?"

Sara turned to see Gloria, the clinic's head nurse. "No, just taking a few deep breaths before I have to make a call I'm dreading."

Gloria slid into the chair next to Sara. The controlled chaos of the internal medicine clinic hummed around them. The buzz of conversations and ringing of phones served as effectively as white noise to mask her next words. "Is it one of your hospital patients? Got some bad news to deliver?"

"Sort of. It's Chelsea Ferguson."

"The teenage girl? Is she worse?"

"Yes. The cultures grew *Staph luciferus*."

Gloria whistled silently. "The Killer. That's bad."

"The only thing that seems to be working in these cases is that new drug of Jack Ingersoll's."

"Oh, I get it. That's the call you don't want to make." Gloria touched Sara lightly on the shoulder. "When will you stop letting what Ingersoll did ruin the rest of your life? I can introduce you to a couple of nice men who go to our church. They've both gone through tough divorces—neither was their fault—and they want to move on. It would be good for you—"

Sara shook her head. "Thanks, but I'm not ready to date. I'm not sure if I can ever trust a man again."

Gloria opened her mouth, but Sara silenced her with an upraised hand. No sense putting this off. She pulled the phone toward her and stabbed in a number.

Dr. John Ramsey found a spot in the visitors' parking lot. He exited his car and looked across the driveway at the main campus of Southwestern Medical Center. When he'd graduated, there were two buildings on the campus. Now those two had been swallowed up, incorporated into a complex that totaled about forty buildings on three separate campuses. Right now he only needed to find one: the tall white building directly across the driveway at the end of a flagstone plaza. The imposing glass façade of the medical library reflected sunlight into his eyes as he wove past benches where students sat chatting on cell phones or burrowing into book bags. He paused at the glass front doors of the complex, took a deep breath, and pushed forward.

There was a directory inside for anyone trying to negotiate the warren of inter-connected buildings, but John didn't need it. He found the elevator he wanted, entered, and punched five.

In a moment, he was in the office of the Chairman of Internal Medicine.

"Dr. Schaeffer will be with you in a moment." The receptionist motioned him toward a seat opposite the magnificent rosewood desk that was the centerpiece of the spacious office, then glided out, closing the door softly behind her.

John eased into the visitor's chair and looked around him. He'd spent forty years on the volunteer clinical faculty of Southwestern Medical Center's Department of Internal Medicine. For forty years he'd instructed and mentored medical students and residents, for forty years he'd covered the teaching clinic once a month, and today was the first time he'd been in the department chairman's office. He swallowed the resentment he felt bubbling up. *No, John. You never wanted to be here. You were happy in your own world.*

John couldn't help comparing this room with the cubbyhole he'd called his private office. Now he didn't even have that. The practice was closed, the equipment and furnishings sold to a young doctor just getting started. John's files and patient records were in a locked storage facility, rent paid for a year.

He wondered how many of his patients had contacted his nurse to have their records transferred. No matter, she'd handle it. He'd paid her six months' salary to take care of such things. What would happen after that? He didn't have the energy to care. Things were different now.

For almost half a century he'd awakened to the aroma of coffee and a kiss from the most wonderful woman in the world. Now getting out of bed in the morning was an effort; shaving and getting dressed were more than he could manage some days. Since Beth died . . . He shook his head, trying to clear the cobwebs that clogged his brain. The knowledge that he'd never again know the happiness of having a woman he loved by his side made him wish he'd died with her. What was the use of going on?

But something happened this morning. He'd awakened with a small spark of determination to do something, anything, to move on. He tried to fight it, to roll over and seek the sleep that eluded him. Instead, he heard the echo of Beth's words: "You're too good a physician to retire. People need you." He remembered that conversation as though it were yesterday. She'd urged; he'd insisted. *Let's retire. I want to get out of the rat race and enjoy time with you.* Retirement meant the travel they'd put off, the time to do things together. Only, now there was no more together.

This morning, he'd rolled out of bed determined that today would be different. It would be the start of his rebirth. As he shrugged into a robe, as he'd done each day since her death he looked at the picture on their dresser of him and Beth. She'd been radiant that spring day so many years ago, and he wondered yet again how he'd managed to snag her.

He'd shaved—for the first time in days—with special care, and his image in the mirror made him wonder. When did that slim young man in the picture develop a paunch and acquire an AARP card? When had the thick brown hair been replaced by gray strands that required careful combing to hide a retreating hairline? The eyes were still bright, although they hid behind wire-rimmed trifocals. "You're too old for this, John," he muttered. And as though she were in the room, he heard Beth's words once more. "You're too good a physician to retire. People need you."

Fortified with coffee, the sole component of his breakfast nowadays, he'd forced himself to make the call. He asked his question and was gratified and a bit frightened by the positive response. John dressed carefully, choosing his best suit, spending a great deal of time selecting a tie. He'd noticed a gradual shift in doctors' attire over the past few years. Now many wore jeans and golf shirts under their white coats. But for John Ramsey, putting on a tie before going to the office was tantamount to donning a uniform, one he'd worn proudly for years. And he—

"John, I was surprised when I got your call. To what do I owe the pleasure?" Dr. Donald Schaeffer breezed into the office, the starched tails of his white coat billowing behind him. He offered his hand, then settled in behind his desk.

"Donald, I appreciate your taking the time to see me. I was wondering—"

"Before we start, I want you to know how sorry we all are for your loss. Is there anything I can do?"

Perfect lead-in. See if you can get the words out. "As you know, I closed my office four months ago. Beth and I were going to enjoy retirement. Then . . ."

Schaeffer nodded and tented his fingers under his chin. At least he had the grace not to offer more platitudes. Ramsey had had enough of those.

"I was wondering if you could use me in the department." There. Not the words he'd rehearsed, but at least he'd tossed the ball into Schaeffer's court.

"John, are you talking about coming onto the faculty?"

"Maybe something half-time. I could staff resident clinics, teach medical students."

Schaeffer was shaking his head before John finished. "That's what the volunteer clinical faculty does. It's what you did for . . . how many years? Thirty? Thirty-five?"

"Forty, actually. Well, I'm still a clinical professor in the department, so I guess I have privileges at Parkland Hospital. Can you use me there?"

Schaeffer pulled a yellow legal pad toward him and wrote a couple of words before he pushed it aside. "I'm not sure what

I can do for you, if anything. It's not that easy. You have no idea of the administrative hoops I have to jump through to run this department. Even if I could offer you a job today— and I can't—I'd have to juggle the budget to support it, post the position for open applications, get half a dozen approvals before finalizing the appointment." He spread his hands in a gesture of futility.

"So, is that a 'no'?"

"That's an 'I'll see what I can do.' Afraid that's the best I have to offer." Schaeffer looked at his watch, shoved his chair back, and eased to his feet. "Coming to Grand Rounds?"

Why not? John's house was an empty museum of bitter memories. His office belonged to someone else. Why not sit in the company of colleagues? "Sure. I'll walk over with you."

As the two men moved through the halls of the medical center, John prayed silently that Schaeffer would find a job for him. With all his prayers for Beth during her final illness, prayers that had gone unanswered, he figured that surely God owed him this one.

2

Jack, this is Sara."

Dr. Jack Ingersoll hunched his shoulder to hold the phone against his ear. He removed his glasses and polished them on the tail of his white coat. The closed door of his academic office couldn't quite block out the noise as one of his fellow faculty members read the riot act to a resident about his choice of a drug for bacterial endocarditis. "Sara, so good to hear from you. How have you been?"

"You can skip the niceties, Jack. This is a professional call."

"I get the picture. So let's keep it professional. What can I do for you?"

"I have a sixteen-year-old girl with generalized sepsis. No response to the usual empiric IV antibiotics. I got the blood culture results this morning. *Staphylococcus luciferus.*"

Ingersoll pursed his lips. "Another case. And, of course, the sensitivity studies—"

"Resistant to every antibiotic tested. So I thought of you and your study."

Ingersoll's pulse quickened a bit. Every patient he enrolled strengthened the reputation he was building as the world's authority on EpAm848. It looked to be a wonder drug, and if he could hitch his wagon to that star, there was no telling where he could go. "Does she meet the enrollment criteria?"

"Yes. I checked before I called you. The mother's anxious to get her into the protocol, and I've laid the groundwork for you. Informed consent shouldn't be a problem."

He found a blank slip of paper in the morass on his desk. "Thanks. What's her name and where is she?"

"She's in the ICU at University Hospital. Name's Chelsea Ferguson." Sara cleared her throat. "Jack, she's just a kid. And the mother's worried sick. Try to upgrade your usual bedside manner. Please."

Ingersoll ended the conversation with a few mumbled assurances. He thought a moment, then punched the intercom button. "Martha, page Dr. Pearson and tell him to meet me in the ICU at University Hospital. Then call over there and get the identifying info on a patient—her name is Ferguson—and give it to Dr. Resnick. Have him make up a set of enrollment papers for the EpAm848 study and bring them to the ICU."

Ingersoll swiveled away from his desk and let his eyes sweep across the horizon. New construction was everywhere at Southwestern Medical Center, girders and columns rising alongside existing massive buildings. Although the economy was rough, there were still more than enough multimillionaires in Dallas who wanted to assure themselves of the best possible care by the brightest minds in the medical field. What better way to do that than to give money to the academic medical center in their hometown? Jack Ingersoll wanted some of that. He wanted to become Dr. Jack Ingersoll, John and Mary So-and-So Distinguished Professor of Infectious Disease, with offices in the Thus-And-Such Building, his salary and research expenses underwritten by the Bubba and Sue Somebody-Or-Other Foundation. And if the EpAm848 study kept going this way, that was exactly where he was headed—if not here, then somewhere.

There were portraits scattered throughout the medical center of some of the distinguished faculty members. He wanted his to join that select group. He'd be wearing a white coat, holding a beaker of brightly colored liquid, looking into the distance, contemplating the discovery that put the medical school—and him—on the map. The artist would have to minimize his developing paunch and maybe enhance his scant brown hair into a handsome widow's peak, but that was the advantage of a painting over a photograph.

He unlocked the bottom drawer of his desk and pulled out a rust-colored stiff cardboard accordion file closed with an elastic cord secured over a large button. Ingersoll unfastened the closure, peered inside the file, and counted the sets of stapled pages. Twenty-one. Twenty-one patients willing to testify that he was a miracle worker. Twenty-one instances where EpAm848 saved a life otherwise doomed because of infection by *Staphylococcus luciferus*—the Devil's own *Staph*, "The Killer."

Patients were dying all over the world from this infection. It was turning into an epidemic, but the success rate of Ingersoll's treatment was 100 percent so far. Conventional wisdom in medicine held that no therapy was 100 percent effective. He felt like a pitcher, taking a no-hitter into the eighth inning. Somewhere out there might be a case that wouldn't respond. But so far, he was throwing a perfect game, and if he could keep it up, there was no limit to how far he'd go.

Martha's voice startled him from his daydreams. She never used the intercom, no matter how many times Ingersoll asked her to do so. He'd finally given up on that fight. "Dr. Pearson just called. He's at the ICU and is reviewing the chart now."

Ingersoll resealed the file and locked it in his desk drawer. "I'm on my way. Page me if there's something urgent."

He transferred his stethoscope, pens, and pocket flashlight to a freshly laundered white lab coat. He slipped his arms in, flexed his shoulders a couple of times to loosen the starched fabric, and buttoned the coat over his pale blue cotton dress shirt, leaving just enough of his rep-stripe tie showing to make a fashion statement. Sometimes a good first impression on the family was the most important part of the consultation.

As he exited his office, he almost bumped into Dr. Carter Resnick, hurrying down the hall, head down, mumbling to himself.

"Resnick, watch what you're doing."

Resnick rubbed his hand nervously over his shiny dome. Ingersoll couldn't understand why some men shaved their heads, but apparently Resnick thought it made him look wiser. It didn't. If anything, it accentuated his geekiness.

"Sorry, sir. I just prepared the packet for Chelsea Ferguson and took it to Dr. Pearson. Would you like me to go with you to see her? Maybe I could help." He brought his eyes up for a millisecond, but dropped them again. Whatever expression they held was hidden behind thick horn-rimmed glasses.

"You know the deal," Ingersoll said. "You didn't get the Infectious Disease fellowship, but I agreed to take you on as a research assistant and promised you the inside track when the second fellowship slot opens next year. Your place this year is in the lab. And the longer you stand here like a schoolboy begging to avoid detention, the less time you're spending in that lab."

Without waiting for a reply, Ingersoll brushed past the young doctor and hurried away to the ICU. *Idiot. He's good in the lab, following orders, but he won't ever be any good at patient care. When I take on another ID Fellow, it certainly won't be him.*

Dr. Roswell Irving Pearson III, generally known as "Rip," scanned his notes one last time. The position of Infectious Disease Fellow under Dr. Jack Ingersoll was a real plum, and Rip had overcome stiff competition to win this appointment. But Ingersoll was a stern taskmaster. He expected his ID Fellow to anticipate his every request and fulfill it perfectly. When Ingersoll said, "Meet me in the ICU at University Hospital," Rip knew that really meant "Find out which patient I'm seeing, review the chart, and be prepared to present the salient facts in the most concise fashion possible." Since this was a case involving *Staph luciferus*, that also meant making sure the teenage girl qualified for the EpAm848 study. Now Rip was ready.

He supposed he shouldn't feel sorry for himself. He could be poor Carter Resnick. Rip wasn't sure how Carter ever got through an internal medicine residency, or why he thought he had any chance at an ID fellowship, much less one as prestigious as this one. Anyone with half a brain could see that Ingersoll was just using Carter, delighted to have a specialty-trained MD running his research lab. Well, the Carter Resnicks of the world would have to take care of themselves. Rip Pearson had his own problems, and the first one on the agenda was presenting this case to his chief.

Rip looked once more at his watch. Martha had paged him less than fifteen minutes ago, catching him already at University Hospital making rounds. He'd sprinted up the stairs to the ICU and rapidly digested the chart information on Chelsea Ferguson. He hadn't introduced himself to Chelsea or her mother, though. He'd made that mistake once, and had learned quite quickly that Ingersoll expected his ID Fellow to be seen but not heard, like an obedient child.

The name of the attending physician on the case made Rip pause. He hadn't done more than nod to Sara as they passed in the halls since their last rotation as internal medicine residents. Now she was a staff member, while his position as an Infectious Disease Fellow meant he was still in training. Would that make a difference? He and Sara had been close until she married Jack Ingersoll. Now all those relationships were topsy-turvy. He wondered—

"What do we have?" Ingersoll's rubber-soled shoes allowed him to approach without warning, something Rip suspected he did, hoping to catch someone bad-mouthing him. The consultant pulled out a chair and took the page of neatly printed notes Rip handed him.

"Chelsea Ferguson, sixteen-year-old Caucasian female, had a dental extraction a week ago, without prophylactic antibiotic coverage. She developed progressive, severe cellulitis of the jaw, and her dentist referred her to an oral surgeon. He tried one change of antibiotics, but when he recognized early sepsis he sent her here. Pending cultures, Dr. Miles began empiric antibiotic therapy for presumed MRSA with IV vancomycin plus gentamycin. Intraoral cultures grew out *Staph luciferus*, and blood cultures have reported the same organism, resistant to all conventional antibiotics. The patient now has generalized sepsis, is spiking temps to between 40 and 41 degrees Celsius, and her condition is deteriorating."

"Eligibility for the study?"

Trust Jack Ingersoll to cut to the chase. Not "What else can we do?" Not "What about the white count, or sed rate, or blood sugar or any other lab test?" No other questions except, "Is this another case I can enroll in the EpAm848 study?" Rip swallowed the retort that was on the tip of his tongue. "Yes, sir. She meets all the criteria. And according to Dr. Miles's notes, her mother has been warned that there are risks and potential side effects."

"Nonsense. None of the patients treated so far have so much as turned a hair. This is really a wonder drug."

"Yes, sir. But there's always a first time."

"Negative thinking, Rip. We'll have none of that." Ingersoll stood. "We have to project a positive attitude. It's important that patients have confidence in their doctors."

A faint buzz issued from under Ingersoll's coat. He pulled an iPhone from his pants pocket, looked at the display, and frowned. "I have to take this."

Ingersoll hurried away from the nurses' station, ducked into the family room, and closed the door. Rip wondered what could have been so important. In his experience, nothing trumped enrolling another patient in the study.

Whatever it was, it didn't take long. In less than five minutes, Ingersoll was back. "Let's talk with these people," he said. "Then I have to leave and catch a plane. I'll be gone for a couple of days, so you'll need to administer the medication and gather the follow-up data. Think you can handle that?"

Rip swallowed the acid that boiled up in his throat. Since the study began, he'd been the one doing just that. He'd mixed every dose of EpAm848 and sat by the patient's bedside while the IV ran in. He'd drawn blood and taken it to Ingersoll's lab for all the necessary tests, made sure the vital signs were monitored, and logged the data that chronicled the patient's response. This might as well have been his study, not Jack Ingersoll's. It bespoke of his mentor's huge ego that he'd even ask such a question. He choked out, "Yes, sir," and managed to sound humble while doing it.

Ingersoll was already moving toward Chelsea Ferguson's room. Rip fell in step behind him like an aide-de-camp trailing a general at a respectful distance. A woman that he took to be Chelsea's mother was sitting at the bedside, systematically shredding a tissue.

"Mrs. Ferguson, I'm Dr. Jack Ingersoll. I believe Dr. Miles told you to expect me."

"Doctor, this is Chelsea." The girl on the bed opened her eyes, managed a weak nod, then closed them again.

The camera of Rip's mind's eye automatically recorded the patient's status: pale, slightly undernourished girl in her late teens, sweating profusely, movements slow and listless. An IV in her left arm was dripping at a regular rate. Her breathing was shallow, and a plastic cannula delivered what he assumed to be oxygen to her nostrils.

"Chelsea is very seriously ill." Ingersoll turned from the patient and addressed his words to Mrs. Ferguson. "She has an infection in her bloodstream that will almost certainly kill her if we can't eradicate it." If he saw the mother's shudder and the girl's grimace, he ignored them. "Our only chance for that is the administration of an experimental medication. We've had remarkable success—actually a 100 percent cure rate—with it. Although side effects and complications are possible, we've seen none of these. I need your permission to proceed."

"What if . . . ?"

"The details are spelled out in the consent forms that Dr. Pearson will go over with you. If you don't wish to sign them, of course, the choice is yours, including responsibility for the consequences. If you proceed with treatment, Dr. Pearson will administer the first dose today." Ingersoll looked at his watch. "I'm afraid I have to leave now, to attend a consultants' meeting. I'll look in again in a couple of days, should you consent to treatment for your daughter."

Rip watched Ingersoll turn on his heel and march out the door as though going into battle. He didn't know what this "consultants' meeting" represented, but he was certain of one thing. As of thirty minutes ago, it had not been on Ingersoll's agenda. It was a result of that phone call. And it was a command performance.

Sara frowned as she searched the chart rack at the ICU nurses' station. The slot for Room 6 was empty. Was it misfiled in the hurry of ICU routine? No, Chelsea's chart wasn't in any of the other slots. Maybe it was on the ward clerk's desk, awaiting execution of an order for lab tests or an adjustment of treatments. But no one except Sara or her resident, Luke Sutton, would have written such an order. And Luke was out today, at home nursing a lower respiratory infection that appeared to verge on pneumonia.

"Dr. Miles?" Sara turned to see Janice, one of the ICU nurses, holding out a chart. "Are you looking for Chelsea's chart?"

Sara took the proffered chart. "Thank you. Is there something new?"

"Dr. Ingersoll and Dr. Pearson were here earlier. They started Chelsea on EpAm848. Dr. Pearson drew her baseline labs himself, and then sat with her while she got the first dose of her medicine. You just missed him."

Sara took a deep breath. The good news was that Chelsea was now getting the antibiotic that could save her life. The double-barreled bad news was the possibility of a side effect or complication—all the reassurances notwithstanding—as well as the likelihood that her ex-husband's bedside manner hadn't improved. Sara hated to think of the psychological damage Jack Ingersoll might have inflicted on the sixteen-year-old girl in that bed.

Sara thanked Janice and carried the chart with her into Chelsea Ferguson's room. In stark contrast with her attitude when Sara left her this morning, Mrs. Ferguson seemed calm and serene. She was brushing her daughter's chestnut hair. Sara wasn't sure—maybe this was wishful thinking—but there appeared to be a bit of color in Chelsea's cheeks, color that had not been there since the day of her admission.

Sara smiled at the mother and daughter. "The nurse tells me that Dr. Ingersoll was here earlier, and that you decided to go ahead with the drug treatment he offered."

Mrs. Ferguson looked up from her task. "He made an appearance, acting like we should be grateful that he spared us a few moments. I know that he must be affected by seeing so many seriously ill patients, but that's not an excuse for just plain rude behavior."

"I'm sorry. Dr. Ingersoll is a very busy man nowadays, and I'm afraid his bedside manner isn't the best. But he's the sole source for . . ." Sara paused and tried to choose her words carefully. "Dr. Ingersoll controls the use of the experimental drug that gives us the best hope of licking this thing."

"He put it a bit more bluntly than that." Mrs. Ferguson gave a particularly vigorous swipe with the brush, and Chelsea flinched. "Sorry, dear."

"But Chelsea's receiving the medication. That's all that matters now."

"Thank goodness for that nice Dr. Pearson. He told us what to expect, answered our questions, and sat with Chelsea while she got her first dose of the medicine. I think he's the one we'll actually be seeing." She laid aside the brush and kissed her daughter's forehead. "At least, I hope that's true."

"Yes, I suspect Dr. Ingersoll will be by from time to time, but you'll see Rip—that is, Dr. Pearson—on a regular basis. If you need anything, ask the nurse to page him or me."

"I'll do that." She patted her daughter's arm, carefully avoiding the IV site. "Chelsea, I'm going to step out for a minute, maybe get a cup of coffee at the nurses' station. Are you okay?"

"I'm fine, Mama." The voice was weak, but these were the first words Sara had heard her patient speak in over twenty-four hours, and to her they were beautiful.

In the hall, Mrs. Ferguson took Sara's arm in a grip that was surprisingly strong for such a frail woman. "Is there anything I can do to report the way Dr. Ingersoll acted? He seemed to have no more feeling for Chelsea or me than he would for a lab animal."

"I'd wait until Chelsea's on her way to recovery. There'll be plenty of time to lodge a complaint with the right people in administration then." Sara thought about it. "I'll be happy to help you do it then."

"All right. But I'll hold you to that. Really, I don't care how important that man is. There's no excuse for being so callous."

Sara nodded her agreement while scenes unfurled in her mind, scenes she'd tried hard to put behind her. *If you only knew . . .*

"What's so important?" Rip Pearson stirred his coffee, even though he took it black. He recognized it as a nervous habit, but in his stress-filled world nervous habits were the norm. He'd deal with them after he finished his fellowship.

Carter Resnick rubbed his head as though checking to see if his hair had grown back. Then he put both hands on the table, leaned forward, and whispered, "We should talk."

Rip put his hand behind his ear. The noise level in the hospital cafeteria was such that even the two nursing students at the next table had no chance of hearing this conversation. "Speak up. We're not exchanging state secrets here. What's on your mind?"

"I think Dr. Ingersoll is lying about that second ID fellowship slot."

Rip shrugged. "How would you—how would anyone know? I mean, he applied for it and now it's up to the folks who make decisions like that."

"I'm getting a lot of computer experience in the research lab. After some digging around, I'm able to get into sites that are supposed to be protected. Anyway, I hacked the records of the Internal Medicine Board and there's no mention of such an application. Ingersoll never submitted it."

Rip was ashamed of the first question that popped into his mind, but he asked it anyway. "What about my slot? Is it approved? Will I be able to take my ID boards when I finish?"

Resnick's grin was almost evil. "I really ought to make you sweat, but I won't. Yes, your fellowship is on the up-and-up. But how does it make you feel, working for a liar?"

Rip didn't know what to think. His first reaction was that the research assistant was getting a little revenge on the man who'd beat him for the fellowship. Was Resnick trying to push Rip toward resigning so he could step into the slot?

The silence hung between them for what seemed like several minutes, although it was probably more like a few seconds. Finally, Rip said, "I don't believe you. And even if I did, I don't think I'd do anything about it. If I were you, I'd keep this to myself, especially the part about hacking into the Internal Medicine Board site. I doubt whether the administration of the medical center would condone such activity."

He left without another word. At the door, he looked back. Resnick was still sitting at the table, grinning.

3

I DON'T SEE WHY THIS MEETING WAS SO IMPORTANT THAT I HAD TO DROP my patient responsibilities and fly out here." Jack Ingersoll slapped the conference table, almost upsetting his coffee cup.

Bob Wolfe sat back in his chair, automatically withdrawing from Ingersoll's "in your face" attitude.

"Did you hear me?" Ingersoll asked through clenched teeth.

Wolfe worked to keep his voice level and his demeanor calm. No need to spook the doctor . . . yet. "Jack, I thought it was important that you understand what's going on. It's been made very clear to me from top-level management at Jandra that the fate of the company is riding on the success of Jandramycin."

"What's Jandramycin?"

"That's another thing. From now on, the drug is no longer to be referred to as EpAm848. We're calling it Jandramycin. The bigwigs want the public to identify the drug with our company when they hear about the preliminary results of our studies."

Ingersoll hit the table again, and this time his cup rocked in its saucer. A few drops of coffee sloshed onto the table. He stabbed at them with a napkin. "The public isn't going to hear about our preliminary results yet. That's why they're called 'preliminary.' Apparently you've forgotten how all this works. We're doing Phase II studies right now, seeing which dose works best, which ones might cause side effects. Then comes Phase III, where we compare EpAm848 with placebo or other drugs. Considering the severity of the disease we're treating, we may be given permission to omit the placebo, maybe even do a case-control study with only EpAm848—I mean, Jandramycin—as the active drug. But this stuff won't be available for general use for a couple of years. Probably longer than that before the FDA approves it."

With the look of Santa pulling one last present, the big one, from his bag, Wolfe said, "I'm way ahead of you. We've pulled a few strings and made a deal or two—the FDA will accept the data from your work and the two European studies as fulfilling both the Phase II and the Phase III requirements."

Ingersoll leaned back as though he'd been hit. "How did you manage that?"

"You don't need to know the details. What you do need to know is that, as we speak, our factory is working twenty-four-hour shifts to produce and package Jandramycin. Our PR department has its best people creating a campaign that will blow the public's mind. And our detail men are poised to hit the streets and spread the word."

"But—"

"Now listen, and listen closely." Wolfe tapped the table in front of Ingersoll with his spoon to emphasize his words. "Up to now, Jandramycin looks like a miracle drug. That's why you're such a fair-haired boy in the medical community." He pointed to the bound journals on shelves that lined one wall of the room. "Your work is going to catch everyone's attention. Lead article in the major medical journals. Lots of interest from the press. That is, if you cooperate."

Ingersoll opened his mouth, then shut it again.

"From this point onward, there can be absolutely no hint of side effects, complications, or therapeutic failures with Jandramycin. It's up to you to make sure that happens." Wolfe's voice dropped to a near-whisper, but the words came out like steel darts: "You may think you're important because you stumbled onto a use for a compound we thought was useless, but if you foul up now, you can kiss that big research grant, your paid lectures, and all the other perks of your relationship with Jandra good-bye. Not only that, we'll see to it that you can't even get a job in an emergency room in Pocatello, Idaho. Provided you're still around to see it happen."

Sara yawned. Even the ultra-strong coffee of the hospital cafeteria wasn't enough to counteract the effects of a sleepless night. She looked at her watch. Time enough to finish breakfast and get a second cup of coffee to take to the conference.

"Mind if I join you?" The question was apparently rhetorical, since Rip Pearson had already pulled out a chair and was depositing his tray across the table from her.

"Actually, I've been wanting to talk with you. This is the second day that Chelsea Ferguson's been on your 'wonder drug'— what is it? EpAm something. She seems to be better, but how does Dr. Ingersoll think she's doing?"

Rip spread salsa liberally over his scrambled eggs, then forked a generous portion into his mouth. He chewed, swallowed, and washed it down with coffee before answering. "Sorry. But you know the drill. Eat when you can—"

"Sleep when you can. Yes, I know. Now, what about Chelsea?"

"I think she's improving. As for Dr. Ingersoll, I can't say. He got some kind of urgent phone call when we were seeing Ms.

Ferguson, and he's been gone since." Rip added more salsa and took another bite of eggs.

"What could make Jack take off like that?" Sara had known Jack Ingersoll as intimately as was possible, and she couldn't think of anything more important to him than his patients and his practice. If he'd only been willing to pay the same attention to his family . . . but that was water under the bridge. "Anyway, how long do you anticipate keeping Chelsea on therapy?"

Rip chewed the last bit of egg, finished his last triangle of toast, and dabbed his lips with a napkin. "For *Staph luciferus* cases, treatment is given daily via intravenous infusion for a total of ten days." He said it as though by rote, and Sara realized he was parroting back the protocol Ingersoll and the drug company had written.

Rip shoved his tray aside and took a satisfied sip of coffee. "Now, how have you been? We don't see much of each other anymore."

Sara remembered when she'd first met Rip. She was sitting with a hundred other freshmen undergoing orientation at Southwestern Medical School. The Dean, resplendent in three-piece suit with a chain draped across the vest to display his Phi Beta Kappa key, had just said, "We didn't ask you to come here. But we may be asking some of you to leave."

She heard a muffled chuckle to her right and looked at the man sitting there. His wavy blond hair was fashionably long. In contrast with the casual dress of others in the class, he wore a button-down collared blue oxford cloth shirt open at the neck. His khakis sported ironed creases that could cut cheese. Top-Siders worn without socks completed the Ivy League look. He leaned toward Sara and whispered, "Sorry. Actually, they *did* ask me to come here. They recruited me, so I doubt they'll be asking me to leave."

After the lecture, he'd invited her for coffee, where she learned he was indeed the product of an Ivy League background. Roswell Irving Pearson III graduated *magna cum laude* from Yale. He broke the family tradition of working in investment banking, choosing instead to come to Southwestern to study medicine. "And please call me Rip. I'm trying to adapt to my new surroundings, and Roswell doesn't fit that image." Thinking back on that encounter, Sara decided that was probably when he began to put salsa on his eggs. It was more Texan.

"Sara? You went quiet on me. How have you been doing?"

"I've been staying busy. Isn't that the recommended method for getting over a loss in your life? I think I recall that from the lecture on depression."

Rip reached across the table and touched her hand. "It's been two years since the baby died and Jack left you. Don't you think you should be over it by now?" Rip's words were soft, his touch even softer.

"Please, let's not talk about it. There's just so much—" The buzz of a pager cut through the din of the cafeteria.

Both of them consulted the tiny boxes they carried. "It's me," Sara said. "The ICU."

"Funny, I've got the same call," Rip said.

They looked at each other for a moment before Sara said, "Chelsea."

They left their dishes on the table and headed for the stairs at a brisk pace.

Rip pushed through the swinging doors of the ICU a half step ahead of Sara. The crowd of people in Chelsea's room confirmed their fears.

The head nurse, holding a chart, stepped out of the room. She addressed both doctors, swiveling her head from one to the other. "We were helping Chelsea out of bed and into a chair so we could change her linens, and she fainted. Now her blood pressure's down to eighty over sixty, pulse a hundred. I paged you both and drew blood for some stat blood work. They're getting her back into bed now."

Rip hesitated. Technically, Sara was still the doctor in charge of the case. But since Chelsea was in the study, Jack Ingersoll would undoubtedly insist he be involved in all treatment decisions. And in Ingersoll's absence, Rip had that responsibility.

Sara made it easy. She turned to Rip and said, "She's your study patient, and she's going into shock. Want to take the lead here?"

"I can't see EpAm848 causing her blood pressure to drop. Never been a problem before, and we've given it to some pretty sick people. Let's have a look at her."

Ten minutes later, Sara and Rip huddled in the hall outside Chelsea's room. "I think it's septic shock," he said. "She's had an indwelling catheter for a while, and my money's on sepsis from a urinary infection." Catheters in the bladder could eventually cause infection, and sometimes those bacteria spread to the bloodstream with disastrous results.

Sara opened the chart she held. "I'll order blood cultures, a urinalysis and culture, along with the lab work Janice already requested, but those will take a while. Why don't we get some urine, spin it down, do a Gram stain, and see what we've got?"

"That's scut work, Sara. You're faculty. I'm a fellow. I'll do it."

Sara shook her head. "If you hadn't decided to get post-graduate training, you could be on the faculty as well. We're equals, Rip. We've been together through four years of med school and three years of residency. I don't want to hear any more of that."

"Okay. You get the sample. I'll speed up the IV's and tweak the medications. Want to start a vasopressor drip?"

"What do you think?"

"Let's piggyback some Dopamine into her IV and run it as needed to get her blood pressure to better levels."

"Do it," Sara said.

There had been a time when every clinical ward in a hospital had a small lab space where medical students, interns, and residents could do simple procedures themselves. At University Hospital, that space had long since been co-opted for other uses, so Rip and Sara ended up in the hospital's clinical laboratory.

"Let me do that," the head technician said. "I do this every day. Neither of you has done it for years."

It seemed to take an eternity, but finally the tech gestured to a binocular microscope. "There it is. Want to take a guess before I tell you what you've got?"

Sara looked through the eyepieces and frowned. When she stepped away, Rip removed his glasses, adjusted the 'scope, and felt his heart skip a beat as red rods came into focus. He couldn't be certain based on the microscopic picture alone, but he'd looked at hundreds of slides with dozens of organisms, and he was almost sure of the diagnosis. "What do you think? *E. coli?*"

The tech nodded. "Yep. *Escherichia coli.* I plated out some of the sample you brought, and in a couple of days I'll have a culture confirmation and some preliminary antibiotic sensitivities."

Rip looked at Sara. They both knew what that meant. They didn't have thirty-six or forty-eight hours to wait before starting treatment. They had to begin antibiotic therapy *now*.

Sara thanked the tech and they both began to make their way back to the ICU. "Does your drug, whatever the name is, have any effect on *E. coli*?"

"It's EpAm848, and the answer is that nobody knows for sure. We've only used it against *Staph luciferus*. But look at it this way. If it were effective against *E. coli*, we wouldn't be having this conversation. This wouldn't have developed."

Sara bit her lip. "I'm at fault here. I didn't keep an eye out for other causes of Chelsea's fever and all her other symptoms. She's probably had that urinary infection for several days. If I'd remembered to do repeated urine cultures, we'd have caught this earlier."

"Don't beat yourself up. We can't be perfect. No doctor can. The important thing is that we've caught it before she went into profound shock and developed multiple organ failures. We can still treat her and bring her through this."

"Okay. You're the ID specialist. What empiric antibiotics would you use for *E. coli* infection like this?"

Rip ran through the index cards of his mind. "I'd go with an IV quinolone like levofloxacin. And, even though we don't see any evidence of anaerobic infection, I'd add clindamycin until we get the results of the cultures, both urine and blood."

"I agree. Do you want to write the orders?"

"Sure."

"Does this mean you have to stop the Ep whatever?" Sara said.

"I don't know. It's never been given with other antibiotics, so I don't know what could happen. But if we stop EpAm848 now, the *Staph luciferus* could start up again."

"I have to leave the decision to you," Sara said.

And whatever I choose will probably be wrong. Putting aside the question of one antibiotic rendering the other useless, what was Jack Ingersoll going to say when he found that one of

43

his precious study patients had been compromised? What if there were complications? How could a researcher tell if they were due to the EpAm848, the other medications, the disease itself? The patient would be dropped from the study. And to Ingersoll, every patient in the study was pure gold.

If he were here, Rip was pretty sure what Ingersoll's decision would be: Don't give anything more. He'd argue that EpAm848 was a strong antibiotic. It might be enough by itself to combat the sepsis. Just give supportive care, use IV fluids and vasopressors, administer oxygen. Give the drug a bit of time and it could pull the patient through. Another triumph for EpAm848. Another feather in the cap of Jack Ingersoll.

Rip could call Ingersoll's cell phone. Tell him the situation. Leave the decision up to him. Doing this on his own would expose Rip to his mentor's wrath big-time. He might even lose his fellowship because of it.

They reached the ICU and pushed through the doors. Both doctors were silent as they approached Chelsea's bedside. Rip nodded to Mrs. Ferguson, who continued to maintain her bedside vigil, one hand lightly touching her daughter's arm. The mother's lips moved in what Rip took to be silent prayer. He added one of his own. *Please, Lord, help me make the right choice.*

He looked at Sara. Then he reached down and smoothed the hair that had fallen onto Chelsea's forehead. He took a deep breath. "Mrs. Ferguson, Chelsea has another infection—a serious one in her urinary tract. It's caused her blood pressure to go down. If the infection is left unchecked, it could put her in grave danger. I think we can get on top of it, but to do that, we're going to have to use some additional medications."

"Does that mean she won't get any more of the drug you've been giving her? Until today, it seemed she was getting better."

"No," Rip said. "I promise you, she'll keep getting the EpAm848 as well." He hoped he could deliver on that promise.

The phone dragged Dr. John Ramsey up from a dream of walking through a field of bluebonnets with Beth. *No, please, I don't want to leave. I just got her back.* The ringing continued, and gradually reality took hold. Beth was gone. He'd never see her again this side of heaven. Sometimes—actually, often—he wished he could go there now. He'd never gone further than the idle thought, but now he understood why men and women who'd lost their spouses after many decades of marriage might find their will to live gone.

He pushed himself up off the sofa and blinked at the TV. The program he'd been watching had long since given way to two people arguing in front of a judge. With one hand he used the remote to silence the set; with the other he lifted the receiver. "Dr. Ramsey."

"Dr. Ramsey, please hold for Dr. Schaeffer." The female voice was much too perky for John. His mood was dark, so everyone's should be. He grunted a response and flexed his aching back muscles.

"John, this is Donald Schaeffer. I hope I didn't catch you at a bad time."

John's nerve endings tingled, and suddenly he was fully awake. "No, no. Just sat down to let my lunch settle and began watching a documentary on the Learning Channel." There was no need to let Schaeffer know the TV had been tuned to a *MASH* rerun.

"I've pulled every string I could, but there's no way I can swing an extra faculty member at this time."

John's stomach did a back flip, and for a moment he was afraid the few bites of grilled cheese sandwich he'd choked down at lunch would come right back up. "Thanks, anyway," he mumbled. "I guess—"

Schaeffer continued as though John hadn't spoken. "But I believe I can manage a part-time position for you. We're short in the GIM clinic, and you could pick up that slack for the next six months or so. By that time, we'll be into the next fiscal year, and I think I can swing a full-time appointment if it works for both of us."

"General Internal Medicine sounds right up my alley, Donald. After all, that's what I did for forty years. How soon can I start?"

"Why don't you come by tomorrow and see Kim, my department administrator? She can work out all the details."

"I don't know how to thank—"John realized he was talking to a dead phone. Schaeffer must have moved on to another of the message slips on his desk. He probably wouldn't think about this one again until he saw John in the halls of the department. But John would think about it constantly. Maybe this was the rope he could use to pull himself out of the depths of depression. He bowed his head. *Okay, God. You came through on this one. But I still don't think we're even.*

4

Ladies and gentlemen, welcome to flight 1084, from San Francisco to Dallas."

Jack Ingersoll ignored the instructions that followed. He closed his eyes and prepared to enjoy the flight. Jandra had sprung for a first-class ticket, and when he got to the gate he was happy to see that the aircraft was a 757. Although there'd been a time when he enjoyed travel, with familiarity had come first boredom and then actual distaste. Now, when travel was necessary, he wanted as many creature comforts as possible for the journey.

As soon as he felt the plane lift off the runway, Ingersoll reclined his seat and settled back. He brushed aside the flight attendant's offer of a drink. He hadn't slept last night, replaying in his mind his conversation with Wolfe, but alcohol wasn't going to be the answer. Besides, he didn't want to be muzzy-headed when he reached Dallas. He'd need his wits about him as he tried to impress Dr. Pearson with the importance of making sure no adverse data crept into the reports of the EpAm848—that is, the Jandramycin cases. He was going to have a hard time getting used to the name, but he supposed it would help remind him of how much was riding on the success of this drug.

He checked his watch. Mid-morning in San Francisco. With the two-hour time difference and the length of the flight, there was no reason to consider going to the medical center after he landed. Even Pearson, never one to punch a time clock, would be gone by then. Tomorrow would have to be soon enough.

Ingersoll pushed the call button.

"Yes, sir?" One nice thing about flying first class. The service was much better than what one got back in coach.

"I've changed my mind. I'll have a glass of white wine."

He really should have called Pearson yesterday afternoon to check on the progress of his latest patient, but after his meeting with Wolfe, all Ingersoll wanted to do was go somewhere and clear his mind. He'd wandered the streets of San Francisco aimlessly for hours, had something totally forgettable from room service, and had fallen into bed to stare at the ceiling for most of the night. At least Jandra had been decent enough to put him up at the Sir Francis Drake. On previous trips, his hotel was a La Quinta in Berkeley. He should have known something was up when they gave him his travel itinerary and he saw first-class travel and a nice hotel. First the carrot, then the stick.

In addition to Wolfe's veiled threats, Ingersoll already had something to worry about, something he had to keep forcing from his consciousness. Even though Jandramycin—there, he remembered the word—Jandramycin was considered a true wonder drug, the Jandra researchers had only been able to postulate its mode of action. Not unusual, since sometimes the mechanism of action of a drug was clarified months, even years after its introduction, as data accumulated. Well, that suited him just fine. He knew exactly why it worked, and that knowledge was something he meant to keep to himself as long as possible. That and a few other things as well. Meanwhile, he would continue to build his reputation.

He reached for his headset, ready to dial in some music, when an announcement rang through the aircraft. It was distorted a bit by a less-than-perfect PA system, but the message was clear. "Ladies and gentlemen, is there a doctor on board?"

Ingersoll was always careful to balance the perks that might go with being recognized as a doctor with the responsibilities that accompanied that recognition. He reached into his shirt pocket and sneaked a glance at the name on his boarding pass: Jack Ingersoll. No MD after his name, no Dr. before it. He was safe.

Five minutes later, there was another announcement, and this time the flight attendant's voice had an edge. "Ladies and gentlemen, this is urgent. If you're a doctor, please make your way to the aft galley. Thank you."

The passengers in the first-class cabin stirred and looked around, each one apparently wondering if there was a doctor among them. No one moved. Ingersoll felt, almost heard, a collective sigh of relief go up. Not just that they were spared the responsibility of tending to someone who'd fallen ill, but that they'd escaped that fate themselves. They'd survived for one more hour, most likely for one more day, God willing for one more month or year. But life was fragile, and never seemed so much so as when someone else's life was threatened.

From his seat in the last row of first class, Ingersoll craned his neck and looked down the aisle. A stocky black man on the aisle ten or twelve rows back beckoned a flight attendant over and said, loud enough for Ingersoll to hear him, "I'm not a doctor, but I'm an EMT. Can I help?"

"Yes, please. We think one of the passengers is having a heart attack. I was about to get the AED and take it back."

Great. A heart attack, and apparently they'd be using the automated external defibrillator. Ingersoll could almost write the scenario that was about to play out.

Twenty minutes later, his fears were confirmed. "Ladies and gentlemen, this is your captain. I'm sorry, but we're diverting to the nearest major city, Las Vegas, for a medical emergency. Please remain in your seats for the balance of the flight. We'll give you more information as soon as it's available."

Ingersoll craned his neck to look at the rear of the aircraft in time to see the lead flight attendant replacing the AED in its case, and the EMT spreading a blanket over a form stretched out in the aisle. Good thing he hadn't volunteered his services. He probably couldn't have done more than the emergency medical technician, and undoubtedly the paperwork at Las Vegas would be a nightmare. He just hoped he wasn't going to be delayed too long. Then again, he supposed a night in Las Vegas wouldn't be all that bad.

Sara scanned the numbers on Chelsea's chart. Fever coming down. Blood pressure holding stable now. Twenty-four hours since adding the additional antibiotics to the girl's treatment regimen, and Sara could hardly believe how much improvement she saw. Had they made a good guess in choosing empiric therapy, or was EpAm848 making a definite difference in the septic shock, as well as the *Staph luciferus* infection?

"How are you feeling?" Sara put her hand to Chelsea's forehead and was gratified to note that it was much cooler.

"Okay, I guess." Was Chelsea's voice stronger, or did Sara imagine it because she wanted to see signs of recovery? No, she definitely seemed better.

As usual, Mrs. Ferguson was at her daughter's bedside. "Whatever that new medicine is, I think it's helped. She seems stronger. And she actually ate a little this morning." She forced out what was probably her best effort at a smile.

"How's the patient this morning?" Sara made room for Rip at Chelsea's bedside and handed him the chart.

"Seems better," she said. "Check out her temp and vital signs."

He nodded his approval. "Looking good."

With a promise to return that afternoon, the two doctors stepped outside and settled into chairs at the nurses' station. Rip said, "I need to get some follow-up labs."

"What do you want? I'll order them," Sara said.

"Nope, I've got to draw them myself. That way, I'll know the blood gets to the right places."

"Places?" Sara asked. "Where will it go besides the hospital lab?"

"Some of it goes to Ingersoll's lab. Those tests are part of the study, and apparently part of his deal with Jandra is that they fund his own private research lab."

"Where is it? I thought I knew where everything was in the internal medicine department."

Rip gestured vaguely to the north. "He negotiated for some space in the Parkland Hospital building. Nobody is allowed in but Carter Resnick and the one tech that works there. I have to call over and let them know I'm coming. Then I knock, hand over the tubes of blood, and have the door slammed in my face."

"Why all the secrecy?"

"Sara, you know Jack Ingersoll as well as I do—probably better. What's his first priority?"

Sara didn't even have to think about it. "Jack Ingersoll."

"Right. And the fewer people who know about his research, the more secure he feels. I maintain the case log, but all I do is chart the patient responses and enter the lab results I'm given."

Sara pondered that for a moment. "That makes me wonder. If Jack wanted to keep any data hidden . . ."

"No, there are two parallel studies going on in Europe. Jandra sends updates to Ingersoll on a regular basis. The results are pretty much the same as the ones we're seeing. Almost identical, in fact."

"But you don't correspond with those investigators?"

"Don't even know their names. Jandra is keeping all that under wraps."

Sara decided not to pursue the matter. For now, it was probably enough that Chelsea was improving. There might be a firestorm when Ingersoll returned and discovered that two antibiotics had been added to his patient's treatment regimen, but she'd deal with that when it happened. She'd handled Jack's tantrums before. As for the secrecy . . . well, if Jack was hiding anything, it certainly wasn't preventing the EpAm848 from working yet another miracle, this time for her patient. And for now, that was enough.

Sara was deep in thought as she emerged from the medical center library. The force of the collision made her head snap up, and she found herself looking into kindly gray eyes that the lenses of wire-rimmed glasses couldn't hide. The hair was a little grayer, a little sparser. But the smile was still there, the one that had calmed her when the world seemed ready to crumble around her. "Dr. Ramsey. I'm so . . . I mean, I . . . What are you doing here?"

"Are you all right?" John Ramsey asked. "I'm sorry I collided with you. I guess I'm sort of preoccupied."

"I'm fine." She paused a beat. "Do you remember me?"

"Of course. Sara Miles. Or is it Ingersoll now? How have you been?"

She flinched inwardly. "It's Miles. I kept my maiden name. Which made it easier when Jack—" She hurried on before he could ask about that. "Never mind. I'm fine. After I finished my residency here, I was invited to stay on as a faculty member. I'm an Assistant Professor in Internal Medicine."

"Wonderful. Then we'll be colleagues. I'm retired, but I'll be joining the faculty part-time, working in the General Internal Medicine clinic."

"That's where I spend most of my time. And I look forward to working with you."

As she watched Ramsey's retreat down the hall, Sara was transported back to her senior year in medical school, to a time when she sat in Ramsey's private office and cried until she thought there couldn't possibly be any more tears in the world.

"I didn't get the residency I wanted," she snuffled. "I thought my interview in New York went really well. My grades are top 10 percent of the class. My letters of recommendation were perfect. Why didn't I get it?"

Ramsey had leaned back in his chair and tented his fingers. "Sara, you matched here at Parkland. That's a fantastic internal medicine residency, and I suspect there are about a hundred medical students who'd give their right arm for the opportunity you now have."

"But I had my heart set on Mount Sinai. That's where Brett's going to do his surgery residency. We had it all planned out."

"If you and Brett are really in love, you'll make the long-distance relationship work. If not, this is the way you'll find out." Ramsey leaned forward across his desk. "God has a plan. It may not always be the one we have in mind, and generally it's not on our schedule, but He's in control."

He'd been right, of course. It had taken Brett six months to become engaged to a socialite in New York, and Sara had met and married Jack halfway through her residency. Now her old mentor would be working with her, and at a time when it appeared that she might need some support. Funny how things work out. *Just like you said, Dr. Ramsey. Just like you said.*

John Ramsey tried to concentrate on what Kim was saying, but his mind wandered. The office he sat in was a marked contrast to the one occupied by Dr. Schaeffer. If the administrator worked in such a small, plain space, why did the Chairman have an office big enough to garage a fleet of cars? John had always pictured working at the medical school as something that was first class all the way. Apparently, that condition was sort of like the spring showers in North Texas—present in one spot and absent in another. And he suspected that the staff sometimes resided in the dry area.

The salary on the sheet Kim handed John was decent, although nothing like what he'd made in private practice. On the one hand, he had no overhead, no personnel decisions. Of course, neither did he have benefits—not as a part-time faculty member—but that could change. He found himself wondering if this would morph into a full-time position. What was it Schaeffer said? "If it works for both of us." In other words, it's a two-way street, brother, and if you don't produce, I'll hire someone else. *Welcome to academia.*

Kim paused, apparently through with what John had already decided was a canned presentation memorized through many repetitions. She looked at him and raised her eyebrows. "Any questions?"

He'd tuned out most of her spiel, but John figured he hadn't missed anything that wasn't in the packet she'd given him.

"Not right now, but I'll call you if I think of any." He got to his feet. "Would it be okay if I wander over to the General Internal Medicine clinic and get the lay of the land?"

"Sure. I'll take you over to GIM and introduce you. Just remember that you can't participate in patient care until we get the last of your paperwork approved."

In the clinic, Kim sought out a middle-aged blonde in nurse's scrubs. "Gloria, this is Dr. John Ramsey. Dr. Ramsey, this is Gloria, our head nurse." And with that, she hurried off.

Gloria's smile lit up the hallway. "We're looking forward to having you with us, Dr. Ramsey. I don't know who'll be assigned as your nurse, but for now, if you need anything, just ask me."

"Thanks. Today I'd just like to see how the clinic is laid out, so I don't get lost when I come back."

"No problem." The pager on her belt let out a muted buzz. "I've got to answer this, but I'll be around if you need me."

John peered through the open door of an exam room. It was clean, compact, and pretty much like one in his private office—when he had a private office. Of course, in that setting, when he encountered an especially perplexing problem he'd often told the patient, "I need to send you to a specialist at the medical school." Now he was that specialist, or at least one of them.

"May I help you?" The woman in the doorway was about John's age. She wore a clean white coat over a simple blue dress. Low-heeled shoes put her eyes at the level of John's chin. Those eyes, behind rimless glasses, were pale blue, the same color as Beth's. He felt tears coming, and fought them back.

"Thanks, but I'm just looking around." He extended his hand. "I'm Dr. John Ramsey."

She tucked a stray lock of salt-and-pepper hair behind her ear. "I'm Lillian Goodman, one of the GIM clinic doctors. I understand you'll be joining us here soon."

"As soon as the paperwork is finished." He made a sweeping gesture. "Apparently news travels fast around here."

"You'd be surprised at how efficient the grapevine is." Her expression softened a bit. "And on a personal note, I was sorry to hear about your loss. My husband died almost ten years ago, so I really do know what you're going through."

John was trying to frame an appropriate response when he heard footsteps in the hall—not running, but definitely moving at a fast clip. Gloria appeared in the doorway and said in a low, urgent voice, "Dr. Goodman, a woman just collapsed in the hall near the elevators."

Lillian was already in motion, and John fell in behind her, not exactly sure what his role should be but anxious to help. People milled around in the elevator foyer. John pushed through and saw an elderly woman crumpled on the floor like a marionette dropped by a careless puppeteer.

John knelt at the side of the unconscious woman. Lillian assumed the same position opposite him.

"Carotid pulse is weak and irregular," he said.

"She's breathing spontaneously, but sort of shallow," Lillian replied. She looked up. "Did anyone see what happened?"

There was a general murmur in the group, a mass shaking of heads.

A rumble of wheels and rattle of equipment announced Gloria's arrival. "Here's the crash cart. What can I do?"

"Give me a second," Lillian said. "Right now she's breathing on her own. John, check her blood pressure. I'm going to do a quick neuro exam."

In a moment, John straightened. "Mildly hypertensive. Heart rate about seventy but the rhythm is grossly irregular. Probably atrial fibrillation."

Lillian didn't look up. "Atrial fib fits. She's probably had an embolic stroke."

John had already reached the same conclusion. A small clot forming on the heart wall had broken loose and made its way to the brain.

"We need to get her out of here so we can start treatment," Lillian said.

"How—?"

Lillian stood and swept her gaze over the small crowd that had gathered. "We've got a medical emergency here, folks. I'm going to ask all you visitors to clear the area. If there are physicians or nurses here, please stand by. All other medical center employees please go back to your positions."

"Do we transport her into the clinic?" John asked.

"It's a nightmare getting through all the hallways between here and Parkland. It works better if we get EMT's up here, take her down in this elevator and around to the Parkland Emergency area by ambulance."

"I'm on it," Gloria said. "I've already called 911. EMT's should be here any minute."

"Her breathing's slowed down considerably," John said. "Want me to intubate her?"

Lillian looked him in the eye. "How are you at inserting an endotracheal tube?"

"Probably a little rusty. I'm due for recertification in advanced cardiac life support."

"I had my ACLS refresher last week. I'll tube her. You start an IV."

John was adjusting the flow of IV fluid while Lillian pumped an Ambu bag to inflate the woman's lungs when the elevator door slid open and two emergency medical technicians wheeled off a gurney. His heart was still racing when Lillian left to accompany the stretcher back onto the elevator and down to the waiting ambulance. He'd hoped joining the medical center faculty would energize him, give him a reason to get out of bed in the morning, but he certainly hadn't bargained for this much excitement on his first day on the job.

Rip felt the buzz of his cell phone against his hip. He saw the number on the caller ID display and thought, "Oh, boy. Here it comes."

He punched the button and said, "Dr. Ingersoll, I'm in a patient room. Hold one second until I can step outside." He excused himself and made for a quiet corner of the nurses' station. "Okay, now I can talk. Where are you?"

"I'm sitting in McCarran Airport, listening to the racket from about a million slot machines and waiting for my flight to take off. We were diverted here for a medical emergency, and then they found some sort of mechanical problem with the aircraft that kept us here overnight."

"What kind of medical emergency?"

"A passenger—Never mind. It doesn't concern either of us. I'm calling to see how that girl we enrolled in the study is responding to the medication."

Rip interpreted Ingersoll's statement about the medical emergency not concerning him as meaning he'd sat on his hands and let someone else handle it. He'd bet he was right. And he hadn't bothered to learn his patient's name. Just "that girl." Typical. "Chelsea's doing better. She's responding well to the antibiotic." He took a deep breath. "But there's a problem that may impact her eligibility for the study."

He waited for the firestorm he was sure would ensue, but instead there was only silence. "Dr. Ingersoll? Dr. Ingersoll?" Nothing.

Rip wondered at what point Ingersoll's phone had dropped the cell. In an ideal world, it would have been right after, "responding well to the antibiotic." He waited for Ingersoll to call back, but his phone remained silent. Finally, Rip decided that his time of reckoning had been postponed for a bit. He didn't know how long—minutes or hours—but he was sure of one thing. It would definitely come.

5

Sara pushed away the remains of her dinner. It didn't matter that she often couldn't recall what she'd eaten or what program she'd watched. The ritual—and that was what it had become—was designed to get her through one more evening. Frozen meals from the microwave, the TV for company, falling into bed, frequently awakening at four o'clock in the morning to the cries of an infant who wasn't there.

Most of the time Sara was halfway out of bed when she realized there was no baby in the house, no source of crying. That had ended almost two years ago when she found her infant son lying cold and lifeless in his crib. She knew about SIDS, of course. Sudden infant death syndrome was the fear of every reasonably intelligent mother, and as a physician she'd made sure she did all the right things. No exposure to smoke. Put the baby to bed on his back, always with a pacifier. But still, it had happened.

She'd tried to lean on Jack for comfort in the days that followed the baby's death, but he withdrew, acting as though Sara was somehow to blame in the matter. It must have been her fault. She'd given him a son who was flawed, unable to survive. Jack came home later and later, usually slipping into bed after she'd cried herself to sleep. Sometimes he didn't come home at all, offering a flimsy excuse or none at all.

Sara begged Jack to come with her for counseling. He refused, and eventually she stopped asking. She wasn't surprised when the divorce papers arrived, citing "incompatibility." That was almost two years ago. Now when they spoke, it was with forced civility. He had his life, and she had hers, such as it was.

Somehow the evening passed, as had all the others since Jack left her. Eventually, it was time for bed. She almost said sleep, but corrected the words as they passed through her mind. Sleep was never a certainty any more.

She padded from the bathroom in her robe, warm from the shower, but not free of the emotional chill that was the undercurrent to her life. She was turning back the covers when the ring of the phone startled her. Who could be calling? This wasn't her week on call. Certainly not family or friends. She had none to speak of.

"Hello?"

"Sara, this is Rip. Did I wake you?"

She glanced at the clock beside her bed. A little after ten. "Not at all. Just settling in for the night. What's up?"

He cleared his throat. "I wasn't sure whether you'd want to know, but I decided—"

"What is it, Rip?"

"Does Jack drink?"

Sara thought back to their time together. "One glass of wine and Jack relaxed. Two glasses and he turned maudlin. Three glasses freed his inner self—belligerent and self-centered."

Rip's sigh came through clearly. "Bingo! He called me a few minutes ago. Apparently, he was pretty upset about all the delays in his trip. He was flying first class, and I'm guessing he couldn't turn down the free alcohol. After he landed here at DFW, he couldn't remember where he'd parked his car, so he called and asked me to come to the airport and pick him up. I suggested he take a taxi. He ordered me to come. I politely declined and told him that wasn't in my job description."

"How did you leave it?"

"I hung up on him. He called back a couple of times but I didn't answer. I wondered if this sort of behavior was unusual."

"Yes and no. Jack didn't drink much at all after we were first married. Then . . . then the baby died, and he started to drink heavily. And when he'd had a bit too much, he got really belligerent."

"Did he . . . did he ever hit you?"

Sara teased a tear off her cheek with her finger. "No, if I stood up to him he'd generally break down and ask me to forgive him. I suspect tomorrow morning he'll try to act like this never happened."

"Well, I hope he doesn't have a hangover in the morning. I have to tell him we may have compromised his study protocol in Chelsea's case, and I'm going to need him to be in the best possible mood."

"Why don't you let me break the news?" Sara said. She thought back to Jack's reaction after she'd shaken him awake to tell him his son was dead. If she could get through that, nothing Jack Ingersoll could say or do would bother her.

Bob Wolfe eased warily into the visitor's chair across from David Patel. Wolfe's shirt was plastered to his skin, held there by the sweat that began to form the moment Patel's secretary delivered this summons. He rolled his shoulders and leaned forward, trying without success to loosen the broadcloth straitjacket. "You wanted to see me?"

"Do you think Dr. Ingersoll got the message?"

Typical of Patel. No time given to social niceties. No wasted words. Down to the nitty-gritty. Wolfe wanted to reach across the desk and shake the man, but instead he pasted a confident smile on his face. "I sat him down and had a heart-to-heart. He understands that the data on Jandramycin has to be good, no exceptions."

"You use the carrot and stick?"

"Sure. The carrot was easy. More research grants. Co-authorship on every paper on the drug. We'll write them; all he has to do is add his name. Jandra will pressure the journals to print them. No problem."

"And?"

"He's our number one consultant, lecturing other doctors about the drug and its uses. Trips to speak all over the U.S. When we release Jandramycin overseas, he becomes a world traveler at our expense. Everything first class, with a handsome honorarium for each lecture."

Patel nodded once, practically an "attaboy" for him. Wolfe decided not to wait for the next question. "And the stick was even easier. If he crosses us up, we pull all his research money. No more lectures. No more papers. We could even—"

Patel held up one finger and smirked. "How's this? If he doesn't perform, he can expect more than the loss of all those perks. We'll get the word out that, although his research was valid, it was the work of others, and he stole it. We'll systematically destroy his reputation."

"Good idea. I'll call him in a day or two, see how things are going, and squeeze him with this."

Patel pulled a stack of papers toward him and began signing them. As Wolfe pushed back his chair, obviously dismissed, the CEO muttered under his breath, "That's what they pay me for, Bob. That's what they pay me for."

"Dr. Ramsey, I'm Verna Wells. I'll be working with you on the days you're here in the clinic."

The woman sitting at the clinic nurses' station smiled, showing a row of white teeth in a face dark as rich chocolate. Her royal blue clinic jacket had a floral pattern, and there was a small gold cross on the lapel. Her only jewelry was a plain gold wedding band and a simple watch with a leather strap.

"Thanks. I'm looking forward to being here. You're probably going to have to answer a ton of questions for me until I get my feet on the ground."

"You'll pick up the routine fast enough. Let me show you which exam rooms you'll be using."

After a half hour, John's head was spinning. "Verna, I give up. Do you think that's enough to let me function for my first day or so?"

She laughed, a hearty sound that seemed to come from deep inside her. Never had the term *belly laugh* seemed so appropriate, because once Verna came out from behind her desk John realized she carried about two hundred pounds on a five-foot-four-inch frame. "I think you'll do just fine. And if you have any questions or problems, buzz for me. Remember where the buttons are in the treatment rooms?"

"I remember. Now how long do I have before I start?"

She glanced at her wrist. "You've got about half an hour before your first appointment. You might want to get some coffee." Verna looked over John's shoulder. "Here comes Dr. Goodman. She generally goes for coffee every morning. Maybe she'll show you the way."

"Verna," Lillian Goodman said, "are you getting Dr. Ramsey squared away?"

"Well, he doesn't seem to know much, but I think he's teachable." She grinned. "Bring me back my usual?"

"Coffee with double cream and three sugars. Got it." Lillian looked at John. "Want to come along?"

John followed her through a maze of corridors, and soon they were walking into a moderate-sized cafeteria. "I give up. Where are we?"

"University Hospital. Really not too far from the faculty clinic where we started, and they have a great cafeteria."

He shook his head. "I staffed residents at Parkland Hospital for years, but I've never been in a lot of these buildings."

"Don't worry. You'll be able to find your way around real soon."

They ordered, including coffee for Verna, and John insisted on paying. "Do we have time to sit down and drink this, or do we need to hurry back?"

"We've got a few minutes." She pointed to a door in the far wall. "That's the staff dining room. It's quieter there."

"What do you hear about the lady who had the stroke outside the elevators the other day?"

Lillian's face clouded over. "She never regained consciousness. Died within an hour. MRI confirmed an embolic stroke, but while she was in the radiology department she had a cardiac arrest. We couldn't resuscitate her."

"Autopsy?"

"The family refused one. And since there were at least two possible causes of death, we chose not to push."

John grimaced. "I guess I've lost my first patient since joining the staff here."

"Not really. All you did was take her blood pressure and start an IV. She wasn't really your patient." Lillian blew across the surface of her paper cup, then sipped. "And I guess you can be glad of that."

"Why?"

"Her family is threatening to file a malpractice suit against the medical center and every doctor who had anything to do with her treatment."

In the midnight darkness, the lamp spilled a pool of yellow light onto the papers strewn helter-skelter over the scarred surface of his desk. The page shook in his hand as he stared at the figures scrawled in the margins. It all came down to this.

The man scrabbled through the mass of documents and pulled another sheet. What was the line from *Macbeth*? "If it were done when 'tis done, then 'twere well it were done quickly." Decision time.

He eased himself from the chair like the unfolding of a carpenter's rule. Do this, and he could say good-bye to this tiny office. He envisioned a corner suite with a view—maybe even a private washroom. But tonight the community restroom down the hall would do.

The man locked himself in a stall and dug in his pocket for the dog-eared match folder he'd carried all day. He struck one match. It fizzled impotently. Two more attempts before one lit. He bent it against its fellows and the whole folder ignited. He touched the improvised torch to the papers he held and watched as they burst into flame.

Would the smoke set off the fire alarm, activate the sprinklers? He cursed under his breath for not thinking of that. He held the flaming mass lower in the toilet and fanned the air furiously with his free hand. The ashes dropped into the water, and he breathed again. He flushed twice, and it was over.

He washed his hands, splashed water on his face, and walked back to his office. For good or for evil—probably a bit of both—it was done.

Jack Ingersoll reached out to punch the intercom button on his phone and was gratified to see that his hands were almost steady. *A lesser man would have a tremor this morning. I should have been a surgeon.* "Martha, page Dr. Pearson and tell him I'll be ready to make rounds in fifteen minutes. We'll start in the ICU."

"Yes, sir," Martha called through the open door that connected her office with his.

Ingersoll ground his teeth. Would that woman never learn to use the intercom? Oh, well. It wasn't worth the hassle of trying to get her replaced. No, he'd just wait a bit. If things went as he expected, it wouldn't be long before he'd have a nice new office, along with an administrative assistant that he didn't have to share with two other doctors, someone who would cater to his wishes. And that day couldn't come soon enough for him.

He swiveled in his chair and turned away from the windows and the bright sun that streamed in through them. The two Advil he'd washed down with black coffee seemed to be helping his headache. Another five minutes with his eyes closed, and he'd begin rounds. He hoped Pearson hadn't fouled up anything in his absence. At this point, every Jandramycin patient was pure gold. And he couldn't afford any slipups.

"Jack, got a minute?"

He opened his eyes and saw Sara in the doorway, one hesitant foot over the threshold. He couldn't recall that she'd come to his office since they'd divorced. Quick encounters on the ward or in the cafeteria, an occasional phone conversation about a patient, but never a personal visit. What was up? "Sure. Come in. Sit down."

She took one of the two visitors' chairs. "I won't keep you. I know you're about to start rounds, but I wanted to let you know what happened while you were gone."

He listened intently as she told him about the girl—what was her name? Chelsea. That was it. She told him about Chelsea's sepsis. What were the odds? Sepsis from *Staph luciferus*, responding to Jandramycin, only to be replaced by a garden-variety but potentially lethal infection from an indwelling urinary catheter. As Sara related the details, his mind raced to parse the implications.

Apparently, Jandramycin wasn't effective against *E. coli*. No harm there. It had a specific niche, and if the drug was never used against any bacteria except *Staph luciferus*, it would still have a secure position in the pharmacotherapy of infections.

The girl was still receiving Jandramycin along with the other drugs for her *E. coli* infection, and all the medications seemed to be working. That meant there was no incompatibility among them. Good to know and not the kind of information that would come up in a normal study protocol.

Would the data from this case have to be excluded because of the confounding factors of the second infection and additional antibiotics? Ingersoll thought back to his conversation with Wolfe. *We may have to be creative in the way we handle our data.* So be it, then. He might have to be creative in the way he entered this information into the database, conveniently ignoring the additional drugs, but he couldn't afford to lose even a single patient from the study. He'd handle it.

Sara seemed to be running down, so he brought his full attention back to her. "So little . . . little Chelsea is getting better. Is that right?"

"Yes. Her temp's down. White count returning to normal. No protein or cells in her urine this morning. I think she's turned the corner."

"Well, that's the important thing," Ingersoll said. "I'll look in on her this morning, but you and Pearson should be able to handle things from here on out. You can call me if there are any questions."

Sara frowned. "Jack, we were really afraid you'd erupt when you heard we had to go outside the study protocol to treat her. I'm glad you're taking it this well."

Ingersoll summoned up his most sincere look. "The patient is better. That's what's important." He rose and walked around the desk. He took his ex-wife's hand in both of his. "Sara, I appreciate your coming by to tell me in person. And I hope you won't be a stranger. I think we had something really good at one time, and I'm sorry I let it slip away while I was depressed about the death of our son. Maybe we can get it back."

6

Sara snuggled beneath the covers. Life was good. She and Jack had a lot of good years ahead of them, and the prospect made her smile. Maybe she'd give up her practice at the medical school to be a real stay-at-home mom. That was something a lot of her female colleagues talked about, and although none of them had actually made that move, it was obvious to Sara that deep down, most of them would like nothing better.

She rolled over and reached across the bed, but a cry stopped her arm in mid-reach. Her mother's instinct drove her out of bed, and in a few seconds she was shrugging into her robe as her feet darted here and there in search of her slippers. Don't turn on the light. Don't want to wake Jack.

The cries were louder now, and Sara quickened her steps. She paused at the doorway of the nursery, and the cries stopped as suddenly as they began. She shuffled across the carpet and peered over the edge of the crib. The bundle it held was jammed up against the far corner. She lifted the corner of the blanket and reached forth a hesitant hand to touch the angelic face. It was cold and unmoving as marble.

Her cry began as a low moan deep in her throat and escalated into a siren-like shriek.

Sara sat up in bed and reached for the light at her bedside. Another nightmare. No, not another one. The same one. The same dream that had tormented her since the original scene played out.

There was no hope of sleep now. She shoved aside the bedclothes, grabbed her robe, and padded on slipper-shod feet into the kitchen. Maybe a snack would help. She passed the bathroom and remembered the bottle in the medicine chest. One at bedtime as needed for sleep. Her doctor prescribed them after the baby died, but Sara refused to take them. No, she wanted to feel the full force of her grief. Jack, on the other hand, took them regularly. She'd watched him lie there in drug-induced sleep and hated him for it. How could he ignore the loss . . . their loss?

The prescription was old now. Would the pills still be good? Why had she kept the half-full bottle anyway? She had no intention of drugging herself to sleep. Of course, there were times when she'd wanted to take all of them and fall into that deepest and most permanent of sleeps. But not tonight. She wasn't that desperate. Not yet.

Sara shivered, even though the house was warm, and hurried into the kitchen. She spread a stack of crackers with peanut butter, poured a glass of milk, and eased into her accustomed chair in front of the TV. Maybe there'd be something on that would help her relax.

Sara munched on a cracker and wondered why she'd dreamed about being in bed with Jack. After the baby died, she'd gone out of her way to avoid him, even made an effort to exclude him from her dreams. Why had she let him back in now? Was it because of what he'd said? "I think we had something really good. . . . Maybe we can get it back."

Then again, Jack seemed different today, more interested in what she said. He actually remembered the name of their mutual patient, asked how Chelsea was doing. Could he have changed? Was it even possible for Jack Ingersoll to change? And was she willing to take that chance?

As she pondered the question, Sara flashed on the end of her meeting with Jack. What was it he said? He was depressed over "the death of our son." Our son! He had a name, Jack. Actually, he had your name: Jack Jr. But you just called him "our son."

What was it the Bible said? "Can the leopard change his spots?" No, and apparently neither could Jack Ingersoll.

Dr. John Ramsey looked for what seemed like the hundredth time at the file folder on his kitchen table. The label read "Malpractice Insurance." A few days ago, he'd rescued it from one of the boxes of files he'd brought home from his office and shoved into a corner of his garage. He'd blown the dust off it and put it on the table, but today he decided it was time to open the folder and face what was inside.

He took one last sip of cold coffee, picked up the phone, and dialed the number he'd printed with a Sharpie on the cover of the folder.

"Insurance office."

"This is Dr. John Ramsey. I need to speak with Mr. Alexander about my malpractice insurance."

"Is this about a claim?" The woman's voice was flat, almost bored. She must have these conversations every day, but to John this was a new, and rather scary, situation.

"It's about a possible claim. I need some information. That's why I need to speak with Mr. Alexander."

"May I have your policy number?"

John figured he might as well talk to a wall. "I've canceled my original policy, but I have tail coverage. And I need to ask Mr. Alexander a question about that policy."

Nothing seemed to faze this woman. "And what is that policy number?"

After giving her the number of his policy and waiting through a series of clicks, followed by three minutes of what passed for soft rock music on hold, John heard a familiar voice. "Dr. Ramsey, I hope you're enjoying retirement."

"Not as much as I was before I began talking with your secretary." John reined in his desire to vent. No benefit there. "I have sort of an unusual question."

Alexander listened without comment as John explained his visit to the clinic at the medical center and the part he'd played in the scenario that followed. "Now I'm hearing that her family may file suit against everyone involved. And I guess my question is whether I'm covered."

The silence on the other end of the line made John wince. What he was hoping for was a quick, "Of course." Instead, he heard only the rattling of paper.

"Are you there?" John asked.

"Yes, I'm looking through your contract. Of course, you canceled your original malpractice insurance when you retired, so that wasn't in force when this incident occurred. However, you bought tail coverage to insure you against claims brought after that original policy ended. But this is a new incident, so in that case . . . Hmmm. Tell you what. I don't want to say anything until I run all this by one of our attorneys. Can I get back to you?"

John gave Alexander his phone number and hung up with a deep sense of foreboding. If the agent had to do that much research, there was a good chance that his position in malpractice litigation arising from the incident at the medical center was going to be pretty much what his patients always complained about when they had to wear a hospital gown: uncovered and vulnerable.

Sara entered the hospital room and her heart leaped when she saw Chelsea sitting in a chair smiling back at her. Gone were the IV's. The hiss of oxygen was wonderfully absent. The only reminders of Chelsea's stay in the ICU were several potted plants that hadn't yet been loaded in the Fergusons' car.

"Ready to go home, Chelsea?" Sara had a hard time believing this was the same teenager who'd seemed at death's door not so long ago.

"Doctor, we can't thank you enough," Mrs. Ferguson said. "Dr. Pearson was by earlier this morning. He said because Chelsea was in the study for that new drug—Jana something-or-other—he'd need to see her in a couple of weeks to draw some blood for follow-up studies. Frankly, if that Dr. Ingersoll had said that, I'd tell him to forget it. But Chelsea says she has no problem coming back if you or Dr. Pearson say she should."

"Is that right, Chelsea?" Sara said. "Will you come back?"

Chelsea nodded. Even after she was out of the ICU and well on her way to recovery, Sara couldn't recall hearing the girl speak more than a dozen words.

"I think it would be a good idea to do that," Sara said. "If you'll call my nurse, she can set up an appointment to see me in the clinic. Either Dr. Pearson or I can draw the blood samples while you're there, so you don't have to spend a lot of time waiting in the lab."

Sara did one last exam of her patient and pronounced her fit to go. "I'll just sign the order, and a nurse's aide will put you in a wheelchair and take you downstairs. Chelsea, are you okay here by yourself while your mom brings the car around?"

"Sure." When she finally spoke, Chelsea's voice was soft, her speech hesitant. Well, a near-death experience would probably do that to you.

Sara was halfway to the nurses' station when Mrs. Ferguson hurried up behind her. "Doctor, I want to thank you again. I'm sure you and Dr. Pearson saved Chelsea's life. If there's ever anything I can do—"

"No need to thank me. The fact that Chelsea is able to go home will be reward enough."

"And when we come back, I want to find out how to lodge a complaint against that terrible Dr. Ingersoll."

Sara hesitated. "We'll talk about that later. After all, it was the medication that Dr. Ingersoll helped develop that saved Chelsea's life. And maybe he was having a bad day when he first saw her."

As she pulled the chart from the rack and began to write discharge orders, Sara wondered why she'd defended a man she'd hated for so long.

Dr. Lillian Goodman passed a steaming paper cup to Verna Wells. "Have you seen Dr. Ramsey this morning?"

Verna took a sip and nodded approvingly. "You always get it right. Thanks, Dr. Goodman." She moved aside a stack of files and set the cup carefully on the desk at the nurses' station. "Dr. Ramsey won't be here today. The schedule Gloria gave me shows him working three days a week."

"Oh. Well, I just wanted to see how he was doing. I know it can be intimidating, getting used to a new practice location."

Verna eased herself out of her chair and followed Lillian down the hall. "I know he'll appreciate your help. He seems to be getting the hang of things just fine, but I'm really glad to see you two becoming friends."

Lillian drained her own cup and tossed it in a wastebasket. "We're just colleagues, Verna. I'd do the same for any new doctor, male or female."

"Dr. Goodman, it's time you thought of getting a life outside these four walls. Dr. Ramsey's a nice man. There's nothing wrong with noticing that . . . or even doing something about it."

Lillian was shaking her head before Verna finished talking. "John Ramsey is trying to recover from the death of his wife. He's vulnerable."

"But you two seem—"

Lillian held up her hand. "I know what John feels right now. I've been down that road. He needs someone to talk with. He needs someone to care about what he's going through. He needs an occasional hug, a human touch. He needs . . . Well, what he needs is a good friend, and that's what I intend to be. But I'm not going to let it get more serious." *I can't. Not right now.*

No one knew he was in New York. He'd used a false ID at airport security, paid cash for his ticket. He traveled from Kennedy Airport via public transportation, spent the night in a cheap hotel under yet another name, walked to this building today carrying his toiletries and dirty linen in an anonymous briefcase. Tonight he'd be back home. And he hoped he'd be much richer for the trip.

The only light in the room where he now waited was the faint flicker from a small black-and-white TV on the table in front of him. A secure feed led to that TV from the fish-eye lens of a camera concealed in the crown molding of the conference room one floor below. The camera let him see all twelve men gathered around the mahogany table, while a microphone transmitted sound from the room. The men fidgeted and whispered to each other, most of them ignoring coffee that grew cold in their cups. He could hear an occasional comment. "What's going on?" "Why all the secrecy?"

He reviewed the security measures on which he'd insisted. The room in which he sat was a vacant office well removed from where the board members of Darlington Pharmaceuticals were gathered. Both rooms had been swept for bugs only ninety minutes ago and pronounced clean. He'd been in place for an hour before the first man arrived. He wouldn't leave until an hour after the last one departed, but first he'd wipe down every surface he could have touched. He didn't think they'd try to identify him by fingerprints, but he wanted nothing left to chance. Tonight he'd leave New York, having never really been there.

There was no camera in his room, but even if there were, his face was shrouded in darkness. He fiddled with the small gadget attached to the microphone on the table in front of him. It would distort his voice, making it completely unidentifiable, even if someone chose to record it and try to match it to a voiceprint later. Ridiculous? He thought not. Just leaving nothing to chance.

One floor below him, the man at the head of the table, the CEO of Darlington Pharmaceuticals, stood and cleared his throat. Conversations died in midsentence. "Gentlemen, I'll get right to it. You all know that we have tried to acquire Jandra Pharmaceuticals. Even in their weakened cash position, they've turned down our offers. I believe we now have an opportunity to snatch up the company for even less money."

"Ridiculous. We have inside information that they're about to launch a new product that will revive the company." The speaker's hands were in constant motion, fiddling with the pencil in front of him, adjusting his tie, centering and recentering a legal pad. He looked around the room before returning his gaze to the CEO. "What's changed?"

"The man whose voice you're about to hear can put a stop to the success of that new product. Matter of fact, he guarantees it." The CEO took a sip of water. "Of course, there's a price. But I can assure you, it's worth it."

In the darkened room, the man leaned toward the microphone and spoke slowly and distinctly: "Gentlemen, Jandra is about to launch a new antibiotic, Jandramycin. It offers the only cure for the deadly epidemic of *Staph luciferus* that is sweeping the world, taking over two thousand lives so far. Jandramycin is, and will be touted as, a 'wonder drug.' However, it has shortcomings and faults. These have been purposefully hidden during the various phases of drug testing. I'm in a position to bring them to light. The result will sink Jandramycin and send Jandra stock plummeting."

He let the buzz around the room die down. Someone would ask the question, and it turned out to be the oldest man on the board, who asked three. "How can you do it, why are you doing it, and how much will it cost us?"

He smiled. "I won't answer the first two questions, but I assure you I have my methods and my reasons. As for the price, it's ten million dollars, wired into a bank account in the Cayman Islands. Four million up front. Another three million when Jandra accepts your offer to buy them. The final three million when your acquisition is complete. These terms are nonnegotiable. You have fifteen minutes to decide."

Everyone wanted to talk at once. Questions flew, and the CEO fought to keep order.

The first question, of course, was "Can we afford this?"

The answer there was simple. The four million was manageable. Everything else was dependent on a successful acquisition, and if that happened, the price was right.

Gradually, the buzz died down. The CEO rapped his water glass on the table. "Gentlemen, it's decision time. Price is not the crux of our debate. At issue is whether we support and underwrite this piece of industrial espionage. If we vote to accept this proposal, nothing that took place in this room can ever be revealed. Not to a spouse, a business partner, even in the confessional. Hands for 'yes.'"

Some hands shot up decisively. Others eased up gingerly. But in a moment, every hand was raised.

7

HOW MANY PATIENTS IN THE STUDY NOW?" INGERSOLL THREW THE QUES-tion over his shoulder as he strode through the tunnel that linked the medical school with University Hospital.

Rip didn't break stride, nor did he reach for the note cards in the pocket of his white coat. He knew the number of patients who'd received Jandramycin, their names and diagnoses, and how they'd been at their last follow-up appointments. "Thirty-nine counting the patient we put on Jandramycin yesterday."

"Oh, that was the woman—"

"It's a man. Mr. Rankin is a fifty-one-year-old school prin-cipal with sepsis from *Staph luciferus*, acquired when a cut on his foot from a camping trip became infected. He—"

"No need for all that. Thirty-nine. That's what I want to know."

The two men walked along in silence, Rip carefully keeping a pace behind his chief. Most doctors in postgraduate pro-grams became good friends with the men and women under whom they trained. By the time a fellowship was over, they had formed a collegial bond. That wasn't the case here, though. From day one, Rip had received the unspoken message: You're

80

here to learn from watching me, but I'm in charge, and don't you forget it.

"How many cases do we need before Jandra can submit their new drug app?" Rip said.

Ingersoll mumbled something.

"Sorry. I didn't hear that."

Ingersoll didn't slow or even turn his head. "I said the application for approval of a new drug was filed with the FDA two weeks ago."

At the doors of the ICU, both men found their way blocked by a cluster of people. The women cried, the men tried vainly to comfort them, and there was about the group an aura of defeat and despair. Rip had seen that scene too many times, but it never failed to move him. Someone didn't make it. For the doctor, the aftermath meant an hour's worth of paperwork. For the family, it was the beginning of a lifetime of "what if's" and "if only's."

Slowly the group moved into the waiting room, opening a path for the doctors. Ingersoll was about to push through the swinging doors when Rip said, "How could they apply two weeks ago? I recall being told they needed at least forty patients from us before they could file the app. Two weeks ago we had thirty-seven."

"Let me worry about that. Your job is to keep the study running smoothly." Ingersoll strode to the nurse's desk, where he stopped and cleared his throat loudly. "I need the chart for my patient—" He looked pointedly at Rip.

"Cletus Rankin. Room eighteen."

"For my patient, Cletus Rankin, in room eighteen," Ingersoll repeated, as though the nurse hadn't heard Rip.

Ingersoll took the proffered chart, scanned it, and nodded with satisfaction. "Defervescing already. Good, good."

Just like Ingersoll. Use a five-dollar word instead of saying, "His fever's coming down." "Yes, he seems to be responding well. I looked in on him earlier this morning, and—"

"I'll just pop in to see him myself."

It only took Ingersoll a minute to make what Rip termed his usual cameo appearance: nod to the family, put a hand on the patient (didn't seem to matter where, it was the touching that counted), assure everyone that things were going well, and exit.

"You have the lab results from yesterday?"

"Aren't they on the chart?" Rip said.

"If they were, I would have seen them. Did you deliver the blood samples?"

"Yes, sir. To both the hospital lab and Resnick."

"Then get the results, and see that they get onto the ICU chart."

"Will do."

Ingersoll pushed back his sleeve and consulted a watch that appeared to have every function except the position of the International Space Station. "I'm leaving this afternoon to attend a meeting in Bermuda, where I'll be speaking on Jandramycin. Take care of things while I'm gone. See you Monday."

Rip ducked back into Mr. Rankin's room to answer questions the family had apparently been hesitant to ask his chief. He checked the chart, wrote a couple of orders, and decided he'd treat himself to a mocha latte before tracking down the errant lab reports.

The Starbucks in the medical center's basement was crowded. Rip had almost decided to sit outside in the courtyard when he saw Carter Resnick at a table for two in the corner. His first inclination was to ignore the research associate, but at the last minute he veered off toward Resnick. "Mind if I join you?"

"Help yourself." Resnick moved his briefcase from the second chair and gestured toward it. "The great one turn you loose long enough to get a cup of coffee?"

Rip eased into the vacant chair. "He's leaving for Bermuda. But there's still plenty of work for both of us to do. What are you doing here?"

"I had to get out of the lab for a bit. You can't believe how boring it is, running lab tests on our patients, collating data. I wish Ingersoll would let me have some patient contact." Resnick sipped his drink—he'd also opted for a latte—then swiped at the foam moustache on his upper lip.

Rip tasted his coffee, found it too hot to drink, and set it aside, spilling a few drops in the process. "What do you know about the new drug application for Jandramycin?"

"Not much. I know Jandra said they wanted a hundred patients before they submit."

Rip toyed with his cup, making wet circles on the table. "And how many patients have we collected?"

"You know that as well as I do. Thirty-nine."

"Ingersoll told me this morning that the NDA has already gone in. Where did all the patients come from?"

"There are a couple of investigators in Germany, but they didn't start collecting patients until after we did."

"So how did Jandra come up with the volume of data needed for a new drug application?"

Resnick finished his drink, this time ignoring the foam moustache. It made his Cheshire cat grin more pronounced. "It's magic, isn't it?"

John Ramsey had been in the medical center's Faculty Club before, but never as a faculty member. The club wasn't what the name implied—no dark wood, overstuffed furniture, and faculty members sitting around sipping drinks and smoking cigars. It was bright and airy and highly functional. Windows on three sides showed views of Dallas or the buildings of the Southwestern campus. Tables were set for groups of diners from two to ten. Steam tables held several entrees. There was a well-stocked salad bar. But for John, the best thing on the menu, and his lunch of choice, was a Reuben sandwich on pretzel bread, and that was what he now held.

"Thanks for meeting me for lunch, Mark." John took a bite of his sandwich, chewed, and washed it down with iced tea.

"Glad to do it," Dr. Mark Wilcox said. "Besides, I don't get invited to the Faculty Club at the medical center very often."

"You can thank my chairman," John said. "He let me charge this to his account. Part-time faculty members don't get this kind of perk."

Mark put down his BLT. "How are you doing? Be honest with me. How long as it been since you lost Beth? Three months?"

"Closer to four. And not a day goes by that I don't miss her. But I'm trying to get my life back together. That's why I begged Don Schaeffer for this job. Unfortunately, I may have gotten myself into trouble before I saw my first patient." John took another swallow of iced tea, then cleared his throat. "That's why I invited you here today. I need some advice."

"Ask away, although I doubt there's anything in medicine I know that you don't. I'm a lowly GP who's fresh out of medical school, and you're a wise old internal medicine specialist."

"Don't sell yourself short, Mark. When I first met you on ward rounds during your third year of medical school, it didn't take me long to realize that tall, redheaded fellow who asked so many questions was pretty sharp. Then one of your classmates told me you were a practicing lawyer before you applied to medical school. That explained your maturity, I guess, but the fact that you chose to leave a good career to start over in medicine was what really impressed me."

"Nothing to it. I just decided I could help people a lot more by trying to cure their ills than by suing doctors who hadn't been able to." Mark frowned at the man who'd become his mentor. "Are you in legal trouble?"

"I may be." John related his story in short, unemotional sentences, much as he'd present a case to a consultant. He finished with, "The family says they're going to sue the medical center and everyone involved. So what do you think my exposure will be?"

Mark tented his fingers and pursed his lips.

Thinking before he talks. No wonder I thought he'd be a good doctor.

"I could give you the standard lawyer's disclaimer. I need more facts. I need to read your malpractice insurance policy, including the tail coverage. I need— Never mind. You just want my opinion. My opinion is that you assisted the physician in charge of the activity in trying to save the life of a patient. You may have done more than the average citizen, but you never went beyond your capabilities and training, never breached the standard of care. The medical center's policy aside, you're probably protected under the Good Samaritan Law of the state."

John let out a breath he didn't know he was holding. "So you think I don't have to worry?"

"Oh, we always have to worry, all of us. Doctors might as well have targets painted on their backs, with signs saying 'Sue me.' You definitely could be named in a suit. If so, your lawyer should be able to mount a good defense. That would cost you some legal fees and some time, but you'd have a decent chance of coming out okay."

"And if I need a lawyer?"

Mark took a bite of his neglected sandwich, chewed, and swallowed. "Lucky for you I'm still licensed to practice law. And I'm running a special right now: defense of one lawsuit in return for lunch. So I guess you've got a free one coming."

John only managed to choke down half his sandwich, but Mark seemed to have no difficulty finishing his, following it with a trip to what John had heard his colleagues call the "sin bar"—a table laden with tempting desserts.

Mark returned with a piece of pecan pie. "Sure you don't want something?" he asked.

"No, I think I'd better just watch you." John waited while Mark took a bite. "Tell me honestly. Do you miss practicing law? Do you ever wonder if it was a mistake to give that up, go to medical school for four years, and have to start all over again building a practice?"

Mark chewed his pie and swallowed. "Sometimes I think that being a lawyer is sort of like being a member of the Mafia. You know, 'Once in, never out.' As it turns out, I'm sort of melding medicine and law. I have a small family practice, but I also review malpractice cases for insurance companies that cover doctors. I do a little consulting for pharmaceutical companies." He grinned. "And I help out old friends who have legal problems."

Mark finished his pie and pushed the plate aside. "Why don't I drop by your clinic next week? You can give me your malpractice policy, and I'll have a chance to see how the faculty operate their private clinics. Remember, all my medicine clinics were at Parkland."

"Honestly, the surroundings may be nicer, but we pretty much practice the same brand of medicine we teach the residents. Anyway, you're welcome to drop by. Monday is my next day in the clinic, and I'll bring the policy then. If you come around noon, maybe I can talk Donald Schaeffer into springing for another lunch at the Faculty Club."

Outside, the two men stood in front of the elevators when John heard, "Dr. Ramsey. How are you?"

John turned and saw Sara Miles standing behind them. "Sara, were you in the Faculty Club?"

"Hardly. I had a sandwich in the food court. I'm just waiting for Rip—er, Dr. Pearson to bring some papers for me to fill out. I have a patient in his drug study." She looked pointedly at Mark, and when neither of the men moved, she stuck out her hand. "I'm Sara Miles, one of John's colleagues."

"Mark Wilcox. Dr. Ramsey was sort of a mentor to me while I was in med school. And it's a pleasure to meet you."

"He mentored me, too, so we have that in common." Sara looked at her watch. "Well, Rip must have gotten delayed. I guess I'll have to track him down." She extended her hand again. "Dr. Wilcox—"

"Please, it's Mark."

"Mark, it was nice to meet you. John, I'll see you Monday."

Mark ignored the ding of the elevator and moved away from the opening door. "So that good-looking lady is one of your colleagues?"

"Yes. But she's a little young for me."

"I wasn't thinking about you," Mark said. He stepped into the elevator. "See you Monday."

It was Monday morning, and Sara was trying without success to get her engine revved up for the week ahead. She slumped in a chair at the doctors' dictation station in the clinic. Her second cup of coffee was at her elbow while she looked over the charts for her appointments that day.

Gloria tapped on the doorframe, entered, and handed her a pink phone message slip. "You have a call from one of your Jandramycin patients. Mrs. Ferguson. She's worried about Chelsea."

"Chelsea's been out of the hospital for over a month. This is probably something entirely different." She dropped the slip on the desk and picked up her pen. "I'll call her at noon, after I've finished seeing patients."

Gloria didn't move. "I'd call her now. Mrs. Ferguson was almost hysterical."

Sara had come to trust Gloria's assessment of situations like this. She nodded, picked up the phone, and punched in a number. Mrs. Ferguson answered on the first ring.

"This is Dr. Miles. My nurse said you had some concerns about Chelsea."

The normally calm woman was obviously distraught. "This morning, she couldn't get out of bed. It was like the muscles in her legs wouldn't work. I had to carry her down the stairs. She's lying on the sofa right now, crying."

"Did this come on suddenly?"

"Yes. She was fine yesterday. This morning, she can't walk."

"And nothing out of the ordinary happened to her yesterday? No injury, even a slight one? She didn't eat something unusual?"

"No. We went to church in the morning. I remember telling friends I was so thankful Chelsea was back to normal."

Sara's mental Rolodex began to flip. "Is she in pain?"

"Not really. She says her legs tingle and feel numb. Mainly she's scared and frustrated."

"Any other signs? Headache? Nausea? Visual symptoms?" She went through a list of symptoms, getting a negative response to all her questions.

"What is it? Is she having a stroke? Could she have been poisoned or something?"

Sara shook her head until she realized the woman on the other end of the phone couldn't see it. "We don't know," she said. "I'll have to see her. Can you get her here, or do we need to call an ambulance?"

"I'll bring her in the car. Shall I bring her to the clinic?"

Sara checked her watch. Her patients for the morning were already arriving. The odds of having to admit Chelsea for evaluation and treatment were pretty good. "No, bring her to the Emergency Room here at the medical center. I'll let them know you're coming so they can call me."

Fortunately, Sara's first few patients were follow-ups that required very little concentration on her part. While she adjusted medication doses, reviewed lab reports, and took care of a few minor problems, her mind churned with the differential diagnosis of sudden and unexplained weakness.

Finally, at mid-morning, Gloria tapped on the exam room door, as Sara was finishing with a patient. "Excuse me, Doctor. The ER just called. They're ready for you."

"Thanks. Would you tell the patients who are waiting to see me that I've been called away for an emergency? I should be less than an hour. Offer to reschedule them if they don't want to wait."

Sara hurried through the tunnels connecting the buildings in the medical center, turning right and left without conscious thought until she reached the Emergency Room. She found Chelsea on a gurney in one of the exam rooms, her mother beside her.

"Can you help?" Mrs. Ferguson asked.

Sara forced a smile. "Don't worry. We'll get to the bottom of this."

A quick neurological exam confirmed what Mrs. Ferguson had said: Chelsea had very little strength in the muscles of her lower limbs, and her reflexes there were diminished. Her upper extremities seemed to be working normally. Sara had been thinking about this and was ready with her decision. "We're going to need a number of tests, and we can get started on those right now. But I'm also going to ask one of our neurologists to consult on the case."

Mrs. Ferguson's face fell. "Neurologist? So is this a stroke? Or a tumor?"

"I don't really know what it is yet. But something has affected this set of muscles. Dr. Pearl is more experienced in this area, so it's a simple matter of two heads being better than one." Sara addressed Chelsea: "They're going to draw some blood from you. Then you'll be going to the radiology department for an MRI. That's sort of scary, because you're in a tunnel kind of thing and have to hold still for about fifteen minutes. I don't want to give you anything to sedate you, because we don't know what's going on yet. Think you can handle it?"

Chelsea bit her lip, then nodded. A frightened child had once more replaced the smiling teenager, and it tore at Sara's heart.

Sara decided not to mention some of the other tests. A spinal tap. Electromyography and nerve conduction studies, with needles in the muscles to check their function. Probably more blood tests—a lot more. Chelsea and her mother had been through so much, and now this. It wasn't fair. *God, why did this happen?*

Sara saw the agony on Mrs. Ferguson's face, and her mind drifted to her own loss. No mother should ever suffer the death of a child, and this woman wasn't going to if Sara could do anything to prevent it. But first she had to find out what was going on.

She answered a few questions, then stopped at the nurses' desk to write some orders. She'd call Dr. Pearl later today, after some of the reports were back. For now there was only one thing Sara could do. There in the midst of the busy ER, clutching Chelsea's chart to her heart, she closed her eyes and voiced a silent prayer.

8

Y̶OU LOOK LIKE YOU'VE LOST YOUR LAST FRIEND."

Rip Pearson's voice startled Sara out of her reverie. She gestured to the empty chair across from her in the hospital cafeteria. "I'm not sure how many friends I have, but you're probably my best one, and I need you now."

Rip settled his tray onto the table but didn't unload it. Instead, he braced his elbows on the table and leaned toward Sara. "I'm here, ready to listen."

"I just saw Chelsea Ferguson in the ER and admitted her. She awoke this morning with severe weakness of both legs. I've ordered some tests. Anna Pearl's going to see Chelsea this evening."

Rip raised his eyebrows. "What's your best guess?"

"Oh, the differential's a mile long, but I'm betting on Guillain-Barré syndrome."

Rip shook his head. "That's too much of a coincidence."

"What do you mean?"

"I've had calls this week about two other patients who received Jandramycin. Their private doctors saw them with some pretty serious problems."

"And they have Guillain-Barré, too?" Sara asked.

"No, one of them has severe headaches and visual disturbances. The other has developed early kidney failure. But the common link is Jandramycin." He pushed his tray aside, untouched. "If you're through eating, let's go somewhere quieter where we can talk about this. I think there's a connection between our 'wonder drug' and these complications."

Sara stood. "I can't eat, especially now. And I imagine that when we let Jack know about this, he'll lose his appetite, too."

"That's another thing we need to talk about," Rip said as they moved toward the exit. "If we tell him about what's happening, is he going to investigate it . . . or deep-six it?"

Jack Ingersoll's fingers lingered over the keyboard as he mulled his next sentence. He was scheduled to present this paper to the World Conference on Infectious Diseases in Frankfurt. Then he planned to submit it to a prestigious journal—maybe the *Journal of Infectious Diseases* or the *Journal of the American Medical Association*—and with a little push from Jandra it should end up as the lead article.

"Dr. Ingersoll, Drs. Miles and Pearson are here to see you." His secretary's announcement carried through the open door like Gabriel's trumpet.

He picked up his phone and punched the intercom button. "How many times have I asked you—Never mind. Send them in."

He rose from behind his desk and gestured his visitors to chairs. "What can I do for you?"

Sara opened her mouth, but Pearson gave her an "I got this" look. "Some of the Jandramycin patients are having some problems. We wondered if you had any information that would help us figure out what's going on."

Ingersoll's smile never wavered. "What kinds of problems?"

"Chelsea Ferguson has Guillain-Barré syndrome," Sara said.

"And two other patients are having problems," Pearson added. "One of them has severe headaches and visual symptoms; the other is in early kidney failure."

Ingersoll spread his hands. "I'm sorry to hear that. Are any of these patients just off the medication?"

Pearson shook his head. "No. Chelsea's more than a month out. The other two have been off the med for six weeks or so."

"Then we can't assume their problems are due to Jandramycin. Sorry."

"Jack," Sara said, "you've kept all the data on this study very close to your vest. And I can't find any information from the animal studies on the compound. Is there anything there that might suggest the likelihood of late complications?"

"That data is proprietary, and until Jandramycin is released, it's going to be available to only a few people on a need-to-know basis." He rose. "Now, if you'll excuse me, I have a paper to write. And, Pearson, I believe you have some patient data to compile."

"Sure, I'll get on that right away." Rip pushed back his chair and took a step toward the door. "But first, can you tell me why Jandra has already filed an NDA? I thought they wanted a total of a hundred patients, forty from us. The NDA was filed before we reached our target number. Where did the others come from?"

Ingersoll didn't need this. He was too close. "Look, you don't have the big picture. Nobody does except me. You just have to trust me. When Jandramycin launches, there'll be enough credit to go around, and I'll be sure you get some." He looked at Sara. "That goes for you, too. I appreciate your furnishing patients for the study. How many of yours do we have?"

Sara rose and moved toward the door. "I know of five. But given what I'm hearing, the number may be entirely different when this is all over."

After three sharp taps on the exam room door, it opened just wide enough for Verna to peep in. "Dr. Ramsey, there's a Dr. Wilcox here to see you."

John didn't look away from the man who perched on the edge of the exam table. "Have him wait in the doctors' dictation room. I'll be out in a minute."

He waited until the door closed before he continued. "Sorry. As I said, your blood pressure's a bit high, but I think we can get it under control. I want you to see our dietitian. If you can lose twenty pounds,.odds are that the pressure will come right back down."

The man's face fell at the mention of a diet. He frowned. "Why don't you just put me on some pills?"

John had heard this a hundred times, but he tried to make his reply sound fresh. "Pills shouldn't be a permanent solution. They're great to attack the problem acutely, and I'll probably put you on something for now, but you need to be concerned with your long-term health." He went on to mention the benefits of a healthy lifestyle, but as the patient's eyes began to glaze over, John decided not to fight the battle right then. There'd be plenty of opportunities later.

"Get dressed and meet Verna outside. She'll have a prescription for your medication. She'll also set up an appointment with the dietitian. I want to see you back in three weeks, and we'll see what your blood pressure is then." The patient smiled, but it vanished when John added, "And we'll check to see how much weight you've lost."

John paused at the door and asked the same question he'd been asking patients for forty years: "Are there any questions I've left unanswered?" There rarely were, but it never hurt to ask.

After giving Verna a few instructions, John moved to the dictation cubicles where he found Mark Wilcox thumbing through a journal. "Sorry to keep you waiting."

"Not at all. I'm just reading this paper by Jack Ingersoll. It's a preliminary report on the use of Jandramycin to treat *Staph luciferus* sepsis." Mark put the journal aside. "Isn't he on the faculty here?"

"Yes, he's head of the Infectious Disease section and apparently quite a rising star. I heard the other day that he's about to be fast-tracked to full professor."

"Well, someday maybe I can meet the great man, or at least touch the hem of his garment."

John frowned. "You sound a little bitter."

Mark pulled a ballpoint pen from his pocket and began clicking it. "I'm not sure that's it so much as just cynical. At the time the article was submitted, he'd treated thirty-two patients with *Staph luciferus* sepsis with 100 percent cure and no side effects. John, we both know that the medication doesn't exist that has both those qualities. It either works most of the time and is very safe, or is effective all the time but there are risks. Call me a doubter, but I won't believe this until I see the work duplicated by another investigator."

"Let's see." John picked up the journal and found the paper in question. "Accepted for publication . . . hmm. They must have rushed this into publication, because it was accepted only three months ago, so the figures have to be fairly fresh."

A hushed, earnest conversation just outside the door made John turn to look. Rip Pearson was talking with Sara Miles.

"Well, you're in luck. There are a couple of people who should be able to give you a little insight."

John stuck his head into the hall and waited for a lull in the conversation. "Rip, do you have just a second?"

There was a moment for an exchange of the usual pleasantries. Then John asked, "Rip, how many patients are in the Jandramycin study now?"

Rip took a deep breath and let it out as a barely audible sigh. "You know, based on what I've heard this morning, I couldn't begin to hazard a guess."

Sara stirred her chef's salad and speared a small piece of tomato. "Mark, it was nice of you to take us all to lunch."

Mark made a deprecating gesture. *If you only knew how happy I am that this worked out.* "My pleasure. I owed John a lunch. And after what you and Rip hinted at, I had to hear the rest of that story."

The four sat in a back booth at one of the trendier eating places on McKinney Avenue. John looked at his watch. "Shouldn't we have stayed on campus for lunch?"

Sara smiled at John. "You're still new on the faculty. In private practice, you were always on call. Here, you're one small cog in a great big machine. None of us have clinic this afternoon, so we can take a longer lunch. As long as you have your cell phone and pager with you, you're fine."

John shrugged. "Guess you're right."

"Enough of that," Mark said. "I want to hear more about how the number of patients in the Jandramycin study is a moving target."

It was impossible for Mark to miss the look that passed between Sara Miles and Rip Pearson. *Who is this guy? Why should they trust him?*

John must have seen it, too, because he spoke up. "I've known Mark since he was a sophomore medical student. I'll vouch for him. He's sharp, he's solid, and you can trust him. I realize you may not want to share this information with either of us. If that's the case, fine. But if you want some input, Mark's got a sharp mind. And I've been around for enough years that maybe I can contribute a little senior wisdom."

Sara and Rip exchanged another look, a different one this time, and apparently a decision was reached. "Okay," Rip said. "Here's what we know. But it can't go any further."

As he listened, Mark found himself wishing for a yellow legal pad so he could take notes. *Once a lawyer, always a lawyer, I guess.* When Rip finished, Mark said, "So the bottom line is that somebody is fudging the data on Jandramycin. Right?"

"It seems that way," Rip said.

"And it's probably Ingersoll?"

"No, it could be his research assistant, a doctor named Resnick. Or I guess it could be coming from the other end, someone at Jandra. And for that matter, there may be others with the opportunity. Ingersoll's kept everything so secret, I don't even know who's involved in the process."

Mark shoved aside his sandwich and took a long drink of his Diet Coke. "This is the lawyer talking now. If someone's submitting manufactured data, what's your liability in it?"

Rip shook his head. "I guess I could say I'm just following orders from the man running the study. But as a practical matter, if this comes to light I'll be tarred with the same brush as Ingersoll and whoever else is responsible."

"What about a responsibility to patients?"

"That brings up another problem," Sara said. "There may be some side effects of Jandramycin that are just now coming to light."

"Explain," Mark said.

"One of the patients in the Jandramycin study has turned up with Guillain-Barré syndrome," Rip said. "There are at least two more that we know of who've developed different problems. We don't know the specifics, but it's enough to make us wonder if there are late effects of the drug that no one suspected."

"Or that they knew about but chose to keep hidden," Mark said.

"Assuming that's true, who are our suspects?" Sara asked.

"Same list we've already named," Rip said. "Ingersoll, Resnick, someone at Jandra, or a person as yet unknown. Right now, all we have is questions. I think it's time to try to get some answers."

Outside the restaurant, John ransomed his car from the valet parking attendant. "Where can I drop you two? Back at the medical school?"

"Yeah, I guess I'd better start making some phone calls," Rip said. "I'm going to have to call every patient who received Jandramycin and find out if any of them have developed problems."

"Can I help?" Sara asked.

"No, a call from me will seem like a routine follow-up, but a call from a doctor not involved in the case would send up red flags. This is going to have to be completely under the radar."

"If you need anything from me, let me know," John said.

After a short drive, the three doctors climbed out of the car in the faculty parking garage. John beeped the car locked and said, "Call me when you know more. We can meet at my house to discuss it."

As a half-time faculty member, John shared an academic office with another part-timer. He decided to go back there and tackle the pile of unread journals on his desk.

When he walked in, his secretary was attacking the keyboard of her computer as though it was an enemy to be subdued. Usually, she greeted him with a smile, but today she kept her head down, barely acknowledging him. Strange.

The mystery deepened as John entered his office: a middle-aged man sat across from his desk. John dropped his briefcase and took his white coat from a hook behind the door. "May I help you?"

The man rose and picked up his own briefcase from beside his chair. "Dr. John Ramsey?"

"Yes."

The man plunged his hand into the case and pulled out a sheaf of papers, which he thrust into John's hand. "You've been served." He took two steps toward the door, turned, and added, "Sorry about that. Have a nice day."

John stood immobile for a few moments, not daring to look down at the papers in his hand. Then he moved slowly to his swivel chair and dropped into it. Like a child peeking out from under the covers, afraid he'd see a boogeyman, John squinted and let his eyes scan the document he held. There, buried in unfamiliar verbiage, was his name, along with Lillian Goodman's and a number of other colleagues. True to their threat, the family of the woman he'd assisted was suing the medical center and every person remotely connected with her brief time there. And blameless or not, he knew the next few months would be terrible.

He sat for a moment with his eyes closed and wished he could turn back the calendar—not a few days or a few weeks, but half a year. Then Beth would be there. And he wouldn't feel as he did now—as alone as a man on a desert island, with no sign of a ship on the horizon.

9

Sara dropped her backpack by the door, kicked off her shoes, and collapsed into the one comfortable chair in her living room. Automatically, her hand found the TV remote, but she let it fall onto the table with a clatter when she realized she didn't need background noise or diversion—she needed quiet and a chance to think.

There was something about Jandramycin that wasn't right, something about the study and the people involved in it that set off alarm bells in her head. She had no proof, but her clinical intuition told her that the "wonder drug" had some late risks that had either been ignored or flagrantly hidden. Who would do it? Who could do it? Of course, this might have begun at the source with the people at Jandra Pharmaceuticals. She'd have to find out who had such access. She picked up a scratch pad from beside the phone, rummaged in the drawer of the small table until she found a pen, and made a note. "Jandra."

Beneath "Jandra," she wrote "Jack." Her ex-husband had control of the study, and its success or failure would have an enormous effect on his career. Then came "Resnick." She'd never liked the obsequious little doctor, and she could see him fiddling data and hiding information if it would benefit him.

She tapped the pen against her teeth, fighting the urge to write the next name. No, he couldn't do such a thing. But he had almost as much access as Jack to the data. Finally, in handwriting that was uncharacteristically cramped, she scrawled, "Rip."

The ring of the telephone startled her. She dropped her pen, reached for it, and kicked it under the sofa. She'd get it later. Sara grabbed the phone just as her answering machine came to life. "Hi, this is—" She stabbed at the button to stop the message.

"Hello. Hello?"

She could almost see Rip's frown from the tone of his voice. "Sara, is this a bad time?"

"No, I just dropped— Never mind. No, this is fine."

"I missed connecting with you at the medical center, and I thought you'd want to know what I found out."

Sara tucked her feet under her and rolled her shoulders to relieve some of the tension. "Sure. Tell me about it."

"I called everyone on the list of patients who received Jandramycin. Of the thirty-nine names I had, I was able to get information about thirty of them."

"Pretty high rate of return for your calls. What did you find out?"

"Interesting," Rip said. "Of the thirty, six have developed some sort of major medical problem."

"Such as?"

"In addition to Chelsea, there's one other young man with Guillain-Barré syndrome. One woman has severe muscle pains and episodes of weakness, another has debilitating headaches and visual problems, a middle-aged man is being worked up for a bleeding disorder, and an older man looks like he's developing kidney failure."

Sara's mind was churning by now. Was there some kind of common link to these problems? And could she be sure they were all related to Jandramycin?

"Still there?" Rip asked.

"Yes. How much detail do you have on these patients?"

"Not much, but I'm going to call their doctors tomorrow and see if I can't get more. Want to meet tomorrow about five to see if we can put this all together?"

"Sure. Let's do it in my office. That way, we have my books and computer if we need to use them."

They talked for a few more minutes before Rip rang off, pleading the same level of fatigue Sara felt herself. This had been quite a day for both of them.

She no sooner put the phone down than it rang again. "What did you forget?"

A voice she didn't immediately recognize said, "I forgot to ask you if you'd have dinner with me tomorrow night, but I thought I'd let you get home first."

Sara smiled. "Mark, I'm sorry. I thought this was Rip calling back."

"Nope, it's me. I really enjoyed our lunch together, even if it did turn into a game of 'What's wrong with this picture?' and I was wondering if you'd like to have dinner together tomorrow, just the two of us."

Sara didn't know what to say. This was all moving much too fast for her, and the addition of another person to the mix was more than she could handle. "I appreciate the invitation, and I hope you'll ask me again, but right now I've got too much going on in my life."

"So much that you don't take time to eat?"

"No, but—" She could see how this man would be good in the courtroom. He obviously thought well on his feet. "Listen, I already have something going on tomorrow afternoon, and I don't know how long it's going to take. Can we talk about this another day?"

"Sure. And while I have you on the phone, have you discovered anything more about Jandramycin's side effects?"

John Ramsey's words came back to her. "He's sharp, he's solid, and you can trust him." Maybe three heads would be better than two. "Listen, are you free tomorrow afternoon?"

"Dr. Ramsey, are you ready to start seeing patients?"

John wanted to tell Verna that he wasn't ready, might never be ready again. You work for forty years and never have a complaint lodged against you, much less a malpractice suit filed, and then one day, *Bam!* You're sued for trying to save the life of a woman experiencing a non-survivable event.

He was ready to walk out of the clinic, go home, forget about practicing medicine. Instead, John did what he'd been doing for years, rain or shine, good mood or bad. He followed his calling. "Sure. Who's first?"

Somehow John made it through the morning, pleased to find that he was still able to compartmentalize, putting his personal worries into quarantine while his professional self handled problem after problem.

"That's it. You had one more patient, but he was a no-show."

"Thanks, Verna. I'm going to return these phone messages, then I'll get some lunch."

John sighed when he saw the pink slips Verna had left in his dictation cubicle, held down by a paperweight advertising the latest wonder drug from some pharmaceutical company or other. But first things first. He dialed the number for Mark's office. After four rings, he heard the rhythm of the rings change and realized the call was rolling over to an answering service or voicemail. *Oh, it's lunchtime.* He hung up without leaving a message and dialed Mark's cell phone.

John let it ring until he heard, "This is Mark Wilcox. Please leave a message."

"Mark, this is John Ramsey. I've been . . . I've been served. I guess we need to talk. Are you available this evening? Call my cell and leave a message."

John had hardly hung up when his cell phone vibrated in his pocket. Was Mark getting back to him already? "Dr. Ramsey."

"Doctor, this is Bill Alexander."

He'd almost forgotten about his earlier call to his malpractice insurance carrier. Maybe his coverage extended to the incident at the medical school. Maybe things were going to work out. A spark of hope flared. "Yes. Thanks for getting back to me."

"You won't thank me after you hear what I've found out." The spark flickered and died, leaving nothing in John's heart but a chill that no sun could warm.

"Let me guess. I'm not covered."

The conversation lasted another five minutes, but the upshot was what John originally feared. His malpractice coverage was not in force for new events. And it was the opinion of the company's lawyers that it was unlikely the medical center would cover the actions of an employee who hadn't even officially gone to work yet. In other words, John was on his own. He thanked Alexander and hung up. He wondered what would happen if he just walked out, packed a suitcase, and took off for parts unknown.

"John, God's in control. Hang on."

Beth's words were as real as though she were in the room with him. Those words seemed to be her solution for everything bad that happened in their lives: an employee who embezzled a huge chunk of money from his practice, the sudden deaths of his parents in a terrible accident, the news that John's brother had terminal cancer. All these were times when he wanted to walk away from it all. And Beth always reminded him—God's in control. So he'd hung on. And sure enough, things worked out. Maybe they would this time, as well.

He squared his shoulders and began to work his way through the message slips. He was wrapping up a conversation with an insurance claims representative, trying to keep his temper in check while convincing her that the presence of asthma in childhood didn't constitute a pre-existing condition in the case of a patient with pneumonia, when Verna appeared outside his door. He held up one finger in a "just a minute" gesture and ended the conversation, gratified that he'd been able to convince the sentry on the other end of the phone to let his patient pass into the realm of the insured.

"What's up?" he asked.

"That no-show is here. I'm not sure how he got into the general internal medicine clinic, though. He's got an infected wound on his arm that looks pretty bad. Probably needs debridement and some antibiotics. Want me to send him to general surgery?"

John was already on his feet. "No, he's here. I'll take care of it. In forty years of practice, I've seen my share of infected wounds."

The patient was a middle-aged man, lean and tough as a buggy whip. He wore a flannel shirt with the sleeves rolled past the elbows. A folded baseball cap peeked out of the hip pocket of his jeans. "Sorry I was late, Doc. Had trouble with those valet parkers out there." He pronounced the word *valett*. "Told 'em I was gonna have to pay to see you, pay for my medicine, and I wasn't about to pay for some guy to park my pickup when I could do it myself."

John smothered a smile. He'd had the same thought a number of times. "No problem. You're here now. Let's see that arm. What happened?"

While the patient related a story of coming out second best in a fight with a piece of rusty machinery at his auto repair shop the preceding week, John slipped on a pair of gloves and examined the man's left arm. It was swollen, hot to the touch, red from the elbow to the wrist. A weeping crust covered a six-inch gash on the side of the forearm. "Thought it would be okay if I kept a bandage on it and used some of that antee-bee-otic ointment. Looks like I was wrong."

"I'm going to clean that up and get you on some pills to fight the infection," John said. "I may have to snip away some dead tissue, but I don't think it will hurt enough to need a local anesthetic. Think you can take it?"

"I've had worse," the man said.

While Verna cleansed the wound with peroxide and painted it with antiseptic, John took the dirty bandage from the treatment table and looked around for a spot to dispose of it. Blood, tissue, pus, and similar material were to be placed in a special container, one that was lined with a red plastic bag prominently labeled "biohazard."

"Over in the corner," Verna said, nodding in that direction.

"Thanks." John opened the container to drop in the bandage, but it hung on the rim. He swatted the dirty gauze into the almost overflowing bag, but when he did he felt a sharp pain in his hand. "Ow!"

"What happened?" Verna asked.

John took a pair of forceps from the treatment table and stirred the top layer of debris in the biohazard bag. His throat tightened when he saw the glint of a syringe and needle peeking out of the container.

He tried to keep his voice calm. "Verna, I'm going to need to talk with someone in Infectious Disease. Could you page them while I finish cleaning up this wound?"

"Sure. Is it about the antibiotic for this wound?"

"No, it's about our needle-stick protocol. It's for me."

"Jandra Pharmaceuticals, how may I direct your call?" The voice was cheery, but the inflection told Sara that this was a message the woman repeated a hundred times a day.

"This is a doctor in Dallas, calling about one of your new drugs. Is there someone there who can give me some details about Jandramycin?"

There was a moment's silence. "I'm sorry. I don't believe we have a drug by that name. Are you sure?"

Sara shrugged to relieve the tension that had become a permanent fixture in her shoulder muscles. "I'm sure. Jandra Pharmaceuticals, Jandramycin. Think about it." She decided on a different tack. "Who's your public relations manager?"

"That would be Mr. Olson, but he's on vacation."

Sara waited, but apparently that was as much help as she was going to get. "Okay, your director of research?"

"That would be Dr. Wolfe. Would you like me to ring him?"

"Please."

If she says, "Have a good day," I'll scream. Just before the tell-tale buzz of a phone ringing, Sara heard "Have a good—" and gritted her teeth. It apparently wasn't going to take much to get on her nerves today. But if she wanted to coax any information out of this Wolfe guy, she'd better be on her best behavior.

"Bob Wolfe." The voice was a deep baritone, the accent definitely East Coast.

"Mr. Wolfe, this is—"

"Dr. Wolfe. I'm a Pharm D."

"I'm terribly sorry. Yes, the operator did give me your title. I apologize."

"No problem. Who's this?"

"This is Dr. Sara Miles. I'm on the internal medicine faculty of the Southwestern Medical Center in Dallas. I have a question about Jandramycin."

This time the pause was long enough that Sara thought she'd been disconnected. Finally, Wolfe said, "If you're at Southwestern, I'd suggest you talk with our principal investigator, Dr. Ingersoll. He's on the faculty there, too. Would you like his number?"

I've got his number. I know more about him than you ever will, you self-important—"I know Dr. Ingersoll, and one of my patients is in his study. That's why I'm calling. She's developed what I believe is a late complication from Jandramycin, but Jack . . . Dr. Ingersoll won't accept that possibility. I need to know if there's anything in the basic research that would suggest an association with—"

"Stop. I don't want to hear about this. Dr. Ingersoll is in charge of the project, and if he doesn't think your patient's problem is related to Jandramycin, the matter's closed."

"You mean—"

"Listen, Dr. Miles, if that's really your name. How do I know you're not from one of our rival companies, sniffing around for dirt so you can sabotage our new drug application? What you're asking for is proprietary information. And you're not going to get it."

There was a loud click. *Why that self-important, self-centered, pompous*—Sara took a deep breath and blew it out slowly through pursed lips. *Who says Lamaze training can't be useful except in labor?* The phone in her hand came to life, and she heard a familiar female voice. "Jandra Pharmaceuticals. How may I direct your call?"

"I think I was disconnected."

"To whom were you speaking? I'll be glad to ring them back."

"Never mind. This time, would you ring your CEO or COO or whoever's in charge there?"

"That would be Dr. Patel. I'll ring his office. Please hold."

This time Sara said it before the operator could get it out. "Thanks. And have a nice day."

Rip Pearson knew this was one of the most-feared situations faced by health care professionals, and he worked hard to keep his voice low and his manner calm. "John, this isn't the end of the world. I've seen this scenario dozens of times, and the odds are so overwhelmingly against your getting infected in any way—"

"I know, I know." John Ramsey squirmed on the edge of the treatment table. "But it makes me so angry that someone, a health care professional, could dispose of a needle and syringe in such an unsafe manner. Besides, it's not even one of the safety units they're supposed to use, the ones you can recap with one hand after using them."

"What makes you think it was one of the staff that did this? You said yourself this wasn't one of the safety syringes we use here. If it were, we wouldn't be having this conversation. This was most likely a patient, probably a drug user. They had the syringe in their purse or their pocket and saw a chance to get rid of it. The cap came off when they dumped it, and it sat there just waiting to bite you."

"Okay. I'll stop fuming over something I can't change. Now what do I do?"

"Have you had hepatitis immunizations?"

"Aren't we going to talk about HIV exposure?"

Rip made a calming gesture. "We'll get to that, but your chances of getting HIV from a needle stick like this are less than 1 percent. What we worry about most is hepatitis, especially Hep B. Have you been immunized?"

"Yeah, the full series."

"Tetanus?"

"Current on that, too."

"There's the possibility of bacterial infection at the wound site, but we don't usually give prophylactic antibiotics for that. We'll just watch."

John leaned forward a bit. "And last, but certainly not least?"

"As I said, HIV isn't much of a risk. As you know, we can't do any kind of meaningful test on the needle or syringe, and we can't HIV test the person who used them last. I'd call this a class 2 or 3 exposure. We'll draw a baseline blood test and retest you periodically. You'll need to be on the standard two-drug regimen for at least a month. The odds are overwhelming that you'll be fine."

John didn't seem to relax despite the reassurance. That would probably take a while. He struggled with what was probably meant to be a smile. "Thanks for coming over so quickly, Rip. I appreciate it."

"Glad to do it. I'm sorry that Dr. Ingersoll wasn't available. We generally like for a senior faculty member to take care of situations like this that involve our staff."

"Actually, I'm glad it's you. I trust you. I'm not sure I can say the same about Jack Ingersoll."

He'd wondered how long it would take for questions to arise. Nothing is perfect, certainly not in medicine. He'd heard it all his life. "When something's too good to be true, it isn't."

There wasn't a drug in the world that worked all the time with no potential for side effects. Penicillin had been a fantastic leap forward after Fleming made the accidental discovery in 1928. But now 2 percent of the people in the U.S. were allergic to this wonder drug, risking reactions that ranged from an uncomfortable rash to a violent death. Aspirin had been in use for over one hundred years, providing relief of mild to moderate pain. But over 5 percent of the population couldn't take it because of sensitivity or ill effects that ranged from minor to fatal. Nothing, however benign it might appear, was perfect. The same was true for Jandramycin.

What he'd told the board of Darlington was true—sort of. Jandramycin had problems, and when they came out, Jandra Pharmaceuticals would go in the tank. But he'd known all along it wouldn't be necessary for him to leak the information. The questions would be asked, and someone would eventually ferret out the truth. Of course, if that didn't happen, he was still sitting pretty on the inside of a multi-billion-dollar enterprise with four million untraceable dollars. If it did, that amount swelled to ten million. Not just a golden parachute—more like platinum or diamond. Enough to let him live for the rest of his life in comfort in a place he'd already picked out.

For now, all he had to do was sit back and let matters take their course. And he was prepared to do just that.

John couldn't hear the ring of his cell phone over the buzz of conversation and clatter of trays in the medical center's food court, but the vibration finally caught his attention. "Dr. Ramsey."

"This is Mark. What's up?"

John Ramsey picked up his venti mocha in his free hand and said, "Let me move outside. I can't hear myself think in here." He walked quickly into the hallway and from there outside into the courtyard. He settled onto an unoccupied bench in a quiet corner. "Better. Can you hear me okay?"

"Loud and clear," Mark said.

John brought him up to date, feeling the lump in his throat grow larger as he worked through the details. His malpractice insurance was no longer in force. It was unlikely that the medical school would protect him from any suit. "And now I've been served with the papers. Can I get you to look at them? Maybe I can buy you dinner tonight?"

"Um, well—" Mark's hesitation told John all he needed to know.

"That's okay. Obviously you have something planned for tonight."

"Actually, I have a meeting at the medical center at five, but I don't know how long it's going to last. Why don't I call you after that?"

John finished his coffee and tossed the cup in a nearby waste container. "That's fine." He rose and began to move slowly back toward the entrance. "What kind of a meeting do you have, if you don't mind my asking?"

"It's about—" John could almost see the gears turning in Mark's head. "You know, you might want to be there as well. Here's the deal."

Sara heard the tap on her office door but didn't look up from the journal she was reading. "It's open."

"Am I early?" Rip said from the doorway.

Sara looked at the clock on her desk. Five minutes to five. "No, you're fashionably on time. Come in and sit down."

Rip eased into a visitor's chair and put a worn leather portfolio on the corner of Sara's desk. "I have some pretty interesting information on the patients who've developed problems after receiving Jandramycin."

"Uh, let's wait just a minute. I sort of invited Mark Wilcox to join us. I hope that's okay."

It seemed to Sara that a frown flitted across Rip's face. "I guess not. And John did vouch for him."

"Did I hear my name?" Mark said. He ambled in, shook hands with Rip and Sara, and took the other visitor's chair. "Is it still okay that I'm participating in this get-together?"

"I was telling Rip that I invited you. And of course it's okay. We can use all the help we can get."

"Good," Mark said. "Because I've asked John Ramsey to join us."

As though on cue, John stuck his head in the doorway. Seeing that the chairs were occupied, he disappeared and returned in a moment with the chair from the secretary's desk in the outer office.

After more explanations and more assurances that everyone was welcome, Sara said, "I'll start, I guess. I decided to call Jandra to see if I could get any information on possible late complications from Jandramycin. I thought they might have seen something in the preliminary animal studies."

"And?" Rip asked.

"No dice. I spoke with their research director, a Pharm D named Wolfe, who stonewalled me. At first he said I should check with Jack, since we're at the same institution. When I kept asking questions, he clammed up. He claimed that what I wanted to know was proprietary information. He even insinuated that I might be a spy from another pharmaceutical company."

"Not unusual. Paranoia is the norm in the pharm industry. They're always looking over their shoulder for a competitor sneaking up on them," Mark said. "Did you talk with anyone else there?"

"I got as far as the secretary of somebody named Patel, who's the CEO or COO, not sure of his title. What I am sure of is that she referred me right back to Wolfe. Wouldn't even let me talk with Patel." She picked up a pen from the desk and began to twirl it between her fingers. "I think Jandra is a dead end."

Mark raised a tentative hand like a fifth grader with the answer to a problem. "Why don't I see if we can get any information from the New Drug Application Jandra has filed?"

"Are NDA's public record?" John asked.

"No. Remember what I said about drug companies being paranoid. Keeping an NDA secret is supposed to prevent competitors from stealing information." Mark grinned. "But in my legal practice I made some contacts in Washington. Maybe one of them has connections with the FDA. I'll see what I can get."

"If we suspect that Jandramycin is causing problems, shouldn't we contact the FDA directly and ask them not to act on Jandra's application?" Sara asked.

Rip shook his head. "And tell them what? We have no proof. All the clinical data here is locked up tight in Ingersoll's lab, guarded by Resnick like a dog watching over a bone. The preclinical trials were done by Ingersoll when he was doing a research fellowship at Jandra, so if there's any useful data in those records we'll never see it. Whatever the FDA has is a sanitized version of the truth, and we have no facts to refute it."

Conversation stopped when John Ramsey's watch beeped. He shrugged and said, "Sorry, got to take my medicine. My doctor tells me it's important that I don't miss a dose." He looked at Rip and managed a weak grin. "Be right back." He pulled two pill bottles from his pocket and ducked out of the room.

As soon as John was back, Rip pulled a sheet of notes from his portfolio. "I've managed to contact most of the patients who received Jandramycin. Of the ones I've contacted, all but three got the drug more than six weeks ago. Out of that group, six have what I consider serious conditions."

Sara rose. "Let's move to the conference room for this."

An hour later, names, symptoms, and pertinent lab data covered the blackboard in the conference room. "To summarize," Mark said, "we have six patients. They've developed various complications: neurologic problems, kidney failure, muscle weakness, excessive bleeding, and headaches with vision loss. Is there the common denominator?"

"Let's put specific diagnoses on the groups where we can," John suggested. "Start with the neurologic problems. Sara tells me she thinks her patient has Landry's ascending paralysis—what you younger doctors would call GBS or Guillain-Barré syndrome."

Sara wrote "GBS" and underlined it.

"Kidney failure can be due to lots of things, so let's put that one aside," John said. "The same with muscle weakness and bleeding disorders. But the visual loss and headaches, associated with an elevated sed rate and some response to steroids suggest—"

"Temporal arteritis," Sara almost shouted. "Everyone agree with that?" There were murmurs of assent, so she wrote "Temp art" and circled it.

"Is there a common thread to those two disorders, one that could also apply to kidney failure, muscle weakness, and excessive bleeding?"

John and Mark looked at each other, and Sara could tell the answer was forming in their minds almost simultaneously. "Autoimmune disorder," they said in unison.

"If we accept that," Rip said, "then let's see if there's a link to the others. Muscle pain and weakness?"

"Polymyositis," Mark said. "It's autoimmune, and it fits."

Sara wrote "Polymyo."

"How about bleeding?" Sara thought for a moment. "Rip, did the patient with bleeding have any purpura?" she asked, referring to the red or purple spots sometimes seen on the skin of patients with blood disorders.

Rip checked his notes. "Yes. And that leads us to—"

"Idiopathic thrombocytopenic purpura," Sara said, scrawling "ITP" on the board. "And that's autoimmune."

"That leaves kidney failure. Which autoimmune disorder can cause that?" John asked.

They kicked that around for a bit and finally settled on kidney failure with an immune cause: IgA-mediated nephropathy. Sara added "Imm neph" to the board. She stepped back, nodded in satisfaction, and put down her chalk.

The discussion continued for a few minutes, but soon it was evident that they were in agreement. The complications from Jandramycin were autoimmune—the patients had literally become allergic to their own tissue. The effects were just manifested in different organ systems.

"Okay," Sara said. "We're dealing with an autoimmune problem. We don't know why, and we need to look at how that happens. But more important, how can we treat it? Steroids can help, of course, but their effect is temporary. Is there something that will reverse the process?"

Rip shook his head and yawned. "We've got more work to do." He looked around the room. "But we're all dog-tired. Let's get some rest and reconvene here tomorrow night."

They straggled out of the building and walked in loose formation across the nearly silent plaza toward the parking garage.

Mark moved beside Sara and said, "I was hoping to take you to dinner. Is that off the table for tonight?"

Sara had to smile at the way Mark phrased his invitation. "I'm afraid so. I'm exhausted, and I'll bet you are." She slowed and half-turned toward him. "As for another night, why don't you wait until things settle down a bit? Then call me."

All three men insisted on seeing Sara safely to her car, and soon she was on her way home. A few blocks from the medical center, she remembered that she needed cereal and milk. Sara was a creature of habit, and cereal for breakfast was one of them. She scanned the businesses around her. She was almost past the grocery store when she spotted it on the right. Sara swerved into the parking lot with only a light touch on her brakes. The squealing of her tires almost covered the sound of breaking glass. She screeched to a stop in the parking lot, looked behind her, and saw the rear window was shattered. Glass shards covered the backseat. To her right, a jagged hole marred the front passenger window. It took a few seconds for the reality of the situation to set in, and when it did, Sara seemed to implode upon herself like a blown-up balloon that's lost its air.

She was vaguely aware of a number of people in the parking lot pulling out cell phones. A few eased toward her car, apparently afraid to approach too near for fear the shooting wasn't over. One man, braver than the rest, shuffled forward and called, "Are you hurt?"

She shook her head. She was still sobbing, gripping the steering wheel in a death grip, when she heard the sirens approaching.

10

In the faculty parking garage, John Ramsey beeped his car unlocked and was about to climb in when he heard someone call, "John, wait up."

"Mark? Where are you?"

Mark Wilcox's head appeared over the roof of a nearby vehicle. "Glad I caught you. I think we need to talk."

"You're right," John said. "I got so wound up in this Jandramycin thing, I almost forgot that I was being sued."

"Then it's a good thing you have a lawyer to protect your interest." Mark gestured to John's Toyota. "I'm parked down in the visitors' lot. Can we climb in here and talk for a bit?"

Once they were settled, John reached into the glove compartment and pulled out a thick sheaf of papers. "Here it is. I didn't understand all the legal language, but it was pretty clear that I was being sued, along with just about everybody else in this zip code."

Mark scanned the first few pages and nodded. "I'll go over this in detail tomorrow, but as I see it, there are several strategies we can employ."

"You mean, other than telling these people they're idiots for bringing this suit in the first place? All I did was offer a helping hand to a woman who was in distress. For goodness' sake, I was just being a good Samaritan."

"Interestingly enough, that's one of the strategies I was going to mention. We could base your defense on the Good Samaritan Law."

"Would what I did qualify?"

"Probably, but I need to research it more. Why don't you try to put this out of your mind for now?"

John grimaced. "Oh, it probably doesn't matter anyway. If they win a judgment, they can just take it out of the proceeds of my life insurance."

"That's not funny. There's absolutely nothing here that's worth considering taking your own life."

"I don't have to do that. Some druggie who dropped a dirty syringe into the trash can in one of our treatment rooms will probably do it for me." He reached into his pocket, held up two prescription bottles, and shook them to rattle the pills inside. "Remember when I excused myself from the meeting to take my medicine?"

"Yes."

"Antiretrovirals. I'm on post-exposure prophylaxis for HIV. And the way things have gone lately, I don't think there's a way in the world I can avoid it."

Bob Wolfe looked around Patel's empty office and tried to relax, but his gut continued to churn. He wiped his palms on the handkerchief balled in his hand. Don't let them see you sweat, they say. Well, that wasn't so easy right now. The secretary's call had been terse: "Dr. Patel wants to see you in his office. He'll expect you in five minutes." There'd been no explanation of the summons then, and none when he showed up. Just "Go in, and close the door behind you."

Now Wolfe squirmed in one of the leather visitor's chairs. This must be how a prisoner on death row feels, waiting for the footsteps of the warden. *Stop worrying. This is probably nothing.* But deep down, Wolfe knew what this was about. It was about Jandramycin. Specifically, it was probably about that nosy doctor who'd called with her ridiculous stories about late complications. He thought he'd stonewalled her pretty well, but maybe Patel had gotten wind of that call. And if he did, there were going to be questions asked. And the answers had better be the right ones.

"Bob, thanks for coming."

Wolfe jumped to his feet and turned to see his boss stride into the office, followed by Steve Lindberg and a man who looked vaguely familiar, but whose name danced at the edge of his memory. "Of course," Wolfe said.

Patel gestured Wolfe back into his chair. Lindberg repeated the move Wolfe had seen before, pulling a visitor's chair to the side of Patel's desk and settling in as though he were an impartial observer in any conflict that might take place.

"I'm Max Berman, chief counsel for Jandra Pharma." The third man shook Wolfe's hand, three quick pumps and release, a politician's handshake. Thousand-dollar suit, hundred-dollar haircut, soft hands with manicured nails. Now Wolfe remembered he'd met Berman once before. He hadn't liked him then, and had a feeling that wasn't going to change.

Unlike Lindberg, Max took the chair beside Wolfe. Did that mean he was an ally? No, more likely it was simply a matter of being in position to watch more closely. Well, watch away, Counselor. *I'm ready for you.*

"I understand you had a call from a Dr. Sara Miles," Patel said. He leaned forward, his hands flat on his desk. "Why don't you tell us about it?"

"How did you know about that?" Wolfe asked.

"Two reasons. After she talked with you, she tried to get through to me. Fortunately, my administrative assistant is well trained and very capable of fending off unwanted phone calls. It seems that I'm out of the country on company business, and my return date is uncertain at this time."

Wolfe knew Patel wanted him to ask what the second reason was, but he sat in silence. *We'll see who blinks first.* After a moment, Patel did.

"As for the other reason, I knew about the phone call while you were still talking with her." He waited like a child eager to explain the magic trick he'd learned.

Wolfe raised his eyebrows, and that was enough for Patel to continue: "I know everything that goes on in this company. Outside calls are monitored and if the content is something that should come to my attention, I learn about it immediately."

Berman spoke for the first time, and now it was fairly obvious why the man was a participant in this meeting. "In case you're wondering, this is all perfectly legal. Like most people, you didn't read your employment agreement carefully. If you had, you'd know that monitoring is carried out on a day-to-day basis. When you signed, you gave the CEO and his designees the authority to monitor telephone, e-mail, and written communications as necessary to protect the company."

"No problem. If you or one of your 'designees'..." Wolfe set the word off with air quotes. "If they monitored my conversation, you know that Dr. Miles got nothing from me."

"Probably true," Patel said. "But the very fact that she called raises a question. She voiced the concern that treatment with Jandramycin may lead to late complications. Is there any truth in that?"

The group remained silent. Patel leaned forward and gripped the edge of his desk hard enough to blanch his knuckles. "Our NDA is moving forward as we speak, and I might add, at great cost to this company. We've put pressure on some of our friends on Capitol Hill, called in every possible favor, and . . . Well, I won't go into detail." He relaxed back into his chair and began to swivel back and forth. "Jandramycin must be brought to market ASAP. We can't have any snags now."

Wolfe decided that there was no question there, so he gave a quick nod and waited for Patel to make his point. This meeting was for a reason, and Patel just now seemed to be getting there.

"David, you know we're all on the same page here." Lindberg's comment was unnecessary, but apparently the man couldn't sit through a meeting for longer than five minutes without saying something.

Patel raked the two men sitting nearest him with a gaze that could cut glass. "I've asked Max to meet with us for a very specific reason. Max?"

Berman rose and cleared his throat. Wolfe and Lindberg turned slightly in their chairs. The attorney addressed them both: "Let me explain. Dr. Miles brought up a scenario that could be very problematic for Jandra Pharmaceuticals. If such side effects exist, it's imperative that we know of them. And if they do not exist, it's equally important that we are firm and forthright in our denial of any such charges. So the question everyone in this room needs to answer is this: Are you prepared to state that you are unaware of any side effects from Jandramycin such as the ones mentioned by Dr. Miles?"

Lindberg almost leaped to his feet. "Absolutely. I'm unaware of any such side effects as Dr. Miles mentioned."

"Nor do you have knowledge of any, and will so state should the occasion arise?" Berman said.

"Correct," Lindberg said.

Berman looked pointedly at Wolfe.

Wolfe nodded, but that wasn't enough for Berman. "Please answer aloud." He smothered a smile. "Sorry, that's a holdover from court. Witnesses have to answer aloud, so the court stenographer can record their responses. Reflex action on my part, I guess."

Nevertheless, he fixed Wolfe with an expectant look. Wolfe took a deep breath and said, "Yes, I'm prepared to state that I know of no such side effects."

As Wolfe made his way back to his office, he wondered how Lindberg could know about the "side effects Dr. Miles mentioned." Maybe he'd been Patel's "designee," monitoring Wolfe's calls in some way.

And why was Patel the only one who didn't respond to Berman's question? Wouldn't he, above all people in the company, have no hesitancy in going on record?

Finally, Wolfe found it strange the way Berman had phrased his question. Not "Are there any side effects?" He'd steered clear of that particular question, as though he already knew the answer. Instead, he'd asked everyone to state their willingness to go on record that there were no such adverse consequences. And despite Berman's attempt to cover his insistence that a nod wouldn't do, Wolfe knew full well the reason for requiring a verbal response. That meeting, especially the responses at the end, was being recorded. He wondered how Berman and Patel might use such a record.

Wolfe tugged at his collar, but the tightness in his throat remained.

The policewoman paused at the end of the walk and looked at Sara. "Are you sure you're going to be okay here by yourself?"

"I'll be fine. Thanks for everything."

"Can you arrange transportation for tomorrow?"

"I'll call a co-worker to pick me up in the morning. How long do you think it will be before my car's available?"

"Depends on how busy the evidence techs are. Couple of days, I'd guess. You say you only heard one shot, and it appears to have gone completely through and out the opposite window. But in case more shots were fired and there's a slug hiding in there somewhere, we want to dig it out, so we have it if there's ever something to match it to."

"Guess I'd better talk with my insurance company about this. I'll need to have the windows replaced and arrange for a rental car."

Like a reluctant beau after a first date, the officer lingered on the front porch. "I know I'd be really shaken if this happened to me. Would you like me to have a patrol car cruise by a few times this evening?"

What Sara really wanted to say was, "Please. And maybe a policeman could sit up in my living room all night, and take me to work tomorrow." Instead, she said, "I'll be fine. Really."

"Okay." The officer took a card from the breast pocket of her uniform. "If there's a problem, call this number, and we'll send someone to check." She pulled a pen from the same pocket and scribbled something on the back of the card. "Here's my cell number, too."

"Thanks again."

The policewoman touched a finger to the bill of her cap, turned, and walked slowly down the sidewalk.

Sara ducked inside to lock and bolt the front door. Soon she heard footsteps fade, followed by the slam of a car door and the sound of a car engine starting. Now that she was alone, the shaking began again. *Why me? Who would do this? Why was someone trying to kill me?*

She almost wished she were a drinker. If this had been Jack, he'd have a glass two-thirds full of liquor in his hand by now. Sara didn't even have any cooking sherry in the house. She supposed she should find something to eat, though. Stress produced adrenaline, and that caused a drop in blood sugar. She snorted. *See how your medical training has come in handy? You were almost killed tonight, but you know enough to look for some peanut butter and crackers.*

Sara made it halfway to the kitchen before dropping onto the sofa with her head in her hands. She fought the urge to start crying again. She'd already done that, sitting in her car, shaking and sobbing. She wasn't going to do it again. *Get hold of yourself. You've faced life-and-death situations when they involved other people and never lost your cool. Pull it together.*

Sara rose, but had to steady herself on the arm of the sofa. In a moment the light-headedness passed, and she was able to walk to the kitchen despite unsteady legs. She managed to put together a couple of crackers spread with peanut butter. She ate them while standing at the counter and washed them down with a few swallows of milk. *Maybe that will take care of the shakes.*

Back in the living room, she pulled a notepad toward her and thought about what she had to do next. The list was a short one, and only one thing required her attention tonight: arrange a ride to the medical center in the morning.

Who should she call? Rip? He was the obvious choice, but for some reason she couldn't bring herself to talk with him tonight, to reveal her vulnerability. True, it wasn't her fault that someone shot at her. And anyone in that situation would be upset. But she just wasn't ready for Rip to see her like this. Silly, but there it was.

Mark? She'd only met him recently. There was no question he was interested in her, but she hesitated to bring him into this. She didn't know Mark well enough, and vice versa.

Jack? Never!

Her administrative assistant? Gloria or some other nurse in the clinic? Another doctor in the department? She chewed on the eraser end of her pencil. No matter how she looked at it, the name she kept coming up with seemed the right one. She picked up the phone and dialed.

"I've got bad news for you. Every one of your HIV tests came back positive, and your T cell count is already dropping. It's like you've been taking placebo instead of zidovudine and lamivudine. We're going to have to ramp up the meds." Jack Ingersoll's face was somber as an undertaker's, his voice somehow an octave deeper than John remembered.

John could already feel the cold dampness of the grave reaching out to him. "There must be some mistake. Those meds are standard treatment. Rip Pearson assured me they'd work."

Ingersoll shrugged. "Rip doesn't know everything that goes on around here." He grinned. "Maybe the pills you've been taking were compounds I've been working on in my lab. You don't suppose one of the side effects could be to kill the immune system, do you? My, my. I'll have to write that down in my journal. My secret journal."

John was drenched in sweat by now. His chest shook with the pounding of his heart. He'd call someone—Dr. Schaeffer, Lillian Goodman, someone to talk with about this. Maybe he could call Beth. She'd know what to do. *Oh, please, God. Send me someone who can help.*

The pounding in his chest morphed into a steady vibration from the cell phone in his shirt pocket. John's eyes sprang open. He was alone in his easy chair, the stroboscopic flashing of images from the muted TV painting the walls of the darkened room.

More by reflex than volition, he answered the phone. "Dr. Ramsey."

"John, this is Sara Miles." His colleague's voice shook a bit, and he wondered what was wrong. "I need your help."

John struggled to come fully awake. His feet explored the area around his chair, searching for his discarded shoes in the near dark. "Where are you? What do you need?"

"I'm at home. But I need you to give me a ride to the medical center in the morning." There seemed to be a catch in her voice that John couldn't explain.

"Sure. But what happened to your car? Mechanical trouble?"

Her laugh had no mirth in it. "Not really. But the police impounded it so they could look for the bullet."

"Whoa. Police? Bullet?"

She told him about the shooting.

"Who's there with you?"

"I'm alone at home with the blinds drawn, the doors locked, and a baseball bat by the front door. But I'm still a little shaky."

John knew the simple thing to do was set up a time to pick her up in the morning, wish her well, and hang up. But that wasn't the right thing. By now he'd found his shoes, and he slid his feet into them. "Would it help to talk about it? Would you like me to come over?"

Her exhalation sounded like a rushing wind in his ear. "I think I'd like that. Would you mind?"

"Not at all. Give me your address."

John splashed some water on his face and combed his hair. He despised the way he'd let himself descend into self-pity. He could almost feel Beth in the room behind him, saying, "John, you can't get bogged down in thinking about yourself when there are other people who need you."

Right now, Sara needed him. He was determined to come through for her. He offered up a silent prayer to that effect, grabbed his keys, and walked out the door.

11

WHEN THE DOORBELL SOUNDED, SARA PULLED THE CURTAIN ASIDE A TINY crack and peeked outside. A gray Toyota sat in her driveway. Unfortunately, she'd forgotten to ask John Ramsey what kind of car he drove, so that information didn't do much to assure her this wasn't her attacker, come back to finish the job.

She moved to the door, but hesitated there. Hadn't she heard about murderers waiting for the peephole to darken, then shooting through it? *You've watched too many crime dramas.*

"Sara, it's me," the familiar voice called.

She released the security chain, turned the deadbolt, and opened the door just wide enough for John to slip through before she reversed the process. "Sorry to be so security conscious, but . . ."

"I understand. Now why don't we have some coffee and talk about this?"

After they took seats at Sara's kitchen table, she told John what she could recall about the shooting. "It was all over so fast. I never noticed a car following me. And if I hadn't swerved into that parking lot, I guess he'd have had a clear shot right through my side window."

"Sounds like you had an angel sitting on your shoulder."

It was an offhand remark, but it triggered a thought in Sara's mind. "You may be right. My mother always said we don't die until we've done everything God put us here for. Maybe I'm not finished."

John drained his mug. He started toward the sink, but Sara stopped him. "Just leave it. I'll clean it up later." She snorted. "You know, we're getting into angels and God, and it sounds like we want to talk about anything except who shot at me and why."

"Then let's get to it." John turned slightly and crossed his legs. "We're both diagnosticians. Look at this situation like it was a patient with symptoms we don't understand. Where do you start?"

"With the history," Sara said automatically. "How is the problem manifested now, what preceded it, and what's been done about it so far?"

"Let's start with the manifestations. Someone took a shot at you. Now the simplest explanation is that it's an isolated incident—in this case, a drive-by shooting, a case of mistaken identity. Unfortunately, nowadays that would be the most common explanation as well."

"Do you think that's it?"

John shook his head. "Doesn't matter. When you're making a diagnosis, do you stop with the most benign possibility?"

"No, you have to consider other causes and rule them out, especially the worst ones. You work your way down."

"Right," John said. "The worst possible scenario is that this was deliberate. If that's the case, we have to consider the *why*."

Nothing was said for a moment. Finally, Sara broke the silence. "I can't think of a reason why anyone would take a shot at me."

"Nothing you've been doing could make anyone angry?"

Sara chewed on her lip. "The only thing is that for the last couple of days I've been trying to get information about Jandramycin. But surely that wouldn't—"

"Let's just follow that line of thought. Who did you talk with yesterday about Jandramycin?"

"This is crazy," Sara said. "We're being ridiculous."

"Maybe," John said. "But are you sure this isn't a valid scenario? If this was a simple drive-by, our discussion just costs us a little time. If it was something more, you may still be in danger. Now who did you talk with about Jandramycin just before the shooting?"

"Rip and I confronted Jack, but he blew us off. Then I called Jandra Pharmaceuticals, talked with a Bob Wolfe, tried to talk with the head man there, and hit a stone wall both times."

"Go back a little further—just before our lunch yesterday. What about the irregularities in the research project? Where did that come from?"

Sara nodded. "Right. Rip told us the numbers weren't matching."

"And he got that information from—"

"Carter Resnick."

John ticked the names off on his fingers. "So if we're going to connect the shooting with your inquiries about Jandramycin, the triggering event could have come from Jack Ingersoll, someone at Jandra, or Carter Resnick."

Sara opened her mouth, then closed it.

"Yes? Take it further," John encouraged.

"Well, we had our meeting yesterday to talk about all this, and Mark Wilcox was there. So I guess we have to include him." Sara frowned. "You know, you introduced Mark to us, but we don't really know much about him. What does he do, anyway?"

"Lawyer, doctor, very sharp, dependable." John ticked the points off on his fingers. "He had a successful law practice, but apparently got tired of it and decided to go into medicine. I get the impression he thought he could do more good that way. Now his practice is sort of a mixed bag: a small general practice, some legal medicine, occasionally consulting for pharmaceutical companies. I've known him since he was in med school, and I think he's okay."

"If you say so," Sara said.

"What about me?" John asked. "I was at that meeting."

"No!" Sara felt as though she were lost at sea, with no land in sight. Only John Ramsey was a fixed point on the horizon. "I have to trust someone, and everything in me tells me I can trust you."

John gave the briefest of nods. "And I'll make sure your trust isn't betrayed. But there's one more person who's been involved in the Jandramycin saga. One more member of our little crew."

"I don't know who—Oh! Absolutely not."

"So how do we eliminate him? Does Rip have anything to gain if Jandramycin moves forward and the side effects stay buried?"

"I can't see any benefit to him."

"I can," John said. "Rip would be co-author of every paper of Ingersoll's on Jandramycin. When he finishes his fellowship, think how much it would improve his chances of getting a plum faculty appointment or research job if he'd worked with Jack Ingersoll on the Jandramycin project."

"I just don't think Rip's that kind of person. And he's been working right beside me to find out more about these side effects. I can't see him trying to stop me now."

"Okay," John said. "I don't think we should totally take Rip off our list, but we can move him down toward the bottom, at least for now."

Sara felt her shoulders slump. "This can't be happening. I don't want to live my life suspecting everyone around me. I can't function that way."

John rose and moved to stand beside her. "Just be careful and watch your back."

"I'd like to think I'm over-reacting. Maybe this has nothing to do with Jandramycin. Maybe it was all simply random."

John patted her shoulder. "That's enough for now. You need some rest. I'll pick you up in the morning, and if you need a ride to pick up a rental car, I'll take you."

Sara rose and took John's hand. "Thanks. It helped to talk about this."

John paused in the living room. "Are you going to be okay alone here tonight? Maybe you should check into a hotel."

"I'm not going to let something like this run me out of my home," Sara said, her words carrying more conviction than she felt.

"We could call one of your female friends to stay with you. And I could ask the police to drive by your house several times tonight."

"They've already offered to do that," Sara said. "No, I'll be fine. I'll lock up after you leave." She gestured at the bat by the front door. "And I have my old faithful softball bat here if I need to deal with an intruder."

"Just remember, a bat won't help if someone starts shooting at you."

"It's what I have tonight, but I'm already thinking of . . . never mind." No need to tell John she'd already made up her mind to buy a gun. The next time someone started to shoot at her, she was determined to return fire.

After she heard John's car pull away, Sara slumped into a chair in her living room. Her mother's Bible was on the coffee table beside her. She'd put it there after her parents were killed in an auto accident, but hadn't opened it. Maybe this was a good time to do so. She reached for the book, and it slipped from her hands, falling open to what was apparently a frequently visited page.

Sara lifted the Bible into her lap and scanned the verses. She stopped when she came to a passage marked with a yellow highlighter. Her lips moved silently as she read: "You will not fear the terror of night, nor the arrow that flies by day, nor the pestilence that stalks in the darkness, nor the plague that destroys at midday." *Thanks, Mom. I could always count on you for help.*

Sara held the phone in a death grip. She dreaded this conversation in the worst way.

"Dr. Pearl."

"Anna, this is Sara Miles. I went by to see Chelsea this morning. Her weakness seems to be progressing. What do you think?"

"I scribbled a quick note, but I dictated a full consultation. You should get it in a day or so."

Forget the paperwork. Give me something. Anything. "But you agree this is GBS?"

"Not much doubt. And, as you know, we don't really have any idea why these things happen. About all I can suggest right now is hitting her with high doses of steroids, and I've already started her on that. You know the routine: an H2 blocker to prevent a stress ulcer, a hypnotic at bedtime to combat the steroid insomnia. I wish we had something else that worked but didn't have so many side effects."

If you only knew that this whole thing probably came as a side effect of another med. "You'll follow her with me?"

"Of course. Call me anytime. And thanks for the consult."

So that was it. Anna agreed with Sara's initial diagnosis of Guillain-Barré syndrome—the silent disease that came out of nowhere. It could resolve as quickly as it came on, or it could leave the patient with permanent paralysis.

"No." Sara was surprised to find she'd spoken aloud.

"Something wrong, Dr. Miles?" Gloria tapped on the door of the dictation room where Sara sat.

"No, just talking to myself." Sara shrugged. "Am I through for the morning?"

"There's a walk-in, but if you're busy I can get one of the other doctors to see her."

"No, I'll take it. But be sure I'm clear for the afternoon. I have to pick up a rental car, then meet with the police."

"I'm so sorry to hear about what happened to you last night." Gloria made a dismissive gesture. "It seems like it's not safe to drive anywhere in this city anymore. Probably some gang-banger who got a new Glock and had to try it out on a moving target."

"Maybe." Sara shoved herself upright. "Which room?"

Forty minutes later she had a diagnosis. Not one that made her happy, especially under the circumstances, but it was clear to Sara. She figured a third-year medical student could make it. The patient was a middle-aged woman with gradual development of muscle aches and weakness, combined with a non-itching rash that covered her cheeks like a mask. Preliminary lab work was suggestive, and Sara was certain that more sophisticated tests would confirm her impression.

"Mrs. York, I'm afraid you've developed lupus."

"Oh, my." The woman's expression made it clear she realized the seriousness of what Sara said. "How did that happen? What can you do for it?"

"There are several medications we can use to slow or stop the progression of the disease. As for how, we don't have the final answer yet. It's one of a group of disorders we call 'collagen diseases.' Doctors think they're due to the body becoming allergic to itself—what's called an autoimmune disorder."

No sooner were the words out of Sara's mouth than she began to thumb through the woman's chart. What medications was she on? What diseases had she had recently? Could it be—

There it was, just as she feared. "You were hospitalized with pneumonia a few months ago?"

"Yes. It was really bad. They tell me I almost died because it was some special infection that none of the usual antibiotics would help. I guess I owe my life to Dr. Ingersoll and that new medicine of his."

Rip Pearson frowned at the insistent buzz of his pager. He silenced the instrument, noted the number, and decided he'd return the call in a moment. He already had more on his plate than he could handle.

Rip sat like a penitent, across the desk from Ingersoll, who frowned at the interruption. "Sorry about that."

"Very well," the great man said. "Now are you clear on the things I want you to do while I'm in Germany?"

"Right." Bite your tongue, Rip. Don't scratch the scab from yesterday's argument. Just get through this meeting.

"Leave the big picture to me, Pearson. I promise that if you keep the Jandramycin study going, you'll get your share of the glory."

Or the blame when it comes out that your "wonder drug" had side effects that someone chose to hide. "I know how you want the study run," Rip had said. "How long will you be gone?"

"Six days, I think. The conference is making the arrangements and covering all my travel expenses. First class all the way." Ingersoll rolled the words on his tongue and seemed to savor them as he would fine brandy. "An invitation to speak to an international meeting like this will mean a great deal of positive publicity for our work."

Yeah, and probably a hefty honorarium. Rip knew that Jandra arranged the invitation to Ingersoll. Pharmaceutical companies could no longer offer honoraria directly to physicians for speaking. But there were ways around those rules. One was to pay the money to a sponsoring organization with the understanding it would be funneled to guest speakers. In the case of an international meeting like this one, it was even easier to find ways around the restrictions.

Ingersoll scanned the list in his hand, nodded with satisfaction, and shoved it into the pocket of his white coat. "Now I have to work on my presentations. Do you have any questions?"

Why should I? I've been doing the work on this study since day one. The only thing I don't know is why the drug I'm giving people may save their lives today and sentence them to a lifelong disease or even death in the future. "No, sir. Have a safe trip."

A few minutes later, Rip was in the cubbyhole of the office assigned to him as a fellow. He checked his pager and dialed the number it displayed. "Dr. Pearson. You paged me?"

"Rip, this is Sara. We need to talk."

"Sure. Go ahead."

"No, I don't think this is something I want to go into over the phone. Can we get together? The sooner the better."

Sara sat on a rolling stool and Rip perched on the edge of the exam table. The door to the treatment room was closed. There were no doctors in the clinic. The nurses and administrative personnel were at lunch, returning phone calls, or otherwise occupied. "We should have some privacy here," Sara said. "Thanks for coming over."

"What's up that's so important?"

"Two things. As of this morning, I only had one to talk with you about, but the last patient I saw made the list longer. Do you remember a middle-aged lady named York? Pneumonia?"

"Sure. She was one of the first in the Jandramycin study. I think it was still EpAm848 then. What about her?"

"I saw her today. She's developed lupus."

She watched Rip's face as he connected the dots. It was almost immediate. "Another disease to add to the list. It's not a controlled study, but it's good enough for me. Jandramycin works to kill *Staph luciferus*, but a significant number of patients develop an autoimmune disorder within a matter of weeks."

"So the question remains: what do we do?"

"We've got to find out the exact mechanism of the drug. Then maybe we can figure out a way to block its ill effects."

Sara hesitated. "I don't want to sound stupid, but can't we just analyze some of it?"

"Sure," Rip said. "We could if we had a month or six weeks to determine the exact composition, synthesize the components, and get the proportions right, then do the lab experimentation to find out the true mechanism of action. Meanwhile, patients are dying all over the world."

"What's the count up to now?" Sara asked.

Rip pulled a wrinkled note from the pocket of his white coat. "The World Health Organization has identified over three thousand cases of *Staph luciferus* infection, all fatal except the patients treated here and the medical center in Germany that's also testing Jandramycin." He crumpled the note and tossed it into the wastebasket. "Sara, we've got to step up our search. Doctors around the world are clamoring for that drug. When it's released, thousands of patients will receive it. We have to find out how to save those patients without exposing them to a potentially fatal side effect of Jandramycin."

Sara took a deep breath. She dreaded reliving the experience, but she needed to tell Rip. "Our search may be putting us in danger, as well. You know that we confronted Jack about this, and he blew us off. Then I called Jandra but got nowhere."

"Right. But I may have thought of another way to get the information we need."

"Don't rush into it. I think I've already stirred up a hornet's nest. Last night, someone took a shot at me."

Rip rose and moved around the desk. She stood to meet him. He grasped her shoulders and said, "Are you okay? Did you call the police? What can we do to protect you?"

Sara didn't try to move his hands. "Yes, yes, and I don't know. But in the interim, we need to be careful who else knows about our efforts."

Rip relaxed his hold on her and moved back to his chair. "That's a pretty limited group so far. Besides you and me, there's Jack Ingersoll, and whoever you talked to at Jandra."

"Don't forget Mark Wilcox and John Ramsey. They were in our little session last night."

"I guess John's okay, but I don't know Mark Wilcox. For all we know, he's on the Jandra payroll."

Sara shook her head. "John brought him in, and I trust John's judgment. But I agree, we probably should be a little cautious around Mark in the future." She picked a pink message slip off her desk and began to fold and unfold it. "But you said you thought you had a way to find out the mode of action of Jandramycin. What's that?"

"Well, it may not be as great an idea as I thought, since your efforts got you shot at. Carter Resnick tells me he's become pretty good at hacking into computer systems. I was thinking about trying to wangle some cooperation from him."

"So you think he could get into the FDA's computer and access the new drug app for Jandramycin?"

"No, I think that information's fabricated. I was going to see if he could get the information from Jandra's system."

"Why wouldn't that be a good idea?" Sara asked.

"Resnick has been sort of off-again, on-again giving information to me. On the one hand, he seems anxious to take down Ingersoll. On the other, he guards the research data from his lab with a passion. I think young doctor Resnick has his own agenda. I don't know what it is, but in light of recent events I think I'd better be careful around him."

Sara leaned back. "I think we'd both better be careful around anyone else until this thing is settled."

12

"Sara, this is Mark Wilcox." Mark braced his phone against his shoulder and reached into his desk drawer for a fresh legal pad. He might be practicing medicine now, but old habits die hard. "Do you have a second to talk?"

"Just about that long. Your page caught me between my last clinic patient and afternoon hospital rounds. What's up?"

"I was wondering if you'd like to have dinner with me tonight. There's a great new restaurant I've heard about, and I'd love to take you there."

Mark wasn't sure how to interpret the silence that followed. Was Sara looking for a graceful way to say "No"? Of course she could be checking her schedule to see if she was free. He began to doodle on the legal pad.

"I . . . I'm not sure how good my company would be tonight."

"Tell you what. If you're a terrible dinner companion, we'll split the check. But I'm betting it will be an enjoyable evening for both of us. Goodness knows, I can use one, and I'll bet you can, too."

Another silence, but a shorter one this time. "Okay. But I have to go by and pick up a rental car after work, so maybe I should meet you there."

"Why a rental car?"

As Sara told him about the shooting the night before, Mark pressed harder with his pencil until it broke, sending splintered pieces flying off his desk. "Are you all right? Did you call the police? And who would do something like this? Why?"

"I'm fine. The police came and took a report. And as for the who and why, I'm still working on that."

Mark was leaning back in his swivel chair. He came forward and his feet hit the floor with a dull thud. "Tell you what. Let me pick you up at the medical center. I'll take you to get your rental car. We can drop it off at your house and go to dinner together. How's that?"

He was getting used to the silences. Obviously, Sara was working on overload right now, and she was thinking through all her responses. Finally, she said, "I guess that would work. And I have to eat sometime. Can you pick me up at the plaza outside the Clinical Science Building about six? No, make that six thirty."

"Six thirty it is. I'll see you then. And in the meantime, be careful."

After he hung up, Mark tore the page off the legal pad, crushed it into a tight ball, and slammed it into the wastebasket. He couldn't believe this was happening.

Lillian Goodman emerged from the treatment room into the hallway of the clinic and almost bowled over John Ramsey. "Oh, sorry," she said. "Afraid I was thinking about this last patient."

"No problem. I think about patients all the time. But it's good to have something to occupy my mind. Keeps me from feeling sorry for myself."

Lillian looked into John's eyes and read the sadness there. "Look, it's none of my business, but I'm a widow. I've been down the road you're walking. I know it seems like you're never going to get past what you're feeling now, but believe me, you will."

"I appreciate what you're saying, but I don't think I'll ever get over losing Beth."

"I didn't say 'Get over,'" Lillian said. "I said 'Get past.' When you lose a spouse, or any loved one, your world never gets back to where it was. But eventually you have to adjust to the new normal."

"I'm afraid I'm not doing very well at adjusting. I thought going back to work would help, and I guess it has, but still there are times when I feel overwhelmed with my sense of loss."

"And those times will continue to come. You can feel sorry for yourself. You can even cry. But the fact remains that you're still alive, and you ought to make good use of every day. Did it ever occur to you that maybe God left you here because there are some things God wants you to accomplish?"

"Beth told me that once. She said that when God said it was time for one of us to go, there was a reason, but we wouldn't have the chance to find out what it was until we got to heaven. I never paid a lot of attention to that. I just figured I'd go first, so I made all these plans to make sure she was cared for after I was gone. But now—"

Lillian looked at her watch. "I have patients, and you do, too. But I think it would do you good to talk some of this out. What say I buy you dinner? If not tonight, sometime soon. As I told you, I've been down this same road, and I remember how it helped to have someone to talk with about what I was feeling." She saw the look in his eyes and hastened to add, "Not a date. You're not ready, and if you were, it probably wouldn't be me. Just let me be a friend."

"Well, guess it would help to talk. And dinner tonight sounds fine. Why don't we touch base after our last patients?" John turned away, then looked back over his shoulder, to add, "Thanks for the offer. I could use a friend right now."

Jack Ingersoll closed the last suitcase. Six days in Germany, presenting his paper at a prestigious international meeting, speaking at lunches and dinners where physicians would hang on his every word, all of it first class and paid for by Jandra. His allotted two pieces of luggage bulged, and he'd already thought of a few other things he might need. No matter. He'd buy it there in Europe. If Jandramycin did well, he need never worry about money again.

His cell phone startled him out of his thoughts. As he pulled it from his pocket, he ran through the short list of people who had the number. Who could be calling? Resnick? No, Ingersoll was sure the detailed instructions for projects he'd left would keep Resnick safely tucked away in the lab for the duration of this trip. Pearson? Just the opposite of Resnick, who'd probably never had an original thought in his life, Pearson was competent to handle any question or problem that might come up.

He looked at the caller ID. "Private Number." No help there. He punched the button to answer. "Dr. Ingersoll."

"Jack, this is Bob Wolfe. All packed for Germany?"

"Just finishing, Bob. My flight leaves in the morning. I assume you're about to be on your way as well."

"I'll have to pack tonight—my duties keep me pretty busy around here, you know—but I look forward to seeing you and hearing your presentation."

Your duties keep you busy. Sure they do. You cull through a mound of data your researchers accumulate and cherry-pick the best projects so you can take credit for them. Oh, well . . . "What can I do for you, Bob?"

"It's what I can do for you," Wolfe said. "I can warn you that a Dr. Sara Miles from your institution called Jandra trying to get information about alleged late effects from Jandramycin. I tried to reassure her, suggested she talk with you, but she was quite persistent. She even called Dr. Patel's office."

Jack felt his intestines knotting. "I trust she didn't get through to Patel."

"No, but the news got to him anyway, and I got called in for a rap on the knuckles by Patel, Lindberg, and the head corporate attorney, a guy named Berman."

"Sorry to hear that. Let me assure you that I—"

"No assurances necessary, Jack, because we all know how important it is that Jandramycin move forward and do well, with no hint of any adverse effects to our miracle drug. And we all know the consequences of any information to the contrary being circulated."

"Of course, and—"

"That's why I wanted to call you and—oh, by the way, I'm recording this conversation. I know you won't mind. I called to ask you the same question Berman asked me in Patel's office. Just for the record, you understand."

"Uh, sure. What's the question?"

"Are you prepared to state that you are unaware of any side effects from Jandramycin such as the ones mentioned by Dr. Miles?"

There was a long moment of silence.

"I need a yes or no answer," Wolfe said. "Please respond, Dr. Ingersoll. Do you understand the question?"

A recorded conversation, a loaded question, and his name tagged to his response. Ingersoll knew he was trapped. "I understand the question."

"And your answer, Dr. Ingersoll?"

"Yes, I'm prepared to state that I know of no such effects."

The chuckle on the other end of the line must have been similar to the serpent's response when Eve took a bite from the apple. "That's all I need, Jack. See you in Frankfurt."

Ingersoll hung up the phone and slumped onto his bed, almost knocking a suitcase onto the floor. He loosened his tie and tugged at his collar, but still couldn't get enough air. His good mood of ten minutes ago was gone. Right now, he needed time to think. That, and a stiff drink.

"I'm sorry it took so long to get the rental car," Sara said. "That's going to make us late for dinner."

"No problem." Mark Wilcox wheeled his BMW into the parking lot of the restaurant and hurried around to open Sara's door. The parking valet hustled up, and Mark tossed him the keys.

Inside the restaurant, the maitre d' greeted Mark as though he were a long-lost cousin. "Dr. Wilcox, so glad to have you with us this evening."

"Thanks, Hugo. I hope you have a nice table for us."

"Of course. Right this way."

As they wove through the crowded room, Mark watched Sara out of the corner of his eye. Even though this restaurant had only been open for a few weeks, it had already become an "in" spot. He was glad he'd come by here earlier and introduced himself to the maitre d', slipping the man a twenty-dollar bill instead of a calling card. Yes, Hugo, the table had better be good and the service fantastic. After that, Mark figured it was up to him.

The spot to which Hugo showed them was perfect, a half-round booth toward the rear, where they could see everything and everyone without sacrificing their own privacy. The maitre d' presented menus with the flourish of a magician producing a silver dollar out of midair and padded away.

"Mark, this is so nice. Do you come here often?"

"First time," Mark said.

"But the maitre d'—"

"When I was practicing law, I defended his brother." Mark had spent some time trying to come up with an explanation other than "I came by earlier and greased his palm." He hoped this one would suffice.

The waiter eased up to the table, introduced himself, and asked what they'd like to drink.

Mark picked up the wine list and looked at Sara. "Would you like a bottle of wine?"

"Just water for me, please," she said.

"San Pellegrino okay?" he asked. When she nodded her assent, Mark ordered and the waiter hurried away.

"You could have had some wine if you wanted," Sara said. "I just . . . I just don't drink."

"No, no. That's fine."

"Aren't you going to ask why?"

He'd wanted to, but Mark figured she'd tell him if she wanted him to know. Apparently she did. "I'm an orphan. My parents were killed by a drunk driver when I was in college. When I got the message, I was at a party and I'd just taken a sip of the margarita my date brought me."

"And you swore that was your last drink. Right?"

"I know. Sounds silly, I guess."

"Not at all. Not too many years ago, there were still people who wouldn't drive a German car because they had bad memories from World War II."

The waiter arrived and poured their water as though it were Châteauneuf-du-Pape or some other high-priced wine. "Would you care to hear the specials?" he intoned.

"Give us a moment," Mark said. He turned back to Sara. "I respect your decision. And I appreciate you not lecturing me about the evils of alcohol."

"I've made my decision, but that doesn't give me the right to make yours." She lifted her glass. "Now how about that relaxing evening you promised me? How many years did you practice law before you gave it up to go into medicine? I'll bet there's quite a story there."

Mark dredged up stories from his law practice, his medical training, and his current situation as a primary care physician. Sara proved to be a great listener, and as the evening progressed he found himself doing most of the talking. "Sara, I wanted to get to know you. Instead, you know almost everything about me and I know next to nothing about you. Help me, here."

"Not much to say, really. Graduated from Southwestern Medical, did my residency here, then went onto the faculty. Got married while I was a resident, but that's over."

"Would I know your husband?"

She took another sip of San Pellegrino water. "Jack Ingersoll."

Wow. He hadn't seen that coming. Drop that hot potato right now. "Any children?"

Sara shivered, and Mark wondered what he'd said. "I'm sorry. Is that a touchy subject?"

"Our infant son, Jack Jr., died of SIDS. It wasn't long afterward that Jack divorced me." She reached for her coffee cup and found it empty. "But that's enough about me. Let's talk about more pleasant things."

Mark beckoned to the waiter, who refilled their cups. Sara lifted hers to her lips and in the action her sleeve fell away from her watch. "Oh, my gracious. I had no idea it was this late. I'd better be getting home."

"I wish we could stretch this out a bit, but I suppose we both have a full day tomorrow." He called for the check and covered it with a credit card, managing not to flinch at the total. No matter. The evening had been worth it, and he would have paid double the tab if it could stretch the night out longer.

At her door, Sara said, "Thanks for a wonderful evening. The meal was wonderful, and I enjoyed getting to know you."

Mark put on his most hangdog look. "Would you take pity on a poor guy and give him one more cup of coffee for the road? You wouldn't want me to fall asleep at the wheel, would you?"

Sara laughed. "Oh, come on in. I'll make us both some coffee. I think caffeine addiction is a universal consequence of medical school."

One cup turned into two as the conversation picked up where they'd left off. The pot was empty when Sara yawned and shook her head. "That's it. I'm kicking you out. I have to go to work in the morning."

"I guess you're right. Thanks for the coffee." Mark followed Sara's lead and rose from the sofa. "I'll give you a—"

"Mark. Did you hear that?"

"What?"

"Listen."

Mark strained his ears. At first he heard nothing. Then he did. Faint at first, gaining in intensity and volume before dying away in a mournful decrescendo. The cry of an infant.

13

It's great to find someone who's as fond of good Tex-Mex food as I am," Lillian Goodman said. "I've never been to this restaurant before, but you can bet I'll be coming back."

John shrugged off the compliment. "Finding a good Tex-Mex restaurant in Dallas is as easy as finding a Starbucks in Seattle."

"Yes, but the hard part is knowing which one of them serves the best food. And you get credit for this one." Lillian looked around the room. "I don't know how they stay in business, though. Only about a third of the tables are occupied. And I can't believe they can serve so much food for such low prices."

"You should see it on weekends. Then the waiting line stretches out the door. As for the price, it's a family business. Dad is the host, Mom is the cook, and the oldest kids are the servers and help in the kitchen."

A teenage girl hurried over with a coffee pot. "Dr. Ramsey, would you and your lady like some more coffee? Perhaps some *flan*?"

Lillian was about to say no when John said, "You really should try the *flan*. It's ambrosia."

Oh, well. Another fifteen minutes on the elliptical tomorrow. "Sure. Why don't we split one?"

When the waitress had left, Lillian said, "You seem to be known here."

"I used to be, but I haven't been here since—" He blinked several times.

"John, it's okay to cry. Men can show their emotions the same way women can. And it's a way to heal." She sipped her coffee to give him time to recover. "So you and Beth used to come here."

He nodded. "You might say this was 'our place.' I haven't been back here since she died. And truthfully, maybe it was a mistake to bring you here. I feel sort of guilty."

Lillian chose her words carefully. "It is guilt, John. It's called survivor guilt, and it's the toughest part of the grieving process. You feel guilty because Beth isn't here to enjoy it. And you feel like you're cheating on her by bringing me here." She opened her purse, rummaged in it, and put a credit card on the table. "You know, I invited you to have dinner tonight. Maybe this will help you accept that this isn't a date."

The *flan* came, and Lillian found it to be worth the calories. She and John ate carefully from either side of the cylinder of custard, their spoons finally meeting in the middle. "That last bite is yours," Lillian said, laying aside her spoon.

"That's what Beth used to do." The words came out almost as a croak. John brought his napkin to his face and blotted tears. "Sorry."

"No, that's good. You can't keep it bottled up. It's not healthy." Lillian decided to plunge ahead. "John, until the dessert came, you hardly touched your food. How much weight have you lost since Beth died?"

"I really don't know." He shrugged. "I know that I probably should get some new shirts. The collars on these are pretty loose."

"But you don't feel like buying clothes. Right?"

"How did you know?"

"I've been down that road. Remember." Time to take the plunge. "Have you thought about antidepressants?"

"No. I want to—"

"You want to experience your grief fully, because it would be disrespectful to Beth not to do so. And, like a typical man, you think that grieving harder will get it over sooner."

His expression told her she'd hit the nail on the head. "You're not eating. You're not sleeping. You're distracted. You descend into self-pity. John, that's clinical depression. It's normal under the circumstances. And I think you should see your own doctor and ask him about taking an antidepressant."

John shook his head. "It's not that simple. I'd also have to see if an antidepressant would react adversely with the medications I'm on."

"What kind— No, I shouldn't pry. Talk with your doctor."

"My doctor is Rip Pearson, and the meds are antiretroviral. I got stuck by a needle that someone left in a waste receptacle." He held out his hand.

Without hesitation, she reached forward and took the hand he held out. "Hmm, puncture wound at the base of the thumb. And it looks pretty red." She pressed and felt the tissue give beneath her fingers. "John, there's some fluctuance here. I think you may be forming an abscess. Are you on any antibiotic prophylaxis?"

"No, just post-exposure prophylaxis against HIV."

"Well, we should needle that area and see if there's pus there." She decided that only a couple of doctors could talk like this while still at the dinner table.

Lillian could see his male ego struggling with his training as a physician. Fortunately, the medical science won. "You're right. I'll ask Rip to look at it tomorrow. He can aspirate it and culture the pus." John dropped his napkin on the table and held up Lillian's credit card to get the waitress's attention. "I guess it's time I began to take care of myself. Beth used to tell me that if I don't, no one else will."

Sara's first reaction to the infant cry was an instinctive tightening in her gut, followed almost immediately by a wave of relief—the cry was real. Mark heard it. This time it wasn't just a product of her tortured mind.

"Where's that coming from?" Mark asked.

"I don't know. It sounded like it came from ... from—" Her throat seemed to close off. She dabbed at her eyes.

Mark appeared bewildered. "Sara, why don't you sit down? Can I get you some water?"

She shook her head. "I'll be okay. It's just that—" Again, she couldn't finish.

Sara felt Mark's hand guiding her toward the sofa. When she was seated, he hurried from the room, returning with a glass of water. "Drink this. Take some deep breaths. Then start at the beginning and tell me what's going on."

In a few moments, the roaring in her ears had subsided and her breathing was under control. "It's sort of a long story."

"I've got as long as it takes." He eased onto the sofa beside her. "What's this about?"

"I told you Jack and I had a baby, a son. He was three months old when I found him dead in his crib, probably SIDS. After Jack left me, I began having nightmares about our son. Once or twice a month I'd hear an infant crying in the middle of the night, but when I rushed to the nursery there was nothing there. No baby furniture—I'd long since gotten rid of that—and nothing else. Just a bare room, one that I never entered."

"And now . . . ?"

"Now you've heard the cries, too. It's not my imagination." She shivered. "But I still can't explain it."

"Where's the room?"

She pointed to a door. "Down the hall, last door on the right."

Mark patted her shoulder. "Stay here. I'm going to check it out."

He hurried away, and Sara felt a cold wind on the back of her neck. She'd never believed in ghosts before, but now she halfway wondered if the ghost of her son inhabited the nursery. What would Mark find in there?

Mark was back in five minutes. "Just an empty room."

She tried to hide her sigh of relief. "I told you."

"Do you have a flashlight?"

"In the middle drawer under the kitchen counter," Sara said.

He rummaged until he found the flashlight. "And where's your attic access?" He turned in a circle. "Never mind. I think I saw it a minute ago."

He disappeared into the hall, and soon she heard the attic stairs unfold. Then a series of creaks and groans announced his movement overhead. Just as she was about to venture into the hall and shout up to him, she heard him coming back down the stairs.

"I don't think you're going to find a baby up there," she called.

He poked his head through the door and gestured with the flashlight in his hand. "No, but I found something even more interesting. Come see."

Sara eased off the couch and followed Mark on feet that seemed to be made of lead. He led her up the attic stairs, directing her to stand in the small space where plywood bridged the rafters. "Stay here. Don't step out into the attic. I don't want you to fall through the sheet rock."

"What am I supposed to see?"

"Look where my flashlight's pointed."

At first, she saw nothing out of the ordinary—just rafters and insulation, all coated with a generous layer of dust. But in the area where Mark's flashlight beam settled, she could see that there was much less dust, fewer cobwebs. And sitting on a rafter she saw a series of small boxes interconnected with wires.

She looked up to see Mark's eyes were fixed on hers. "There's your crying baby. A digital recorder with a separate speaker, connected to a timer, and all neatly wired into the house's electrical current. I suspect that it's set to go off on random nights, playing just long enough to get you out of bed."

Sara couldn't believe it. This was something you read about in detective novels or saw in a James Bond movie. It didn't happen to divorced women living in a nice neighborhood in Dallas. The questions flew through her mind. Why? Who?

"Would you happen to have some wire cutters? Or even a pair of pliers with wire-cutting jaws? I'll cut this thing loose. We can talk later about who did it and how. Right now, I want to assure you that you're not going to be awakened by those cries anymore."

Sara's heart sank. No, she wouldn't hear the electronic cries anymore. But neither would she hear the cries of her own baby. He was dead. As dead as the love she'd once had for Jack Ingersoll.

The man behind the hotel desk wore a dark suit, a gleaming white shirt with a conservative tie, and a smile as false as Grandma's teeth. His English was only slightly accented. "Welcome, Herr Doktor Ingersoll. Or do you perhaps prefer Herr Professor?"

"Either will do," Ingersoll said. He dropped his passport and American Express Platinum Card on the registration counter. "I'm quite tired from the overseas flight and would like to go to my room as quickly as possible."

"Of course." The man beckoned to a bellman and said something in German. The bellman gave a curt nod and hurried away for a luggage trolley.

"We have for you a very nice room on the Executive Level. *Zimmer sieben funfzig.*" He paused and translated. "Room seven fifty." The clerk pushed the credit card back toward Ingersoll, along with a few other pieces of paper. "Here is information about our services. All your expenses will be direct-billed to Jandra Pharmaceuticals. I will return your passport as soon as I have completed your registration form."

Ingersoll scooped up the credit card and other papers. One of them, a business card, fell to the floor, and when Ingersoll picked it up he saw that engraved letters identified the Hotel Hessischer Hof, with an address in Frankfurt, Germany. At the bottom, smaller script spelled out the name and phone number of Wilhelm Lambert, Generaldirektor. *Not bad. Business class on Lufthansa. Quartered on the executive level of a first-class hotel, met by the general manager.* So far, Jandra was treating him right. Then again, he knew that all this would vanish like the morning mist if Jandramycin failed to live up to corporate expectations.

"Please go with Kurt, Herr Professor," the manager said, and Ingersoll fell in behind the bellman. Apparently the Germans respected him more as a professor than as a physician. Then again, there were several kinds of "Doktor" here. Most of them were nonmedical and many of them honorary titles, but to be a true "Professor" was a horse of a different color. He made a mental note to identify himself in that fashion in the future.

"Professor Ingersoll. Is that you?" He turned to see a stout, middle-aged man in a wrinkled blue serge suit of European cut hurrying after him. "Please forgive me, but I recognize you from your pictures. I believe it's important that we meet."

Ingersoll frowned. "Yes, I'm Professor Ingersoll. And you are. . . ?"

"I am Doktor Heinz Gruber. From the University of Ulm Medical Center." Seeing Ingersoll's puzzled expression, the man continued, "I lead the research studies being done in Germany on your compound, EpAm848. Or should I say, Jandramycin."

"Oh, I didn't recognize the name." He extended his hand. "Pleasure to meet you."

"I know you are just arriving, and must be tired, but I think it's very important that we talk. I believe we have much to discuss. Much."

Ingersoll weighed the alternatives. He decided he'd better get this out of the way. He pulled a bill from a roll in his pocket and handed it to the bellman, who'd stood patiently by during this exchange. "I'm sorry I haven't had the opportunity to change any money into Euros. Please take my bags to my room."

The bellman's confused expression told Ingersoll that he was dealing with one of the small minority of Germans not fluent in English. Unusual for a four-star hotel, but there it was.

Gruber addressed the man. "*Nimmst Du die Säcke zum Zimmer.*" The bellman nodded and trundled off.

"Thank you," Ingersoll said. "I didn't think I'd need any German for my visit."

"In most instances, you won't. I suspect he understands more English than he lets on." Gruber flashed a grin. "Bellmen and servants learn a great deal that way."

"You said we needed to talk. Can we do it quickly? I'm really jet-lagged," Ingersoll said.

"Of course." Gruber scanned the lobby and pointed toward a quiet corner. "I believe we will have some privacy there."

Ingersoll dropped into an overstuffed chair and settled his briefcase on the floor beside him. "Now, what's so important that it can't wait?" He heard the impatience in his voice, but didn't really care. This was some German doctor doing grunt work for Jandra, and he probably wanted approval. Ingersoll hoped to give him a quick "attaboy" before heading for a well-deserved bath and nap.

"As you may know, along with my colleague, Dr. Rohde, I have been carrying out the German arm of the study on Jandra's new antibiotic. We have been following the protocol they set up and forwarding the results to their American office as we accumulate data."

This didn't seem to call for a response, so Ingersoll nodded and tried to look interested.

"The drug was completely successful in treating infections with *Staphylococcus luciferus*, and we noted no side effects while patients were receiving it. But . . ." Gruber looked around and beckoned a waiter. "*Zwei Kaffee bitte.*" He waited until the waiter hurried away to continue. "You seem a little unfocused. Perhaps some coffee would help. I believe you will find what I have to say important."

Gruber seemed content to sit in silence until coffee was served. He dropped a few bills on the tray, added cream and sugar to his cup, and took a sip. He smacked his lips. "Good coffee is truly one of the forces that keeps doctors and scientists going, is that not true?"

Ingersoll ignored his own cup. "Can we get to the point? I'm quite tired."

"I apologize," Gruber said, while looking anything but sorry. "The point is that we have heard rumors, nothing certain but definite rumors, about . . . " He spread his hands. "*Komplikationen*?"

"Complications, I suppose." Suddenly Ingersoll was alert. "What about these rumors?"

"We are happy to carry out this research. The money supports much of our other work. But it is of concern when we learn that perhaps we are putting our patients at risk for troubles that come later." He leaned forward. "What can you tell me about these rumors?"

Ingersoll remembered his conversation with Wolfe. Was this a trap? Had Jandra set this up to test him? Or was this a well-meaning researcher, simply seeking information? In either case, he knew what his answer would be, and he recited it, just as he'd recited it less than thirty-six hours earlier. "I know of no such effects."

Gloria stuck her head into the dictation room and waggled the chart in her hand. Sara covered the phone mouthpiece and whispered, "One minute." She removed her hand and said, "What did you ask?"

Mark repeated his question. "How did you sleep?"

Sara thought she'd never heard a sillier question. She felt like she'd been put through a wringer. "I'm afraid I didn't sleep too well."

"Oh." Mark's disappointment was obvious. "I was hoping that getting that digital recorder out of your attic would let you sleep through the night for a change."

Didn't he realize that the cries that triggered her nightmares weren't the only thing disturbing her sleep? She had so much weighing on her that the removal of one factor didn't make everything all well. "Mark, I have to get back to patients. Can we talk later?"

"Sure. How about lunch?"

This was going much too fast. She'd thought dinner would be a nice change, but dinner had turned into a time of sharing for which Sara wasn't ready. Better slow it down. "Not today, Mark. Why don't I call you?"

The disappointment in Mark's voice was obvious. "Sure. And if you don't call—"

"I'll call. Now I have to go."

Sara noticed that the phone receiver was damp when she cradled it. Wasn't a phone conversation with a good-looking man who was interested in you supposed to be an enjoyable experience? She should be thrilled that Mark was obviously interested in her. Instead, she was a little afraid.

"What's going on?" Rip Pearson stood in the doorway, a quizzical expression on his face. "Whatever the problem is, you can tell me. I'm a pretty good listener, and you look like you could use a friend."

"That's my problem," she said. "Maybe I don't really have any friends—at least, any I can trust."

"Whoa!" Rip held up his hand. "You and I've known each other for . . ." He counted silently. "For eight years. We've been friends all that time, although admittedly after you married Jack you didn't seem to have time for anyone else. But I've never stopped being your friend." He eased into the chair beside her. "Want to tell me about it?"

Gloria appeared in the doorway, but Sara motioned her away. "Give me five minutes, please. And close the door. Thank you."

She took a deep breath, then launched into her tale of finding the digital recorder in her attic. Rip, to his credit, listened without interruption, although the expression on his face when she mentioned her evening with Mark reminded Sara of someone who'd bitten into a lemon.

When she finished, Rip said, "So who do you think left it there? And why?"

"I've thought about this. Matter of fact, I was up all night thinking about it. I thought about the when, and the who, and the why."

"So what did you come up with?"

"It started a few months after the baby died—about the time Jack moved out and announced he wanted a divorce. At first I thought it was just another manifestation of my guilt. My baby was dead. Therefore I had to be a bad mother."

"But now that you know about the recorder, you think—"

"I think Jack left it in the attic."

"Why would he do that?"

"I have no doubt he did it to torture me. It was simply a gesture of pure evil."

"What can you do about it?" Rip asked.

"That's the problem. I have no proof. He'd deny it and accuse me of being paranoid."

There was a tap on the door. Without opening it, Sara called, "Okay, Gloria. I'll be right there."

"So what do you intend to do?" Rip asked.

"Nothing—except be very careful around Jack Ingersoll." She paused with her hand on the doorknob. "And I'd advise you to do the same."

14

John, how's that hand doing?" Rip Pearson motioned John Ramsey to a seat on the edge of the exam table.

"That's what I wanted to ask you. It's getting pretty sore," John said. "Do you think I should be on an antibiotic?"

"Let's take a look." Rip swung a lamp away from the wall on its hinged arm and focused the light on John's hand. "If that's your primary question today, at least you don't seem to be worrying about HIV with every breath."

If you only knew. "Oh, I'm worried about that, too. I'm just trying to live with it." John winced as Rip pressed on the soft tissue at the base of his right thumb.

"Well, this looks like it's getting a bit red. Feels warm. It's swollen, and I think there's a little fluctuance here."

John knew what that meant. For years he'd taught medical students the four cardinal signs of inflammation. *Calor, dolor, rubor, and tumor.* Heat, pain, redness, and swelling. "So where do we go from here?"

Rip was already reaching for a pair of latex gloves. "I think I'd better stick a needle into that area and see if I can aspirate some pus for a culture." He opened a cabinet and extracted a large syringe, a needle, and several sealed foil packets contain-

162

ing antiseptic swabs. Rip's hand stopped and hovered over a rubber-stoppered vial. "Want a local anesthetic?"

"No, I'll be fine. Besides, the fewer times you stick a needle into that area, the less chance of spreading the infection."

"Right, of course. You haven't lost a step, have you?" Rip said.

"Maybe one or two, but I think I can still remember a few things." John tried to relax as he felt the cool antiseptic on his skin.

"Little stick."

John thought about what a total misrepresentation those two words were. They could mean anything from the mosquito bite of an immunization to the searing pain he was currently feeling in his hand. He hazarded a look and saw that Rip was moving the needle around, looking for a pocket of pus. John winced as he felt the grinding of needle tip against bone.

"We may not have any—Oh, there you are. Come to Daddy." Rip pulled back on the plunger of the syringe and a tiny amount of reddish-yellow pus oozed into the tip of the barrel. "Not much, but it should be enough to culture." He pulled the needle out and applied a sterile gauze pad to the puncture wound. "Hold pressure on that for a minute, will you?"

"I don't like the looks of what you got," John said.

"No, but let's wait until we see what the culture shows." He put a few drops of pus on two swabs and plunged them into tubes containing culture medium. "I'll get an aerobic and anaerobic culture, and . . ." Rip forced the last drop from the tip of the syringe onto a clean slide, then used the edge of another slide to create a thin film of pus on the glass. "Let's get someone to stain this so we can have a look."

Soon the two men watched a lab tech put the stained slide on the stage of a binocular microscope, apply a drop of oil to one of the lenses, and rack the assembly down until the lens barely touched the slide. John remembered how many slides he'd cracked before he mastered the technique of using the oil immersion lens. For the tech it appeared to be old hat, though. He brought everything into focus, stepped back, and gestured for Rip and John to have a look. Rip bent over the 'scope, and after a few seconds of moving the slide back and forth, his face tightened. He stood up and gestured for John to take his place.

John removed his glasses and applied his eyes to the scope. He fiddled with the knobs to bring the field into focus, and when he did, he knew why Rip's expression had changed. Amidst the debris of dead white blood cells he saw round blue organisms. Most were single or in pairs, but many formed chains and grapelike clusters. A second-year medical student could have made the diagnosis: *Staphylococcus*.

John straightened. "It's *Staph*, all right. Think it's *Staph luciferus*?"

"Too soon to tell. Could simply be a coagulase-negative *Staph*, a non-pathogen. We'll have to wait for the culture results."

"So what do we do?"

"I don't think we need to get out the big guns until we have confirmation. Why don't I just put you on a broad-spectrum antibiotic now? We can change it later if we need to."

John tried to keep his expression neutral, but his insides were churning. *What else, Lord? And why me?*

The man's nametag said he was Wes, the owner of this gun store. He looked pointedly at his watch. Five o'clock, time to close. But he couldn't ignore a potential sale.

"This one?" Wes reached into the glass-topped case. His hand hovered in midair over the rows of handguns displayed there and settled on a small revolver.

"Yes, that one," Sara said.

"You know, you don't want to just pick one that's pretty," Wes said. "I mean, this one's nice—blued steel, rubber grips and all. But—"

"May I see it, please?" Sara held out a hand that was rock-steady. Wes handed her the revolver butt-first.

She balanced it in her hand, snapped the cylinder out and checked that the gun was unloaded, snapped it back into place and dry-fired the weapon four times rapidly. "Trigger pull's not too bad. Good balance. I like the weight—about a pound, isn't it?"

Sara enjoyed seeing the startled look on Wes's face. She was a woman. Women weren't supposed to know about guns. Well, she did. She knew that the Taurus Ultra-Lite weighed seventeen ounces, had a two-inch barrel, held five .38 caliber bullets, and was a favorite among off-duty policemen. After a couple of phone calls to the policewoman she'd met after the shooting incident, followed by a little research on the computer, Sara knew just what she wanted.

"How much?" she asked.

Wes scratched his head. "That one's four hundred and eighty dollars, but I might be able to do better than that."

Sara waved the pistol back and forth in a "no you don't" gesture, enjoying the look on the man's face as she used the weapon to make her point. "You will definitely do better than that, since this tag hanging from the trigger guard says four hundred thirty."

"Oh, I must have misremembered," Wes said. "I guess that's the price, then."

"Do you really want this sale? I can go to any of the stores around here, drop a credit card on the counter, and buy this gun for that price with a box of .38 caliber cartridges thrown in." With the revolver still in her right hand, she opened her purse and reached in with her left, coming out with four crisp one hundred dollar bills. She put them on the counter, but kept her hand on them. "I'll give you four hundred cash, and I want the Taurus, a box of ammunition, and a cleaning kit."

Wes was silent for a moment, but she could tell by the expression on his face that she'd won. "Okay, I guess I can do that. And I'll be glad to keep it for you until you get your concealed handgun license. I've got the forms here somewhere."

Sara put the gun on the counter, opened her wallet, and produced a laminated card about the size of a driver's license. The upper left portion carried the word *Texas* in flowing script, with the words *Concealed Handgun License* centered along the top. Sara's picture smiled out from the left side of the license. Wes checked the expiration date and said, "Okay, looks like this is good for another year."

She tapped the four bills. "So is it a sale?"

The bills disappeared into Wes's pocket. "Sure. Let me get you a box of ammo and the cleaning kit."

A peculiar double-buzz beside him brought Jack Ingersoll awake with a start. He opened his eyes and looked around at unfamiliar surroundings. This wasn't his bedroom. The walls were done in a subtle print of plum on a gold background. The bed where he lay was smaller than his own king-sized one. The source of the buzzing was a phone on a bedside table to his left, not in its familiar position to his right. Heavy drapes were half-open, revealing deep twilight outside.

He fumbled the receiver off its cradle. "Dr. Ingersoll."

"Herr Professor, you wished to be awakened at seventeen thirty hours."

"Thanks. Er, *Danke*." He hung up the phone and let his thoughts settle. He was in Germany, for the international conference. This was a five-star hotel, the Hessis . . . something or other. He had an important presentation to make tomorrow, but tonight there were a cocktail reception and by-invitation dinner for the speakers and VIP's.

His head was still fuzzy, the combined effects of an overnight transatlantic flight, too much complimentary champagne on the aircraft, and the worst jet lag he'd ever experienced. He stumbled out of bed and found that he'd slept in his shirt and pants. He pulled a plastic laundry bag off a hanger in the closet and consigned his wrinkled clothes and dirty linen to it.

Half an hour later, fresh from a shower and shave, Ingersoll adjusted the knot in his red paisley tie, tugged the cuffs of his white shirt from the sleeves of his dark blue suit, and prepared to leave his room. He had one hand on the doorknob when the peculiar ring of the phone stopped him. He checked his watch and found it was still on U.S. time. The bedside clock showed five minutes until six. Oh, well. It wouldn't hurt to be a few minutes late to the cocktail party. He expected it to be a bore, but as a speaker he supposed he should put in an appearance.

He lifted the receiver and answered.

"Jack, is that you?" Bob Wolfe's voice betrayed none of the fatigue Jack felt.

"Yes. Is this Bob?"

"Right. I presume you're going to the *Messe*."

"What?"

"The conference center. Sorry. I get over here enough that I've picked up some German, and I tend to lapse into it." Wolfe chuckled. "I was headed over for the cocktail party myself, and wondered if you'd like to walk over together."

Ingersoll's immediate reaction was "No." Wolfe probably wanted to squeeze him some more, make sure he hewed to the company line. Then again, Wolfe was the direct line to Jandra's purse strings, and Ingersoll needed to make sure they didn't suddenly tighten. "Sure," he said. "Are you at the Hess . . . the main hotel?"

"The Hessischer Hof. Yes, I'm in the lobby right now. I'll wait here for you."

"See you in a few minutes." Ingersoll depressed the cradle, dialed the operator, and arranged for his laundry and dry cleaning to be picked up from his room while he was gone. He rummaged through his briefcase until he found his registration slip for the conference. Then, as reluctant as a boy on his way to school without having done his homework, he stepped into the hall and looked for the elevator.

Wolfe rose from one of the sofas in the lobby as Ingersoll approached. "Would you like a drink in the bar here before we face the crowd?"

Ingersoll looked at his watch, which told him it was a quarter past noon in Dallas. "I've got to reset that," he mumbled.

"It's six fifteen local time," Wolfe volunteered. "Your dinner is at seven thirty. It'll take you fifteen minutes to pick up your registration packet and badge. Unless you then want to stand around at the cocktail party for an hour, talking to doctors whose accents make it impossible to understand them, I'd suggest we have a drink here first."

They found a quiet corner in the bar and ordered. A patron two tables away lit a cigarette, and Ingersoll waved his hand in front of his face. "I keep forgetting how many people in Europe still smoke."

"It makes me appreciate my non-smoking room," Ingersoll said. "By the way, thanks for the upgraded accommodations. If

I read the signs correctly, all the rooms on that floor are non-smoking."

"No problem. We just want you to be happy," Wolfe said.

And you want me to keep you happy, too, I'll bet. "So far I have no complaints."

"Have you finished the PowerPoint for your presentation tomorrow?"

"I put the finishing touches on it during the flight over. I think it'll go well."

"You have it on your laptop?"

"Uh, of course." Ingersoll was uncomfortable with the way this was going.

"Tell you what." Wolfe drained the last of his drink. "Let's pop back upstairs to your room for a minute and I'll copy it onto this." He produced a small keychain drive from his pocket. "I'll review it while you're at the VIP dinner, and if I see any errors I can let you know in the morning."

Ingersoll sat stunned. "I, I . . ."

"You don't mind, do you?" Wolfe signaled for the check. "After all, we're all in this together."

Ingersoll had already finished his drink. He lifted the glass to his lips, tapped it, and crunched the single ice cube that slid into his mouth. *Yeah, we're in this together. But it's pretty clear now who's calling the tune.*

Ingersoll sneaked a look at his watch, now set to the correct time. Only another half hour until the cocktail party for all the conference attendees would be over. Already those who'd been here since the party began were drifting out to have dinner. Most of those remaining wore nametags with one or more colored ribbons that proclaimed they were a speaker, moderator, panelist, or officer of one of the sponsoring societies.

169

"Entshuldig."

Someone jostled his elbow, but fortunately the glass he held was almost empty. He supposed he'd just heard the German word for "excuse me."

"No damage done," he said, and turned to find Dr. Gruber standing there with another man. Gruber's companion was a red-faced man who seemed to be stuffed into his ill-cut brown suit like a sausage in a casing. He wore horn-rimmed glasses and an expression of concern.

The man stuck out his hand. "Professor Ingersoll, I am Dr. Rohde. I believe my colleague, Dr. Gruber, mentioned me." Rohde continued to pump Ingersoll's hand. "It is an honor to meet you."

There was a tap on his shoulder. "Professor Ingersoll, we'll be leaving in a moment. Please meet us at the doorway."

"Well, gentlemen, I'm sorry not to be able to visit with you," Ingersoll said, relieved at his rescue. "As you see, I have to leave now."

Disappointment clouded Rohde's face. "I understand," he said. "I had several questions for you. But I will ask them during the open discussion after your paper tomorrow. *Auf wiedersehen.*"

As Ingersoll moved toward the door, he wondered if he'd avoided an uncomfortable conversation this evening, or been set up for a potentially disastrous public grilling tomorrow.

"Put that thing away." Rip's words were almost lost in the noise of the medical center's food court as medical students, residents, and staff snatched bagels and pastries to augment their breakfast coffee. He looked around but no one seemed to be paying attention to him and Sara, tucked away at a corner table.

Sara had told him she had something to show him, but when she opened her purse the last thing he'd expected to see was a revolver. She closed her purse and dropped it onto the floor beside her chair, where it settled with a slight thud.

Rip flinched at the noise. He leaned closer to Sara. "What are you doing with a gun? Where did you get it? Do you know—?"

Sara patted the air in a calming gesture. "What am I doing with it? The next time someone shoots at me, I plan to shoot back. Where did I get it? You might be surprised to learn that they sell these things in stores all over the city. And as for your next question, I already have a current concealed carry permit, and I know how to shoot."

"Why would you have a gun permit?"

Sara glanced to either side of them and confirmed that the adjacent tables were empty. "When Jack and I were married, he insisted we both have guns for protection. His argument was that sometimes we had to come out at night for an emergency, and hospitals aren't always in the best part of the city. He bought a gun for each of us. We both took the classes, got the permit. I carried the gun in my purse when I went out at night. He used an ankle holster for his. But when nothing happened, we gradually stopped carrying them, and I was glad. I hated to have them around. When we divorced, I told him to take my gun with him. Now I wish I'd kept it."

"Is it safe for you to carry that around? What if you drop your purse?"

"The cylinder holds five cartridges. I keep the hammer down on an empty chamber. I make sure the safety's on. The gun's a one-pound paperweight until I need to use it." She pointed her finger and dropped her thumb like the hammer of a gun coming down. "But when I need to use it, it'll be there."

Rip shook his head. "I don't know what's happened to you. Right after that shooting, you told me you were scared to death. You were ready to jump at your shadow. Now you've turned into a gunslinger who's itching for a fight. What made the difference?"

Sara had wondered that herself. Was it the aftereffects of the shooting that changed her? Was she ready to fight back because, all around her, patients were developing serious, potentially lethal illnesses from medication she'd agreed to give them? Had her attitude hardened after Mark found the recorder in the attic? Maybe it was the cumulative effect of all these events. Whatever the reason, she had to agree with Rip. She'd changed.

15

Bob Wolfe closed his laptop computer and rubbed his eyes. He'd been over Jack Ingersoll's presentation repeatedly, running it again and again last night until he literally fell asleep at the computer. He awoke long enough to set an alarm for 5:00 a.m. and fall into bed, fully clothed. His biologic time clock was all fouled up, so this morning he was dependent on a combination of strong, black coffee and nervous energy to keep him going.

At 7:00 a.m. he picked up the phone and dialed the number for Ingersoll's room. The call was answered after two rings, and Wolfe silently cursed Jack for sounding so chipper this morning.

"This is Bob Wolfe. How are you this morning?"

"Fine, fine. The dinner last night was shorter than I'd expected—I guess most of the attendees were as jet-lagged as I was—so I managed to get a good night's sleep." There was an audible gulp, followed by the clink of china on china. "I'm just having a room service breakfast before I get dressed and leave for the conference."

"I suppose I'll see you there." Wolfe swallowed some of his cold coffee. "I just wanted you to know that I've been over your presentation, and I think you've nailed it. No inaccuracies that I can see."

"That's good." Another pause, another clink. "I guess I'd better get moving."

"Good luck—" It took a second for the click on the other end of the line to register. Wolfe dropped the phone into the cradle and stared into space.

Up until now, Ingersoll had been eager to cooperate with Jandra, striving to keep the carrots coming while avoiding the stick. Maybe the dinner last night had convinced him that he truly was a VIP, that he didn't need Jandra's approval and backing. If that was the case, a dose of the stick might be in order. And it ought to be administered before Ingersoll made his presentation at the mid-morning general session.

Wolfe grinned with self-satisfaction as he picked up the phone, dialed "0," and asked in passable German for Herr Generaldirektor Lambert. He was told that Herr Lambert wouldn't be on duty for another two hours.

"Then reach him at home. I expect him to call me in my room within five minutes."

"Begging your pardon, Herr Wolfe—"

"I represent Jandra Pharmaceuticals. Herr Lambert knows the value of our business. Give him the message!" Wolfe slammed the receiver into its cradle and began to pace. He checked his watch every few seconds. This had to be done before Ingersoll left for the conference.

Three minutes after he'd bullied the desk clerk, his phone rang. "Dr. Wolfe."

"Herr Doktor, this is Wilhelm Lambert," the general manager said in flawless English. "How can I help you?"

"Thank you for calling back so quickly. As soon as we hang up, I want you to phone Professor Ingersoll's room and give him this exact message."

Sara hurried down the hall, already late for the internal medicine department's not-to-be-missed meeting, Grand Rounds.

"Got a minute?" Rip fell in beside her.

"Not really," she said. "I want to hear this lecture. The guy won a Nobel Prize in medicine for his work."

He matched her stride for stride. "I think when you hear what I have to say, you'll agree it's more important than hearing a lecture by a Nobel Prize winner."

Sara made a sharp right into a side hall where they'd have a bit of privacy. "Okay, what is it?"

"Does the name Ed Drummond mean anything to you?"

"Not off the top of my head. Why don't you tell me what you've got, instead of playing twenty questions?"

"Ed Drummond was one of our earliest Jandramycin patients," Rip said. "Septic shock from *Staph luciferus* pneumonia. Ring a bell?"

"Vaguely. What about him?"

"He developed kidney failure."

"So he's the one," Sara said.

"Right. And it was hard to treat him because of his age and all his other medical conditions." Rip paused like a quiz-show host about to announce a winner. "He died yesterday."

Sara took a step back, stopping when she felt the wall's cold tile against her. "So now . . ."

"Now Jandramycin is killing patients."

"Are you sure his death was due to the kidney failure?"

"His doctor signed the death certificate that way. There were other factors, of course, but that was the primary cause of death."

Sara pointed back the way they'd come. "We need to speed up our efforts. Let's go back to my office and work on this."

"What about Grand Rounds?" Rip asked.

"If we solve the Jandramycin puzzle, we might win a Nobel Prize ourselves." She shrugged. "And if we don't, more people are going to die."

Jack Ingersoll checked his appearance one more time in the bathroom mirror. He frowned when he heard the phone ring. Was that Bob Wolfe, calling again to remind him that his presentation today was important . . . to both of them? As if he needed a reminder. He looked around at the room he'd been given, thought about first-class travel and nice honoraria paid discreetly through the program committees of international meetings. He knew what was on the line, knew it better than the man who was bullying him.

"Doctor . . . er, Professor Ingersoll."

"Herr Professor, this is Wilhelm Lambert, the *General-direktor* of the hotel. I hope I'm not inconveniencing you by calling." Despite the words, there was no apology in the tone.

"Matter of fact, I was just leaving for my meeting," Ingersoll said.

"Then I will be brief. We've had a bit of confusion about your room. It seems that Jandra Pharmaceuticals may not, after all, be paying your expenses. I will attempt to contact Herr Doktor Wolfe later today to clarify this. Perhaps it will even be necessary for me to call the company's office in America, but that will take several hours because of the time difference."

"I—"

"In the meantime, please stop by the front desk on your way out and leave your credit card information, so that your bill can be covered." A click signaled the end of the conversation. Message delivered.

Ingersoll hung up the phone and turned to stare out the window of his room. The sun was up now, and he had a great view of the city, but his mind failed to register those images. Instead, he focused on the conversation he'd just had. He'd spoken with Wolfe only yesterday about Jandra covering his expenses. There was no mix-up. This was a means of applying pressure, plain and simple.

He grabbed his computer case and started for the door, where he paused and looked at the room rates posted there. Of course, no one paid these rates, there were always discounts, and he had no doubt that the meeting organizers had arranged one. But the Hessischer Hof was a five-star establishment that housed only the VIP's, their tab picked up by companies with deep pockets, and the rooms, especially this one on the Executive Floor, weren't cheap. If Ingersoll had to pay for this himself, he could count on dropping a couple of thousand dollars for a few days' stay.

He pulled the door closed behind him. *Okay, Bob, you've shown me the stick. It's time to go after the carrot.*

Ingersoll peered into the semidarkness of the lecture hall and tried to read the faces of his audience. He was on the next to last slide of his PowerPoint presentation, emphasizing probably his most important and most controversial point: that Jandramycin was 100 percent effective against the until-then lethal scourge, *Staphylococcus luciferus*, with absolutely no adverse effects noted.

Unfortunately, the combination of a dark lecture hall and the spotlights aimed at the podium made it impossible for him to see beyond the first row. In his limited field of view,

Ingersoll didn't see any frowns. No one was shaking his head. But he knew the reactions of the attendees in his field of view didn't constitute a representative sample. At any meeting, the population of the first row consisted of those waiting to present, plus a smattering of speakers who'd already been on the podium but hadn't been able to escape in a timely fashion. The acid test would come when the lights went up and the questions began.

Most speakers were given ten minutes to present their work. Ingersoll was allotted twenty, with an additional ten for questions and discussion. Not only that, his paper was the last one before a midmorning break, during which he would undoubtedly be held captive in the front of the lecture hall by individuals wanting a private word with him.

Ingersoll pushed the button to project his last slide, one with a picture of an aerial view of the campus of the medical center with the seal of the university superimposed in the lower right corner. "I would like to thank my colleagues at the Southwestern Medical Center for their cooperation and assistance in obtaining patients for this study."

He pushed the button again, and the screen went dark. He paused a moment to emphasize the separation of professional from commercial, then acknowledged the research grant from Jandra Pharmaceuticals that made the work possible. "My thanks also to the organizing committee for this invitation. Now I'd be pleased to answer any questions from the audience." The applause began immediately. In a few seconds, the volume rose as the translators in a glassed-in booth at the rear of the auditorium rendered his final words in German, French, and Spanish.

Ingersoll looked to his left, where the session moderator sat at a table at the side of the stage, and asked with a lifted eyebrow and a gesture toward the podium whether he wished to take the microphone and direct the discussion session. The moderator, a French physician, gave a Gallic shrug and waved away the invitation. Ingersoll wasn't sure whether this represented confidence in the speaker's ability to handle whatever came up or a desire on the part of the moderator to distance himself from the presentation.

The questions followed a predictable pattern, and Ingersoll had the answers readily available, either off the top of his head or in one of the slides he'd presented, a set still displayed as a series of thumbnails on the monitor in front of him.

A young doctor in an ill-fitting blue suit stepped to the microphone that had been set up in the aisle. "In your dose-ranging study, what did you find to be the optimum dose?"

Ingersoll moved his mouse over the appropriate slide and double-clicked. A graph filled the screens on either side of him as he discussed the dose-response curve, concluding his answer with, "Even though there were no ill effects from the drug, we elected to use the lowest dose tested because the response was a 100 percent cure with it."

There you go, Bob Wolfe. That's twice I've said it.

An older doctor took his turn at the microphone. "Perhaps Dr. Clément can answer this. Will the recordings of this session include the discussion? "

The moderator leaned into the table, pulled his microphone toward him, and said, "*Oui.*"

Ingersoll's amusement at the taciturn response died as he realized the implication of the question, something he'd totally forgotten. He ran his mind back over all the forms he'd completed and signed to confirm his invitation. He clenched his teeth when he realized that buried among them had been permission for his talk to be recorded.

A few more questions followed, and Ingersoll answered them with no difficulty. He glanced at the clock on the podium.

Time to wrap it up. He made a show of pushing back his sleeve to look at his watch. "We have time for one more question."

Two men stood at the microphone in the aisle. The first in line was a young man with neatly styled black hair and a small Vandyke beard. The man behind him, who looked vaguely familiar to Ingersoll, wore a poorly cut blue suit that badly needed a pressing. The second man in line leaned forward and whispered urgently in the ear of the younger man. Whatever was said must have worked, because the man shrugged and gave up his position without a word. Blue suit moved forward to the microphone. Ingersoll recognized him and felt his heart rat-a-tat in his chest.

"*Ich bin* . . . sorry. I'll speak English. I am Dr. Herman Rohde from Ulm, Germany. Like you, Professor Ingersoll, I have had the privilege of participating in the study of Jandramycin. My colleague and I have treated a number of patients, and like you, we have been pleased that there are no instances where the *Staphylococcus luciferus* failed to yield to the drug. But we are concerned that you are reporting no adverse effects to the drug."

A low murmur swept through the auditorium. Ingersoll opened his mouth, but Rohde apparently wasn't finished.

"I would like to ask you this specific question. Are you aware of any adverse consequences, either during the treatment or afterward, that can be attributed to Jandramycin?"

Ingersoll wasn't sure whether this man was a plant or a fellow clinician asking an honest question. In either case, he had the answer ready almost before the words were out of Rohde's mouth.

"I am unaware of any such adverse effects." Without waiting for a reply or a follow-up, he said, "That concludes our session. Again, thank you all for coming."

Ingersoll reached down to retrieve his briefcase from its position beside the podium, and flinched as he anticipated running the gauntlet of people already forming up in the aisles to ask him questions. He was about to head down the steps when he felt a hand on his shoulder.

"Great presentation, Jack," Bob Wolfe said. He pointed to a small door offstage to their right. "If we duck out that door, we can avoid the crowd."

Wolfe led the way into a small hallway. "Oh, by the way. Sorry about that mix-up about your hotel bill. I've got it straightened out now. Jandra is covering all your expenses, just as we promised. So enjoy your time here."

Ingersoll didn't feel very grateful, but he managed to choke out a "Thanks." *Well, they've got me on tape twice. I guess they really do own me.*

John Ramsey scanned the crowded lecture hall and saw Lillian Goodman with an empty seat beside her. Judging from the PowerPoint slide on the screen, John figured he'd missed at most five minutes of the talk. He eased down the aisle, but hesitated when he saw something in the seat next to Lillian. She glanced toward him, smiled, and lifted her purse from the seat, gesturing him to sit.

"Thanks for saving me a place," he whispered.

She settled her purse onto the floor at her feet. "I thought you'd want to hear this."

At first, John was interested in the presentation. But as the speaker went deeper and deeper into the molecular and genetic basis of his theories, he appeared to lose the attention of most of his audience, John included.

"I thought this was going to be practical," Lillian whispered.

"It was, for about fifteen minutes. Then he tried to show how smart he is." John glanced at the clock on the back wall. "If we can survive another twenty minutes of this, want to have lunch with me?"

"Sure, but it'll have to be fast. I have clinic this afternoon," Lillian said.

Half an hour later, they eased through the doors outside the food court into the patio beyond. "There's a table," John said. "Let's grab it."

As they settled in with drinks and sandwiches, Lillian said, "This is nice. It's rare for me to get outside while the sun's still up."

"Me, too," John said. He went to work on the twist-top of his soft drink, trying to ignore the pain in his hand.

"Can I help with that?" Lillian asked. Without waiting for a reply, she took the bottle and twisted the top free. As she set it back down, she looked at John's hand and said, "That doesn't look good. Did you see Rip about it?"

John took a sip of his Coke, obviously embarrassed at having someone else open it. "He needled it and cultured the pus. The smear looked like *Staph*."

"So are you on an antibiotic?"

John shook his head. "He put me on cephalexin, but I don't think it's helped much."

"Won't the lab have a preliminary culture report by now?"

"Probably, but the antibiotic sensitivities will take another day or so." He took a bite of his sandwich and washed it down with more Coke. "Let's forget my hand for now."

"Fine. But don't ignore it. Do what Rip suggests."

John nodded, anxious to leave the subject. "I really enjoyed talking with you the other night. And if you wouldn't mind, I'd like to do it again." He held up a hand. "Not a date, mind you. I just need someone to talk with."

Lillian smiled. "John, we both know these aren't dates. I also know you feel guilty spending time with another woman. That's natural. But the more you can talk out your feelings, the better your healing will go. Believe me, I know. I've been there."

"So maybe dinner tomorrow night?"

"Sounds fine. We'll discuss it tomorrow. Maybe I'll cook for you," Lillian said. "How long since you've had a home-cooked meal?"

John's throat tightened. He tried to blink away the moisture from the corners of his eyes. "Not since . . . since Beth—"

"But surely one of your children—"

John had to swallow hard before he could get the words out. "Beth and I couldn't have children. We thought about adoption, but somehow things kept getting in the way." He decided he'd better get all of it out. "And before you ask, I'm an only child. My parents have been gone for several years. When Beth died, it left me—"

"That's okay. We don't need to talk about it."

They were leaving the table when John's pager went off. "I guess I'd better answer this."

"I'll see you back in clinic, then," Lillian said.

John pulled out his cell phone and dialed the number on his pager.

"Dr. Pearson."

"Rip, this is John Ramsey. You paged me?"

"Um, right. Can you come to Sara Miles's office? I was with her when the lab paged me with a preliminary report on your culture."

John screwed up his courage to ask the question he dreaded. "What's the verdict? Is it MRSA? Do I need IV antibiotics?"

"That's what we need to discuss," Rip said. "Yes, the treatment for this is giving IV. But you don't have MRSA. The culture grew *Staph luciferus*."

16

JOHN RAMSEY WASTED NO TIME GETTING TO SARA'S OFFICE, WHERE HE found her and Rip talking in low tones. He pulled up a chair and winced at the pain that shot through his hand. He took a deep breath and said, "Whoever dumped that syringe in the trash gave me a really nice gift, didn't they? *Staph luciferus.* Where do we go from here?"

"Until recently, I think the decision would be clear," Rip said. "Jandramycin is the only antibiotic that works against it. No other drug can touch it."

John nodded in agreement.

"But a certain percentage of patients receiving Jandramycin develop late complications—autoimmune disorders that are potentially fatal."

"I know about the late problems," John said. "We've discussed them a bit already. But fatal?"

"One of the Jandramycin patients, one who'd developed nephropathy, died with renal failure. There are other autoimmune disorders that can be lethal as well. We don't know how many treated patients have developed them already. The risk is real, and it's significant," Rip said. "So we have a big decision to make."

Four decades of practicing medicine had made John a realist regarding treatment decisions. "We have three options: do nothing, try another antibiotic, or use Jandramycin. Option number one would undoubtedly allow a spread of the infection, necrotizing fasciitis or gangrene, and amputation of the hand if I didn't die first of sepsis. That's out."

Rip started to speak, but John held up his hand. "We'll have the sensitivity reports tomorrow, but barring a miracle, none of the antibiotics tested will be effective against this organism. So trying another antibiotic would be an expensive way to get the same result as doing nothing."

He waited to see if Rip or Sara had anything to say, but they simply nodded in silent agreement. He took a deep breath. "Jandramycin will work. I'm not sure any of us truly believe that it's been 100 percent successful, but that's what the studies show so far. And not every patient who received it has developed an autoimmune disorder . . . yet."

"And suppose you're one of the unlucky few who do?" Sara asked.

"There's always the option of treatment with high-dose steroids. That may not be a lifetime solution, maybe they won't work at all, but at least there's a chance. And in the meantime, someone may come up with the key that can reverse the process." John sat back in the chair, not particularly happy with the course of action to which he'd committed himself, but relieved that he'd been able to divorce his decision making from emotion and agree to what appeared to be the only viable solution.

"Ordinarily, patients with this infection would be hospitalized," Rip said, "but unlike our other patients, you weren't treated unsuccessfully with one or two other antibiotics. There was no delay in administering proper treatment. You're not toxic with the infection. I think we can do this as an outpatient." He lifted a sheaf of papers from his lap. "We might as well get you enrolled in the study, get some baseline blood work, and give you the first dose of Jandramycin. Let's go to the clinic and get started."

As they filed from the room, John realized that Rip had held the papers for the Jandramycin study all along. It was truly the only option, but John was the one who had to decide to take that step. With his full knowledge of all that was involved, what he'd given was the very definition of informed consent. Very informed.

Carter Resnick opened the door to his lab a crack and peered out at Rip with one eye. "What do you need? I'm collating data right now."

"We need to talk."

"I didn't think you had time to talk with a lowly research associate."

Rip bit back the reply that came to his lips. He needed this information, and maybe Resnick had it. "Carter, that's not true. I've always had time for you. Surely you can spare five minutes for me."

Resnick's visible eye blinked several times. Rip could almost hear him thinking. Finally, the door opened wide enough for Resnick to slip through, then closed behind him with a solid click. Resnick jiggled the knob to confirm the door was locked. He turned to face Rip and crossed his arms.

"Okay, talk."

"Carter, be reasonable. Can't we sit down somewhere like two colleagues and have a discussion? Why don't we go into the lab?"

Resnick was shaking his head before Rip finished talking. "No way. Dr. Ingersoll only allows two people in that lab: himself and me."

"I thought there was a lab technician, too."

"No. When we got to a critical point, Dr. Ingersoll discharged the tech. I do all the work now. It's a matter of security."

"Carter, most of that data you're collating came from me. What could be in there that I don't already know?"

Resnick grinned. "That's for me to know and you to find out."

Rip decided that Resnick's schoolboy response effectively closed the door—quite literally—on any hope of his getting into the lab. He leaned against the wall and fired his first salvo. "I need to know what exactly is in Jandramycin. I have to find out what its exact mode of action is."

"The main thing anyone needs to know is that it kills *Staph luciferus*. Some people postulate that Jandramycin works by attacking the bacteria's cell wall. Its real mode of action probably won't be revealed until Dr. Ingersoll and I publish that information."

There it was. Resnick figured that his work would get him co-authorship of the papers that were sure to come, papers certain to be the lead articles in *JAMA* and the *New England Journal*. Until that happened, Resnick would move heaven and earth to stay on Ingersoll's good side, and if that meant standing guard on the laboratory and the data it contained, so be it.

"Look, Carter, it's important that we know how the drug works. People who received it are turning up later with auto-immune disorders that are disabling and potentially fatal."

Resnick didn't seem surprised. "Everyone?"

"No." Rip did some quick calculations. "It seems like maybe 15 percent of the patients are at risk. But we don't know which ones they are."

There was a muted buzz from the pocket of Resnick's lab coat. He held up one finger to Rip. "I'd better get this."

It was a brief and mainly a one-sided conversation. Resnick said, "I can't tell you that" a few times and punched the button to end the call. He dropped the phone into his pocket and said, "That was Dr. Miles. She asked me the same question you did. You all should coordinate your efforts."

"Carter, listen to me. Lives are at stake here. Why won't you give me this information?"

"Actually, you already have enough clues. You're the diagnostician. Figure it out." With that, Resnick executed a quick about-face, opened the lab door with a key he produced from his pocket, and disappeared inside.

Lillian grabbed the chart from the plastic rack and tapped on the exam room door. Without waiting for a reply, she opened it and walked in. "I'm Dr. Goodman. What kind of—"

Her usual greeting to patients died in her throat as her eyes registered the scene before her. John Ramsey lay on the exam table with an IV running into his arm. "John, what—"

"Easy, Lillian. I'm fine. I'm just getting my first dose of Jandramycin."

She glanced down at the name on the chart she held: John Matthew Ramsey, MD. Lillian had her finger inside the cover, ready to open the chart, when she stopped. No, John would tell her what he wanted her to know. She pulled over a stool and sat down beside John, covering his hand with her own, careful to avoid the small plastic cannula that carried medication into the vein in his forearm. "What's going on?"

"It all started when this lady doctor I know thought I might be getting an infection around a puncture wound of my hand and insisted I see someone about it." He grinned, trying to rob the words of any sting. "The culture grew *Staph luciferus*. So, now I'm on Jandramycin."

"John, I'm so sorry. But I'm glad Rip did the culture," Lillian said, "and even happier that we have something that will knock out the bacteria. I mean, just a few months ago we had nothing, and these infections were potentially fatal."

"Right. The drug should take care of the *Staph luciferus* infection, and that's good. What you don't know, and I guess it's okay to let you in on the story, is that some patients who received Jandramycin are turning up with various autoimmune diseases, most of which can be fatal. So there's a chance that I may save my hand at the risk of developing something just as bad—maybe worse—down the line."

That brought a dozen questions to her mind. "I thought Jandramycin was supposed to be so wonderful. One hundred percent effective against the most dangerous pathogen we've seen since the black plague, but with no side effects. Why didn't someone warn us before we began to use it?"

"It's an experimental drug, Lillian," John said. "When we get informed consent to administer those compounds, all we have to go on is the information the manufacturer gives us. And in this case, that didn't include the whole truth."

"Surely Jack Ingersoll had some inkling about all this." John winced, and Lillian realized she was holding his hand tightly. She relaxed her grip, just lightly covering John's hand with hers. "Sorry."

"No problem. At least the drug is painless going into the vein. To address your question, we don't know what Ingersoll knows about all this. At first, everyone involved was happy that Jandramycin worked so well and had no apparent ill effects. That's why he and Jandra Pharmaceuticals were rushing to get FDA approval. Thousands of people have already died from *Staph luciferus*. Every day's delay condemns more."

189

"Surely Jack suspected something," Lillian said.

"When Rip and Sara first suspected that it might cause autoimmune problems, they confronted Ingersoll about it, but he denied that any problems exist. Now it's as though he has blinders on."

Lillian squared her shoulders. "Let me do some reading. Maybe there's something we can do to prevent these complications."

"We're already working on it, but we haven't had much luck so far."

"Who's 'we'?"

"Sara, Rip, and me. Oh, and another one of my former students, Dr. Mark Wilcox. He practiced law before he went to med school. Now he's an FP."

"Well, like it or not, you just added another member to your group. When and where are you going to get together next?" She rose and gave John's hand a final, gentle squeeze. "You and I can supply something none of the other three have."

"And that is?"

She forced a smile. "Experience. I've been practicing medicine for thirty-five years. I guess with you it's closer to forty. We've seen situations those young pups have only read about. They don't know it yet, but they need us."

"How are you today?" Sara Miles did her best to put a smile in her voice as well as on her face as she approached Chelsea Ferguson's bedside.

"About the same," Chelsea said, her tone flat, her face expressionless.

Mrs. Ferguson, seated on the other side of Chelsea's bed, shook her head and mouthed the words, "Not good." She took a tissue from her pocket and wiped the corners of her eyes.

Sara's neurologic exam bore out Mrs. Ferguson's words. The weakness in Chelsea's legs was much worse, and the reflexes there were virtually absent. Even more worrisome, the girl was losing strength in her arms. This was the reason clinicians had originally given GBS the name Landry's ascending paralysis. The paralysis might progress upward until the patient was unable to move and required the assistance of a ventilator to keep breathing. Sometimes the symptoms resolved, although it could take weeks or months. But sometimes they were permanent.

Still at the bedside, Sara flipped open the chart and scanned it. Anna Pearl's last note was brief, and not at all encouraging. "Progression of weakness in lower extremities, early signs in upper extremities. Will discuss adding further Rx to steroids." Sara racked her brain to come up with something more to add. She'd have to call Anna and see what the neurologist had in mind.

Sara gave Chelsea's hand a final squeeze. "You hang in there. We'll lick this yet."

As she'd come to do, Mrs. Ferguson followed Sara into the hall. "She's getting weaker. Can you do something?"

"I'm about to talk with Dr. Pearl about adding another medication for Chelsea. You heard what I told her. We'll lick this thing." Sara patted the woman's shoulder and turned away, hoping she'd done it quickly enough that Mrs. Ferguson didn't see the tears that strained for release from her own eyes.

Anna Pearl answered her page within a few minutes.

"Anna, this is Sara Miles."

"Oh, yes. We need to talk about Chelsea Ferguson. Her paralysis is progressing."

"I know. I just saw her. What do you suggest we do?" A name jumped into Sara's mind. "Could we add something like methotrexate?"

"Interesting that you should suggest that. I thought about an antimetabolite, but when I did a literature search, these compounds have been tried and don't add much."

Ideas were coming to Sara fast and furious, and she didn't try to filter them as they entered her mind. "What about immune globulin?"

"That's what I was considering. Not every study supports its use, but sometimes it helps. And one dose IV should be sufficient . . . if it's going to work."

"A milligram per kilo?"

"Make it two," Anna said. "If we're going to hit this, let's hit it hard. And keep your fingers crossed."

I won't just keep my fingers crossed. I'll be praying this works— because if it doesn't, I don't know what I'll do. I'm out of ideas.

17

John, you're a hard man to track down." Mark Wilcox pulled out his bottom desk drawer and rested a polished cordovan loafer there. He switched the phone to his other hand and began to doodle on a legal pad. "We need to talk about your malpractice case."

"I'm sorry I haven't returned your calls. There's been a lot going on."

"I'd love to hear about it. When can we—"

"Just a second." There was a muffled exchange. "Sorry. I'm still in clinic and had to answer a question for my nurse. Can we meet this evening sometime? Come by my house and we can talk over coffee."

Mark scanned through the possibilities. "I've got a better idea. I have to see a few more patients, then go by the hospital for a bit. Why don't you come by my office a little after six? If Sara Miles and Rip Pearson are free, we could all meet somewhere for dinner and pool information on the Jandramycin front." He scrawled a note on the pad in front of him. "Del Frisco's has a private dining room. I can have my secretary reserve it for seven thirty. My treat."

"I guess I could check with Sara and Rip."

"That would be great. When you know for sure, call my office and Karla will take it from there." Mark smiled at the prospect of seeing Sara again, even if he did have to share her with others at dinner. This time, maybe their evening together wouldn't end when the meeting broke up. "See you around six."

Mark was smiling when he shrugged into his white coat and walked out of his office to see his next patient.

"Why the worried look?" Lillian Goodman pulled out a chair and joined Sara Miles in the clinic's break room.

"Thinking about a patient," Sara said. She held her Diet Coke to her forehead and closed her eyes. "Why is it always the nice ones who have the complications?"

Lillian's first thought was John Ramsey. If she had anything to do with it, he wasn't going to be one of those nice ones who didn't do well on treatment. She made a mental note to ask Rip Pearson for more information on the Jandramycin late effects John had mentioned. "Which patient is this?" Lillian asked.

"Chelsea Ferguson. She almost died from *Staph luciferus* sepsis, but we pulled her through with Jandramycin. Then she developed Guillain-Barré. We think the drug produces auto-immune disorders in some patients who receive it."

No need to go to Rip. This was all the opportunity Lillian needed. "And now John is one of those patients. What can we do to protect him and the others from those side effects?"

"We're checking into—Wait a second. Who's this 'we'?"

"The other day I found John in a treatment room getting his IV meds. He told me that you, Rip, and another doctor were trying to solve the problem, hopefully before he gets one of those complications." Lillian sat up a bit straighter. "I'm inviting myself into the group."

"But why—"

"Because as a doctor, I'm dedicated to healing people, not making them worse, and I've contributed a couple of my patients to the Jandramycin study. So I feel an obligation to look out for them." She pushed back her chair. "And because, frankly, I'm growing fond of John. He's been through a lot, and I think right now he needs a friend. I've volunteered for the position."

John Ramsey rattled the knob of Mark Wilcox's office door, but it didn't budge. Repeated taps on the door brought no response. He had his cell phone out when he heard footsteps in the hall behind him.

"John, sorry to keep you waiting." Mark hurried up and pulled a set of keys from his pocket. "I got tied up at the hospital. Come on in."

When they were settled in Mark's office with soft drinks, John looked around at the office. Simple and functional, much like the one he'd had for years. "You seem to have a nice setup here."

Mark leaned back and propped one foot on his desk drawer. "I like it. As I told you, I have a limited family practice but still manage to do a little law as well."

"Do you think that as your medical practice gets more active, you'll do less law?"

"I don't see that happening," Mark said. "Things have settled into a pattern, some medicine, some law, sometimes a combination of the two. For instance, I'm a consultant to the in-house counsel at one of the private hospitals in the city. The reason I was delayed was because he and I were meeting with the administrator and the chief of staff. There's a rather sticky problem with one of the physicians who has privileges there."

"So what's new with my case?" John asked.

"I've been in touch with the attorney representing the plaintiff. Frankly, he's never handled a malpractice action, and I think he filed this as a favor to the guy who brought the suit. They move in the same society circles." Mark lifted his can of soda, found it empty, and put it down. "If it looks like we're going to trial, he'll probably turn it over to someone who does this kind of thing all the time."

"If it comes to trial? So it may not?"

"Filing the suit is only the first step in the dance. This is what I used to call an 'I'll get you for this' suit. From what I can tell, the son of the woman who died thinks everything around him should be perfect, and if it isn't, someone has to pay. Never mind that his mother refused to follow her own doctor's advice and wasn't taking her medications. Matter of fact, she was visiting the faculty clinic at the med school for a second opinion because her daughter insisted on it." Mark picked up a pen and began twirling it between his fingers. "The daughter, by the way, opposes this suit."

John's heart hammered against his sweat-soaked shirt. "What happens now? Can you get the court to remove me from the suit? All I did was start an IV."

"Not likely to happen. A suit like this is filed against every person and entity involved. The plaintiff—that is, the person who sues—could amend the suit, but I doubt that will happen while there's a possibility of getting something out of you. And the courts probably wouldn't allow it anyway. They prefer one trial for everyone."

"And if it comes to trial?"

"One thing they teach us in law school is to always try for a settlement, because there's really no way to predict what a jury will do. A trial is the last thing we want, and my goal is to avoid one."

"Does this mean I might end up paying to settle a suit against me that has no merit?"

Mark spread his hands. "I'm going to do my best for you, John. I'll let you know what happens. And I'll warn you, these things can drag out for months, sometimes a year or more."

So there it was. John had come here hoping to hear good news, but there was none. Just like everything else that happened to him lately, the only thing to do was wait. John wondered how much more of this he could take. And as quickly as the thought flashed into his mind, the answer came. The same answer he and Beth had given each other when the tough times came over four decades of marriage. *I don't know. But God's in control.*

Mark looked at his watch. "We've got a few minutes before it's time to head to the restaurant. May I ask you a question?"

"Sure."

"Is Sara Miles seeing anyone?"

John ran that through his mind and came up blank. "I'm not sure I'd know if she were, but I've never heard her mention anyone. I think she's still hurting pretty badly from the loss of her baby and her divorce."

"But that was . . . how long ago? A couple of years?"

"About that. But people heal at different rates. Why do you ask?"

Mark cupped his chin in his hand for a moment. "You may recall that when I was in medical school, I was married." He held up a hand that bore no ring. "Now I'm not."

"I didn't want to say anything, but yes, I noticed."

"My wife died almost two years ago in a head-on crash with a driver who was going the wrong way on Central Expressway."

"Mark, I had no idea," John said.

"I've never even looked at another woman until I met Sara. And ever since then, I can't get her out of my mind."

"So the fact that she was the target of a shooter—"

"It almost killed me to hear about it. And if she feels about me the way I do about her, I don't plan to let her get away. I feel like this is a second chance for me. Maybe it's a second chance for both of us. And I'm not going to waste it."

Sara looked at her watch for what must have been the tenth time in the past half hour. Where was Rip?

"We'll wait until everyone's here to order," Mark said.

The waiter nodded, deposited drinks on the table, and walked away. The group sat in a small private dining room, centered at a table that would accommodate eight, with Mark and Sara on one side, John across from them. A fourth place setting marked the spot where Rip would sit.

"I guess we'll wait until Rip gets here to start sharing information," Sara said, "but I'm sorry to say I don't know a lot more than I did when we met last."

John fiddled with the silverware in front of him. "The same goes for me."

"I have a few things to—" Mark stopped as Rip hurried into the room.

"Sorry to be late. It appears that my attempts to find out more about Jandramycin stirred up a hornet's nest." He dropped into the vacant chair and drank deeply from the glass of iced water in front of him.

Sara leaned across toward him. "What happened? Are you all right?"

"Yes, but no thanks to whoever drove the SUV that sideswiped me and pushed me into a concrete abutment." Rip pulled a handkerchief from his pocket and wiped his brow.

"My car will need some body work, but I managed to keep it under control. Otherwise, I'd have bounced out into the road and been broadsided by another vehicle."

"Could it have been an accident?" John asked.

"I saw the SUV in my rearview mirror just before he hit me. I'm pretty sure he was aiming right at me, trying to sideswipe my car."

Mark leaned back in his chair. "So there've been attempts aimed at Sara and Rip. John, I guess you've been spared."

"Because I haven't been asking around. There's the difference."

"So who have we asked?" Rip said. "Jack Ingersoll, Carter Resnick . . ."

"The higher-ups at Jandra," Sara added.

"And, of course, there could be someone else who knows what we're doing, someone we don't even know about," Mark added.

"What do we do about it?" Sara asked.

Mark tented his fingers under his chin. "Rip, I suppose your accident was investigated by the police."

"Yeah, they came out. Said they'd file a report, put out a bulletin to body shops. I don't look for anything to come of it, though."

"And we know the shooting involving Sara was reported," Mark added. "I could talk with the police and try to tie those together, see if they're willing to investigate further."

"But that's not likely. Right?" John said.

"Not really," Mark replied.

"Forget it," Rip said.

Mark nodded his agreement. "So I guess we either stop digging—"

"Never!" both Sara and Rip answered in unison.

"Or be careful," Mark said.

"You started to tell us what you've found," Sara said. "What was that?"

"One of the guys in my law school class ended up at the FDA. He sort of owes me—I coached him through his last year—so I gave him a call. Could he get a copy of Jandra's NDA for Jandramycin? No way. Apparently they've pulled some strings with the FDA and gotten it not only fast-tracked but protected from everyone but the small group that's due to review it."

"Makes no difference," Rip said. "The mechanism of action they quote for the drug is probably cell wall destruction, and we know that's just a smokescreen. We need the real mechanism if we're going to figure out how to block the late complications."

Mark nodded. "And we can't get that from Jandra."

"Never going to happen," Rip said.

"Or from the investigators," Mark concluded.

"And I understand that we don't have time to analyze the compound we have on hand, then do the animal experimentation to show its mechanism of action," Sara said.

Mark shook his head. "I believe we've tried every legal means available to get the information we need."

As she pondered that last phrase, Sara decided that maybe it was time to think outside the box. She had a couple of ideas—but she decided she'd better keep them to herself for now.

Mark signed the bill, retrieved his American Express card, and closed the folder. "Thank you all for coming."

John dropped his napkin beside his empty coffee cup. "Thanks for dinner. It was good to throw around some ideas and share information, but I'm afraid we're no closer to a solution of our problem than we were before we started."

One by one, the group pushed back their chairs and stood.

Rip declined a ride with John, saying that although his car looked terrible it was still drivable. "I'll call my insurance company in the morning and see about getting a rental while mine's in the shop."

Mark was happy to see that Sara was the last in the group to move toward the door. He touched her on the shoulder. "I was wondering if you might like to go somewhere for a—I was about to say a drink, then I remembered—for another cup of coffee? We haven't really had a chance to talk with each other tonight."

He could see Sara consider the offer. Her frown told him the answer before she spoke. "Mark, I like you. Under more normal circumstances, I'd say yes. But I'm really in turmoil about this whole Jandramycin thing. Until it's settled, I'm not ready for any kind of a relationship. For now, can we just stay friends?" She smiled, obviously trying to take the sting out of her response.

"Sure. I understand." He fell in step beside her. "Any more strange noises in your house?"

He knew it was a low blow to remind her of what her ex-husband did to torment her after he left her. During Mark's classical education he'd memorized the oft-misquoted words of John Lyly, Renaissance poet and playwright: "The rules of fair play do not apply in love and war." On rare occasion, he'd applied that strategy in the courtroom. After all, weren't most legal battles a form of war? But he'd never had occasion to use it with respect to love . . . until now.

Sara turned on the living room lights and double-locked the front door behind her. She wondered why she'd turned down Mark's invitation to extend the evening. Did she sense a danger in letting him get too close to her? Was there something about him that triggered her response? Something John said about Mark tickled at the edge of her memory—something about his consulting for pharmaceutical companies. Could one of those be Jandra?

She dropped her purse on the entryway table, wincing at the muted clunk it made. She unzipped it and pulled out the revolver. A Taurus Ultra-Lite—one pound of metal that could be either a harmless paperweight or an engine of death.

Sara made sure that the safety was on before she swung the cylinder open and dumped the bullets into her palm. She admired the way the copper noses shone in the light from the table lamp. She tried to visualize one of them ripping through flesh, putting an end to a human life. Finally, Sara carefully reinserted the bullets one by one. She clicked the cylinder into place with an empty chamber under the hammer, re-engaged the safety, and dropped the gun into her purse. It was ready. Was she? She wouldn't know the answer until the situation arose. And she prayed that it never would.

At her computer, Sara logged on to PubMed. In the search box, she entered Jandramycin, and was surprised to find no hits. Then it dawned on her. She was looking for preliminary work, and the name, Jandramycin, had been applied only recently. She searched her memory in vain for the initial designation of the compound.

She dialed Rip Pearson's home number. "Rip, hope I didn't wake you."

"Not at all. I was about to sink into a hot bath. That collision shook me up a bit more than I initially thought, and I'm getting a little sore. What's up?"

"What was it you called Jandramycin before Jandra applied that name?"

"EpAm848. Does that help?"

"It may. Enjoy that hot soak." She rang off before he could ask more questions. This might be a total waste of time, but she had to try it.

Back at her computer, she opened the PubMed search box, typed in "EpAm848," then hit "enter." There were only four citations, three of them papers with Jack as a co-author along with Bob Wolfe and some others whom she took to be Jandra research staff. She struck pay dirt with the fourth. It was a preliminary report detailing the design of a study to investigate a potential new antibiotic. She ignored the abstract that followed. It contained nothing she didn't already know. Instead, Sara found a slip of paper and wrote down the names of the authors: Gruber H., Rohde H.

18

Rip watched Jack Ingersoll walk onto the general medical ward as though he owned it. The man was an absolute egomaniac. The words of a Carly Simon song came immediately to mind. Something about being so vain. Rip hummed a few bars under his breath while Ingersoll paused to speak with another faculty member, undoubtedly telling him how successful his presentation had been and recounting some of his experiences in Germany.

"Pearson, what do you have for me?" The musky scent of a popular—and very expensive—aftershave almost overpowered Rip. Ingersoll's white coat fairly crackled with starch. A single pen, probably a Mont Blanc, peeked from the crisply pressed breast pocket. The side pocket bulged ever so slightly with what Rip guessed was the latest version of smart phone.

"While you were gone, we acquired two more patients with *Staph luciferus* infections. All have been placed on Jandramycin and seem to be responding well."

"Very well. Take me to their rooms and let me meet them. I trust you explained to them the reason for my absence."

Sure. I told them all you were on an expense-paid junket to present a paper that was probably full of fabricated data. "Yes, sir. They understand that you were an invited speaker at a prestigious international conference." The words burned Rip's tongue like a mouthful of scalding hot coffee, but he managed to spit them out with a straight face.

The next half hour was spent meeting the patients, both of whom were indeed recovering, thanks in no small part to Jandramycin. Neither showed any evidence of side effects or complications from the treatment. Then again, it was early. Unless Rip could somehow find the true mechanism of action of the antibiotic and, even more important, come up with a treatment to prevent late autoimmune reactions, one of them, maybe both, might eventually be afflicted with such a problem.

The two doctors stopped in the dictation room, and Ingersoll made a few brief notes on each chart. Rip knew this was more to document his presence than add anything to the treatment plan.

"Any new orders?" Rip asked.

"No, no. You've done well. Followed my protocol to the letter. I presume Resnick is getting the material for lab studies on a regular basis."

"Right. I draw the blood myself, take the tubes to your lab, knock on the door, Resnick opens it a crack, I pass them through to him, and he slams it in my face."

"I know it grates on you that you're not allowed in there," Ingersoll said. "But we're dealing with a revolutionary drug, and it's important that our data not get into the wrong hands."

Rip figured he'd never have a better opening than that. "But I'm your colleague, your Fellow. I'm supposed to be a part of this study, but Resnick won't even share the mechanism of action of the drug with me. And it's important, because—"

Ingersoll held up a hand like a traffic policeman. "You already know the mechanism. I told you this early on. Jandramycin breaks down the bacterial cell wall. I can't go into details, but there's a great deal more data in the New Drug Application."

Which is probably a remarkable work of fiction. Rip decided to take a different tack. "You recall that Chelsea Ferguson, one of the patients in our series, was admitted with Guillain-Barré syndrome before you left."

"Terrible when that happens. Refresh my memory about her."

Rip gave Ingersoll a brief review of Chelsea's case, ending with, "It seems to me that this could be a late consequence of Jandramycin therapy. Would you like to see her?"

Ingersoll shook his head. "No, no. I'm sure she's in good hands. And too much time has passed since her treatment to implicate Jandramycin in the problem. It's undoubtedly just one of those unfortunate circumstances."

It was clear to Rip that Ingersoll wasn't going to admit Jandramycin could be responsible for any adverse effects. There was no need to prolong the conversation. But there was one more thing he wanted to say, and he thought he'd figured the best way to say it.

"Dr. Ingersoll," Rip said, "I was helping Dr. Miles clean out her attic recently, and we found something you left behind when you moved out."

"Oh? I don't recall anything being missing. It couldn't be very important. She can just keep it."

"I'll tell her that, although neither of us could figure why you'd move out and leave a very expensive digital recorder behind. And why was it in the attic?"

Rip was sure Ingersoll flinched for just a second before the mask dropped back in place, and he said, "I don't know what you're talking about."

Bob Wolfe had been expecting the summons, but it came from a different source. Not David Patel this time. Instead, he was told that Mr. Lindberg would like to see Mr. Wolfe in his office at his earliest convenience—in other words, now. Wolfe thanked Lindberg's secretary, hung up the phone, and turned to look out his office window.

It wouldn't hurt Lindberg to wait a few minutes. Wolfe was sure he was being called in to report on how things went in Frankfurt, and he wanted to be certain he had the answers clear in his mind. He reran the reel of the last couple of days through his mind and smiled when he could find no fault with what he'd done or the results. He buttoned his collar, cinched up his tie, and took his jacket from a hook on the back of his office door.

Wolfe paused at the open door when he saw Lindberg on the phone. Lindberg's desk faced the huge windows that gave him a spectacular view. Some people might turn their desk away from such a distraction, but Wolfe had heard Lindberg say he kept that perk visible to remind him of how hard he had to work to retain it. In a down economy, people might be fired, but Lindberg was apparently determined to be the one doing the firing, not the one on the other end.

Lindberg's conversation was animated, to say the least. "I don't care how you do it, but I want those mock-ups on my desk tomorrow. Jandramycin is the drug that's going to save this company, and that won't happen if no one knows about it. I want those ads ready for the front part of every major medical journal in the U.S. I want them to hit at the same time our reps are knocking on doctors' doors to tell them about our wonder drug. One hundred percent success against the worst infections in history, with absolutely no side effects."

Wolfe faintly heard the murmur of words rattling forth from the phone when Lindberg broke in. "No, you can't have more time. The FDA is moving this thing forward triple speed, and you don't want to know how we managed to get that done. When they give their approval—and they will—I want those ads ready to roll with the next issue. Is that clear?"

Apparently it didn't matter whether it was clear, because Lindberg slammed down the phone without waiting for an answer.

Wolfe tapped on the doorframe. "You wanted to see me, Steve?"

Lindberg swiveled his chair around and in that split second managed to go from hard-nosed boss to jovial colleague. "Bob, come in. Sorry to keep you waiting." He waved at one of the chairs across the desk from him. "Have a seat."

Wolfe pulled up a chair but decided to let Lindberg take the conversational lead. He didn't have to wait long.

"Tell me about the meeting in Frankfurt."

"Huge attendance, representatives from the U.S., the UK, Germany, France, Belgium—"

"Okay, it was well attended. And our people had a booth where we reminded people of all the great products we have and told them we are coming out with a blockbuster. And so forth. You know what I want to hear."

Not much question there. Wolfe decided to be equally direct. "Ingersoll toed the company line perfectly. I stayed up all night before his presentation reviewing his slides, and they were perfect. Figures matched the ones we sent to the FDA in our new drug app. Conclusions in line with ours, including the lack of adverse reactions."

Lindberg nodded. "And—"

"And the Q&A ended with him being asked if he was aware of any complications associated with Jandramycin. He parroted back what we gave him." Wolfe smiled, remembering the way he'd reminded Ingersoll who was buttering his bread. But there was no need to mention that to Lindberg. Such actions were expected. He figured the marketing director had done similar things in his time, and probably a lot worse.

"Now to another part of our problem. We've had no more calls from that snoopy Dr. Miles, but I understand she's still convinced Jandramycin is responsible for a number of severe late complications in some of the patients receiving it. Now that you're back from enjoying sauerbraten and beer, why don't you contact your source and get an update on that situation? And let me know what you find out."

Lindberg rose and extended his hand, as close to a "thanks for a job well done" as Wolfe expected to receive. Before he was out the door, Wolfe heard Lindberg on the phone once more. "What do you mean, our reps can't get in to see the doctors? Tell them to bring lunch for the staff. Hang around with them while they eat. I've never known a doctor who wouldn't drift back and nosh a bit. That's when—"

"How are you today?" Sara plastered a smile on her face as she approached Chelsea Ferguson's bed. For a change, the girl's mother was not at the bedside. "Your mother not here?"

Chelsea's reply was so weak Sara had to ask her to repeat it. "My sister's sick. Mom kept her home from school and had to stay with her."

"No problem. If you need anything, ring for the nurse. They'll be right here for you." Sara flipped open the chart. "How are you doing after the immune—I mean, that medicine we gave you the other day?"

"Not much different." Chelsea's lower lip trembled. A tiny tear formed at the corner of one eye. "I . . . I still can't move my legs. And my arms are weak."

Sara pulled a reflex hammer from the pocket of her white coat and checked Chelsea. No reflexes in the legs, and definitely weakened responses in the arms. The immune globulin was reported to work most of the time in cases of severe GBS. But so far it hadn't seemed to help. There must be something different about the syndrome that Jandramycin triggered. And she had no idea what that difference was.

"Well, we have a few more tricks up our sleeve. I'll see you again this evening when I make rounds. Meanwhile, you keep your chin up."

Chelsea nodded weakly, then turned her face to the wall. Sara eased from the room, feeling lower than she'd ever felt as a physician. *God, I absolutely don't know where to go from here. Got any suggestions?*

Lillian Goodman paused outside the treatment room door. This time she was well aware of who was inside, but still she hesitated to enter. John was getting his daily IV dose of Jandramycin.

She held up her hand to knock, then dropped it to her side. Would John appreciate some company during the time he received the IV? Or would he prefer to be alone? *This is silly. I'm just visiting a friend.* She tapped on the door.

"Yes?"

Good enough. Lillian entered and closed the door behind her. She tried to put a smile in her voice as she approached the treatment table where John lay. "How are you?"

"Not too bad." He held up the arm that wasn't receiving the IV and wiggled his fingers. "My hand is pretty much back to normal. No redness. No swelling. Not even a little tenderness. Rip thinks it's healing fine, and I agree. So the magic medicine is doing its thing, even against the superbug."

The words hung in the air as they both considered the possible late consequences from the drug now running into John's veins.

Lillian tried to find words to change the subject, but they wouldn't come. Negative thoughts crowded out anything positive about the situation.

John must have sensed her struggle. "Look, I know everyone's worried that I might be going from the frying pan into the fire with this treatment," he said. "But look at it from my side. If we do nothing, we know what would happen. We've been over that. It's either accept a 100 percent chance that the disease will kill me, or at least make me lose my hand, versus a 15 percent chance of some sort of autoimmune response that could possibly be controlled with steroids or something else." He shrugged. "It's a no-brainer."

Something clicked in Lillian's mind. "You came out with that 15 percent figure awfully quickly. Where did that come from?"

"Rip was able to contact almost all the thirty-nine patients in Ingersoll's study. Of those, six had complications we think are due to the Jandramycin. Simple math. Six of thirty-nine. Fifteen percent chance of problems."

"Which poses the bigger question. What is it about that 15 percent of patients that makes them vulnerable to this sort of response?" Lillian pulled a straight chair to the side of the treatment table and sat down. "Has your group come up with any answers?"

John recounted what had been done and the dead ends they'd encountered. Every time Lillian suggested a possible avenue of investigation, John countered with the roadblock that stopped them getting the information they needed.

She stood and began to pace. "So it appears that we need to know how Jandramycin really works before we have any realistic chance to figure out how to prevent that 15 percent of patients getting late complications."

"Right. And if you have any ideas, you're welcome to contribute them." He raised himself on one elbow. "And would you please sit down? I'm getting dizzy watching you pace."

Lillian eased into the chair again. She reached into the pocket of her white coat and extracted a small notebook with a pen stuck into the ring binding. "I'm going to do some investigating of my own. Do you happen to know the original name of the compound? Not Jandramycin. What they called it in the beginning."

"Not really. Why do you ask?"

"Because I may be able to backtrack from there and get information about the mode of action of the drug. There's usually a reason for the names investigators give these compounds." She put the notebook back into her pocket. "Besides, unless you have a better idea, it looks like we don't have anywhere else to go short of holding Ingersoll or Resnick at gunpoint until they give up their secrets."

John said something, but Lillian only half-heard it. Her mind pictured the scenario she'd mentioned so off-handedly, and wondered if it just might work. After all, her late husband's gun was still at home in the back of a drawer under her winter sweaters. And how difficult could it be to use it?

19

Does anyone there speak English?" Sara realized she was shouting into the phone and made an effort to moderate her tone. Although reason told her that talking louder didn't increase the chance the person on the other end of the line would understand her despite the language barrier, the longer she talked the more frustrated she became and the louder she spoke.

The woman seemed calm enough, not at all flustered by the conversation or lack thereof. Neither her tone of voice nor her answer changed. "*Bitte, Ich verstehe nicht.*"

By now, the phrase was familiar to Sara. The woman didn't understand. This was the end of a tedious process, and it looked like it would be wasted effort.

Sara had dug deep on the Internet to find that Drs. Gruber and Rohde were internal medicine specialists on the faculty of a medical school in Ulm, Germany. Then it was a matter of finding the contact information for that medical center, looking up the process for making an international call, calculating the time difference between Texas and Germany, and finally placing the call from her home phone because Southwestern Medical Center would undoubtedly look askance at an unauthorized transatlantic phone call from her office phone.

Completing the call was only half the battle, though. She was transferred from person to person until she finally reached the proper department. Now, for the first time in the series of exchanges, she encountered someone who apparently spoke no English.

For the past five minutes, a calculator in Sara's mind toted up the charges for the call. This must be costing her a fortune, and she was getting nowhere. She was about to hang up when a new voice came on the phone.

"Yes, may I help you?"

"Oh, thank you. This is Dr. Sara Miles at Southwestern Medical Center in Dallas, Texas. Who is this?"

"I am Frau Schilder. I am the *Chefsekretärin* . . . the head secretary for the *Medizinklinik*."

"And you speak English?"

"I speak a little, yes."

Sara rolled her shoulders to relax the tension there. Maybe this would work after all. "I'm a doctor, calling from the United States. I need to speak with Dr. Gruber or Dr. Rohde."

"I am very sorry, but the doctors are both with patients today. Shall I give them a message?"

Would they really call back? It was a transatlantic call, and they had no idea who she was. Then it occurred to Sara that the mention of one word in her message might get a response. "Yes. My name is Dr. Sara Miles. And we need to discuss some important information about Jandramycin."

"Yes, and your phone number please?"

Sara gave it and rang off. She found it interesting that the woman hadn't asked to confirm the spelling of Jandramycin. Apparently the word was familiar to her. Perhaps she'd even been called upon to type reports and collate data. Maybe the work of Gruber and Rohde wasn't shrouded in as much secrecy in Ulm, Germany, as Jack's was here in Dallas. Sara permitted herself a bit of hope.

Funny. She couldn't get the information she needed from her ex-husband whose office was less than two hundred feet from her own, but she might be able to get it from two perfect strangers who carried out their medical practice and research five thousand miles away.

She'd done what she could. Now there was nothing to do except wait, hope, and pray.

Her visit with John as he received his Jandramycin took most of Lillian's lunch time, so she decided to pick up a sandwich in the food court and snatch a few bites between patients this afternoon.

Lillian made her purchase and was on her way out when she saw Jack Ingersoll and Carter Resnick at a table by the wall, deep in conversation. As she watched, she realized it wasn't really a conversation. It was a monologue, as Ingersoll held forth and Resnick listened, occasionally jotting a note in a dog-eared notebook.

Lillian approached their table, but neither man appeared to notice. "Having a little instruction time, Jack?"

She was surprised when Ingersoll turned, recognized her, and stood. Apparently his egocentric personality hadn't totally overwhelmed principles of courtesy undoubtedly learned as a child. Maybe it was because she was a woman. Maybe it was the touch of gray she allowed to remain at her temples when she put the Clairol to work. At any rate, it was good to see a glimpse of humanity in Jack Ingersoll.

"Lillian, good to see you," he said. Ingersoll looked pointedly at Resnick, who struggled to his feet. "You know Dr. Resnick?"

"We've met," Lillian said. "Please, sit down. I have a question for you both."

Both sat and looked up at her expectantly.

"I believe you have three or four of my patients in your study of that new antibiotic. Of course, I'm grateful, as I'm sure they and their families are. After all, you cured them of an infection that would otherwise be a death sentence."

Ingersoll nodded gravely. "Happy that we could do it."

"But now I'm hearing rumors of some very serious late reactions in some of the patients that received Jandramycin." Lillian hurried on, ready now to appeal to Ingersoll's ego. "I don't believe in rumors, of course, and I thought that if anyone could give me the straight word, it would be you."

"Thank you for your confidence. Yes, I'm probably the world's authority on Jandramycin, so I'm glad you came to me instead of paying attention to those silly rumors that keep floating around." He pulled a chair from the next table and motioned to her. "Please sit. This may take a moment."

Lillian looked at her watch and decided that being five minutes late for clinic was a fair trade for information that might save patients from some pretty terrible consequences. She sat.

"As you may know, after I left Southwestern, I took an infectious disease fellowship at UC Berkeley. While I was there, I did some research with a pharmaceutical company in the area. I was working on . . . Never mind, it isn't important."

Lillian leaned forward to signal her interest. *Get on with it, Jack. I don't have time for your life history.* "Go on."

"Anyway, some of the compounds that were supposed to be effective in that area turned out, at least in my lab experiments, to have a marked antibacterial activity. Specifically, they were effective against *Staph.*"

Lillian saw her chance and took it. "What compounds were those?"

Ingersoll shook his head vigorously. "Sorry, Lillian, I can't say. Anyway, I put some of them together in various proportions and tried them out."

"In lab animals, I presume."

"Er, oh, yes. In lab animals at first." Ingersoll took a sip from the almost empty glass in front of him. "I have to admit, there were some unpleasant results at times, but I kept modifying the preparation until I came up with what we now know as Jandramycin. When the epidemic of *Staph luciferus* broke out, I got permission to try the drug on some patients. Since the infection was tantamount to a death sentence without treatment, there was no objection. Imagine how gratified we all were when it was 100 percent effective in eradicating the infection, with no side effects."

Lillian nodded and sneaked a peek at her watch. "So you never encountered any adverse reactions to the drug? Either during treatment or afterward?"

Ingersoll rubbed his chin, and Lillian could see he was choosing his words carefully. "Not once I developed the final compound. None at all."

"Does that hold true for the earlier compounds you put together?"

He waved away the question. "Oh, that's ancient history. As I recall, your question was about the safety of Jandramycin." Ingersoll pushed back his chair. "I really need to go, and I'm sure Carter should get back to the lab. Have I answered your question?"

"Yes, thank you." *And raised a bunch more.* Lillian grabbed her purse and the bag with her sandwich, and hurried away, more determined than ever to find out what Jack Ingersoll was hiding. Somehow she had the feeling she'd just heard a clue, but she had no idea what it was.

"Okay, let me flush this out, and you can sit up." Rip Pearson disconnected the IV tubing that had carried the Jandramycin into John Ramsey's vein, then injected a small amount of solution into the tiny plastic catheter that remained in the vein, its end taped to John's forearm. "You've got four more doses to go. Want me to change the site of your heparin-lock?"

John touched the skin around the site. "No tenderness or redness. Let's leave it for now." He perched on the edge of the exam table and rolled down his sleeve. "My hand feels pretty much back to normal. Is there any chance we can discontinue the Jandramycin early?"

Rip shook his head. "None of us know for sure how effective a shorter course would be. I'll admit that ten days is an arbitrary number, but it's worked in everyone so far. I'd hate to change that." He took off the thin rubber gloves he'd worn and flipped them into a waste container. "Besides, do you want to be the one to tell Jack Ingersoll that we changed his protocol?"

"Don't you think Ingersoll would just report that I'd had the full ten days of treatment? I mean, it sounds like he's not above fudging his reports anyway."

"If you quote me I'll deny it, but you're probably right." Rip gestured for John to roll up the sleeve on his opposite arm. "Let's get your lab work drawn, then you can be on your way."

"What are all these labs, anyway? I know this is a study, but isn't this overkill?" He pointed to the test tubes lined up on the treatment table beside the equipment for drawing the blood to fill them. "And why do you need lab work after every dose of the drug?"

While Rip pulled on a fresh pair of gloves and busied himself with the blood draw, he considered John's question. "You know, in the time I've been an infectious disease fellow I've probably helped run half a dozen of these studies. I get so used to doing things that are specified in a protocol for a study it never occurs to me to question them."

"To get back to my original question—" John flinched as the needle pierced his vein. "Ow, that one stung. Anyway, what lab studies are you doing?"

"Honestly, I don't know. The hospitalized patients get the routine stuff—CBC and chemistries mainly. Those are done in the hospital lab and the results go on the patient chart, but there's another set of tests that go to Ingersoll's lab. I take the tubes to Resnick; he runs the tests and records the results. Then I guess he forwards the data to Jandra."

"And no one will tell you what the tests are?"

"Never asked, but I suspect that I'll be told I don't need to know right now." Rip removed the needle and put a square of sterile gauze over the puncture site. "Hold that for a minute, then I'll put a bandage on it."

"You know, every one of those tubes is used to collect blood for a specific set of tests. I know that in our lab a red-top tube is for serology, a lavender-top is for hematology. Think we could figure it out from the tubes you collect for Resnick?"

"Nope. These are special tubes sent from Jandra. The colors of the tops are different from any I've seen before." Rip lifted the gauze from John's arm. Satisfied that there was no bleeding, he applied a bandage. "That should do it." He tossed the gloves in a waste container and washed his hands.

John shook his head. "So much for that. I was hoping that the lab tests would give us a clue to what the drug does and what can go wrong in patients receiving it. I mean, we're pretty sure the problem is autoimmune, but we don't know why some patients get it and others don't. And we have no idea about prevention or treatment."

Rip shrugged. He eased the test tubes into the pocket of his white coat with a dull clank. "I'm trying to find out more, but so far it's not working out. Maybe our best bet is to break into Resnick's lab one night and get the data off his computer."

Rip smiled at his attempt at humor. Then he looked at John, and noticed that he wasn't smiling at all. "John, I wasn't serious."

John slipped into his white coat. "I am." He opened the door and strode away like a man on a mission.

Sara hurried down one of the main halls of the medical center, deep in thought and only peripherally aware of the people around her. It was ten minutes after one, and like most of them, she was running late. She opened the back entrance into the general internal medicine clinic and almost ran over Lillian Goodman as she retrieved a white paper bag from the floor. "Oh, sorry."

"No problem," Lillian said. "I was hurrying to get here and dropped my sandwich." She straightened and the two doctors proceeded side by side toward the physicians' dictation room that served as their office during clinic hours.

"No time for lunch?" Sara asked.

"No, I was talking with Jack Ingersoll. When we have a break, I'll tell you about it." Lillian dropped her purse and the sandwich at the far end of the low communal counter where the doctors sat and dictated, made phone calls, wrote chart notes, and occasionally huddled in informal consultation.

Sara followed suit. She glanced at the patient list Gloria had placed at her usual station. Busy afternoon, and she hadn't helped by being late. She threw the clinic's head nurse a look of apology before she entered the exam room where her first patient awaited her.

"Mrs. Truman, I'm Dr. Miles. So very sorry to keep you waiting. How can I help you?"

For the next few minutes, the woman sat on the edge of the exam table and related a set of symptoms that immediately set off alarm bells in Sara's head: slight weight gain, increasing fatigue, vague aches and pains, difficulty swallowing at times. Years ago, these would have been passed off as due to nerves, perhaps given the tag of "neurasthenia." But now they suggested a definite diagnosis to Sara.

"Have you noticed any change in your hair or skin?" Sara asked.

"Actually, yes." The woman seemed surprised that Sara would ask this, and happy that her symptoms fit. "My skin is dry. My hair is harder to manage. Matter of fact, my last perm was a disaster."

Sara stepped around behind the woman and put her hands on the front of her neck. "Please swallow . . . Again."

A glance at the vital signs recorded by the nurse on Mrs. Truman's chart reinforced Sara's preliminary diagnosis: slow pulse, blood pressure a bit lower than normal.

"Mrs. Truman, I think your problem is due to your thyroid. It's not producing the amount of thyroid hormone that it should, even though it's enlarged to try to keep up with the demand. That enlargement is pressing on your esophagus, making it difficult for you to swallow."

"Do I need an operation?" The woman's fear was reflected in her voice and on her face.

"I don't think so. We'll need to do some lab work, and if it confirms my diagnosis, we'll get you on some medicine to supply the hormone your own thyroid isn't making."

Mrs. Truman's shoulders relaxed visibly. "Oh, thank goodness. First I thought I was going to die two months ago when I got blood poisoning from that cut on my foot. And now this. I—"

"Where were you treated for that 'blood poisoning'?"

"Why, right here at the University Hospital. The infection was from some sort of super-bacteria that nothing would touch. But they gave me an experimental antibiotic that cleared it right up. It was like a miracle."

Sara bit her lip and picked up the paperwork that lay on the side table. In the block for diagnosis, she crossed out "Hypothyroidism," substituting "Hashimoto's thyroiditis." She'd already noted the lab tests she wanted, but now she added "anti-TPO," a measure of antibodies formed against the patient's own thyroid. She had no doubt this was another autoimmune complication after Jandramycin. How many more would there be? How many patients would have their lives turned upside down, even die, as a result of Jack's wonder drug?

Almost an hour later, Sara slumped in a chair in the dictation room, catching her breath before she moved on to her next patient. Lillian Goodman eased in behind her and took the next seat. "Tough afternoon?"

"I just picked up another patient with a late complication after Jandramycin," Sara said. "Autoimmune, of course. This was thyroiditis." She gave Lillian a quick summary of the story. "And I've done about everything I can to get Jack to admit there's even a chance that Jandramycin is at fault here. We could go to the FDA with our suspicions, but while all that plays out, more people are going to be affected. Some of them may die, just like that man with autoimmune kidney failure. I don't know what to do."

"Personally, I've had visions of breaking into Ingersoll's lab and holding him and Resnick at gunpoint until they give us the true story," Lillian said.

"So have I," Sara said. She stifled a giggle. "Can you imagine us doing that? Just like Thelma and Louise, two gun molls." She shook her head. "Sorry. I'm punch-drunk. Not enough sleep. Too much frustration about this Jandramycin thing."

"Was your last patient allergic?"

Sara frowned at her colleague. "You mean was she allergic to any meds?"

"No, did she have hay fever or asthma? Anything like that?"

Sara thumbed through the chart until she came to the history sheet Mrs. Truman had filled out. "She has seasonal hay fever, on shots once, off them now. Both parents had hay fever and asthma. Why?"

"John told me about 15 percent of patients get a late complication after Jandramycin. For some reason, it popped into my head that about 15 to 20 percent of people in the U.S. have clinical allergy. I just wondered if there was a correlation."

Sara took a second to think about it. "Autoimmune disorders are basically situations where some of the patient's tissues become allergic to themselves. It makes sense that underlying allergy might let Jandramycin trigger that kind of response." She looked at Lillian with new respect. "You may be onto something."

"What was the original name of the compound before it became Jandramycin?"

"I had to call Rip last night to ask him about that. It was . . . . Give me a second . . . It was EpAm848. Why?"

"Two reasons." Lillian ticked off her points on her fingers. "First of all, experimental compounds are sometimes named for the components in them, so we should see what Ep and Am and 848 might stand for. It could give us a clue to the mechanism of action of the drug. And if we know that, we might know how to prevent these late complications."

"And second?"

"Second, we don't have anywhere else to go, John is getting Jandramycin right now, and the clock is ticking toward the time when he might have a potentially lethal late effect."

20

John's cell phone buzzed, but he ignored it and continued to talk with the patient who sat in his exam room. Twenty minutes later, he finished his dictation, laid the chart aside, pulled his phone from his pocket, and checked the number of the missed call. There was none. Instead, the caller ID showed "private number." There was no message. He decided to ignore it, thinking they'd call back if it's important.

He was putting his phone back in his pocket when it rang. Once more, the caller ID showed "private number." Might as well find out what this is about. He pushed the button to answer. "Dr. Ramsey."

"John, this is Mark Wilcox. I have some news about your malpractice suit. Do you want to get together tonight to talk about it?"

John felt his stomach clench. "If we wait until tonight, I'll develop an ulcer while I worry about it. Just spill it."

"Okay, I'll have to make it quick. I'm between patients, and I suspect you are as well."

John didn't feel the need to respond to that. He sent up a silent prayer that this would be good news, but his gut told him otherwise.

"I told you the lawyer that filed the suit initially was a society lawyer, probably doing it as a favor for Randall Moore."

"Who's Moore?"

"Read the paperwork, John. That's the name of the man suing you. Anyway, that lawyer has now turned the action over to Lewis Robinette. Recognize the name?"

"I think I've read it somewhere. Isn't he some sort of hotshot lawyer?"

"You might say so. He specializes in malpractice cases, with an occasional class action personal injury suit thrown in for variety."

"Is he good?"

"Sort of like Ted Williams was a good baseball player. Yeah, he's very good."

John massaged his temples. "So now what?"

"I'll give him a day or two to contact me. If he doesn't, I'll call him. He might still be reasonable and agree to drop you from the suit."

"Think that's likely?"

A long pause gave John the answer, even before Mark spoke. "No."

Sara was about to enter an exam room when she heard Lillian Goodman call softly, "Sara, hang on a second."

She turned and watched Lillian walk swiftly down the hall of the clinic, a chart held at arm's length in front of her like a stick of dynamite about to explode. "I don't think I'd better see this patient. Would you take him?"

"Sure. But why—"

"Recognize the name on the chart?"

Sara looked. "No. Should I?"

"Let's just say it's someone I don't want to establish a professional relationship with." Lillian shook her head. "You know, maybe I should call Don Schaeffer. It would probably be best for the chairman to see him anyway."

"Don't be silly." She looked at the history form. Chief complaint: cough and fever. "Probably bronchitis. I can handle that. And maybe later you can tell me why you didn't want to see him."

Without waiting for Lillian to respond, Sara tapped on the door and entered the exam room. A middle-aged man in a well-cut gray pinstripe suit sat in the patient chair in the corner of the small room. His white French cuff shirt was spotless, and she recognized his tie as a Gucci. He rose when she entered the room.

"I want to tell you that I'm here despite grave misgivings." His tone was mild, but there was no mistaking the emotion behind the words. "I have severe doubts about this institution in general, but my family doctor is unavailable and both my wife and sister insisted that I would receive good care here." He bowed slightly. "Please don't take that as an indictment of you or your capabilities. I don't know you. But—"

Sara waved off his comments. "Never mind. You're here, so we'll just move on," she said. "Have a seat and let's talk a bit. What kind of problems are you experiencing?"

The story was one she'd heard a lot in recent weeks. An upper respiratory infection that worsened and morphed into a persistent cough productive of green to yellow sputum. Fever and chills. Fatigue and loss of appetite. If the history didn't suggest it, the man's persistent cough and the perspiration on his brow gave her clues to his problem.

He shed his coat and shirt when requested to do so, and perched uneasily on the edge of the exam table. When Sara placed her stethoscope on his chest and listened, her clinical suspicion was verified. Crackling rales and diminished breath sounds in both lungs, maybe a little worse on the left. Classic signs of pneumonia.

"Just a chest cold, right?" the man asked. "So you can give me something and let me go."

"Afraid not," Sara said. "I need to get some lab work and a chest X-ray, but I think you have pneumonia."

"But I don't have time for that. I'm a busy man. Can't you just give me a shot of penicillin or something like that?"

She'd heard it all before, heard it so much that her response was almost a set speech. "This could be something quite simple or very serious. I won't know how to treat you until I see the results of these tests. They won't take long, and there's a very good possibility we'll be able to treat this on an outpatient basis." She looked pointedly at her watch. "And the less we argue about it, the sooner we get the information I need to treat you."

He acquiesced, but it was obvious he was used to simply telling doctors what he wanted instead of letting them determine what he needed. Sara hated that attitude, but she'd learned that trying to educate these patients was often an exercise in futility.

While the patient donned his shirt, Sara stepped outside and handed the chart to Gloria. "PA and lateral chest. CBC. Sputum culture. And, oh, have them do a smear and Gram stain of the sputum right now. That will help me pick an antibiotic while the culture's working."

Almost an hour later, Sara was leaving an exam room when Gloria motioned to her. "Got the lab on your patient." She handed a chart to Sara, then fanned out three Post-It notes like a card player considering what she'd been dealt. "CBC showed a high white count with left shift."

Sara nodded. She'd expected this, evidence of a bacterial infection.

Gloria shifted to the second note. "You may want to look at the films yourself, but the radiologist read them as bilateral bronchopneumonia, almost total consolidation of both lower lobes, with a small pleural effusion on the left."

Sara breathed a silent thanks to John Ramsey, who'd taught her and hundreds of other medical students the art of physical diagnosis. *I made that diagnosis with my stethoscope.*

Gloria moved to the third note. "Saved the worst for last. The chief microbiology technician did a sputum smear. Gram-positive cocci, clusters, and chains. She says it looks a lot like *Staph luciferus.*"

Sara took a moment to collect her thoughts. There was no way this patient was going home. She needed to admit him to University Hospital for pulmonary treatments, supportive care, and antibiotics. That raised the big question. Consider Jandramycin therapy immediately, or wait until the culture and sensitivity studies were back? That would take at least two days, maybe three, and if this was really *Staph luciferus,* the man could be almost dead by then. But if this turned out to be another type of *Staph,* even MRSA, Jandramycin would be the wrong antibiotic. And the final kicker—Jandramycin would put the patient at risk for a late autoimmune complication, possibly a lethal one.

Ask Jack to consult? Not with what she knew about him now. There was one person whose opinion she trusted. She'd consult him. "Please page Dr. Pearson and ask him to call me back as soon as possible," Sara said to Gloria. "Then get the papers ready to admit Mr.—" She found the name on the chart Gloria had handed her: Randall Moore. "Admit Mr. Moore to University Hospital with a diagnosis of bilateral bronchopneumonia."

"Mr. Moore, I'm Dr. Pearson. Dr. Miles asked me to consult on your case."

Moore glared at Rip. "I don't need a bunch of doctors poking around on me and running up a big bill. I told—" He doubled over with a paroxysm of coughing and took a moment to recover his breath. "I told that woman I just had a bad chest cold. I think I'll leave and go to an emergency clinic somewhere. They'll give me a shot of penicillin, and I'll be fine."

Rip took a deep breath and tried to get his emotions in check. Maybe the best thing would be to let this guy sign himself out against medical advice. No, Rip remembered the oath he'd taken. Some members of his medical school graduating class had laughed at the process of repeating the Physician's Oath, an updated version of the old Hippocratic oath. But he had sworn to abide by these words: "The health of my patient will be my first consideration."

"Mr. Moore, look at this X-ray." Rip pointed with his pen. "Your lungs are operating at about half-capacity because of the infection. Fluid is already building up in them. If we don't do something about it, you'll die. And it won't be pleasant. You'll suffocate." Maybe a little drastic, but judging by the expression on Moore's face, effective.

"So what do you need to do?"

"Admit you to the hospital. Give you breathing treatments. Control your fever. And pump you full of strong antibiotics."

"How long do I have to stay?"

Good question, and one to which Rip had no answer. "As long as it takes to get the infection under control and make sure your lungs are clearing." He forced a smile. "Believe me, we'll get you out of here as quickly as we can."

"Well . . ."

Rip fired his last possible shot. "I'll have the chairman of our department look in on you later today. And I can ask the head of our infectious disease division to take over your case if you'd like."

Rip was surprised when Moore shook his head. "Not necessary. I want you and that woman doctor to take care of me."

"Why?" Rip blurted.

"Because you didn't let me bully you. Usually my money and position in the community get me whatever I demand. You didn't give in."

"I'm sorry, Mr. Moore, but I was unaware of both of those. I treat everyone the same, whether they live in Highland Park or under a bridge."

"I'll bet you do," Moore said. "But there's another thing. Both of you seem genuinely interested in treating me, even though . . . I don't know if I should even mention it."

"Mention what?"

"That I'm currently suing the medical center and a number of its doctors for several million dollars."

Lillian Goodman settled into the chair in front of a computer terminal in the medical center library. She could have used her office for this, but this way she was away from any distractions. Her cell phone was silenced, her pager set to vibrate, and no one but her secretary knew where to find her. She was determined not to give up until she'd broken through some of the mystery that surrounded Jandramycin, the compound that began life as EpAm848.

She decided that her first order of business would be to figure out what Jack Ingersoll's original area of research was when he stumbled onto his wonder drug. For instance, if the components were substances that might cause lysis of a cell wall, it was reasonable that they could be combined in such a way as to cause bacteria to swell and pop like balloons blown up too much. If they were involved in cell reproduction, the combination might act to keep bacteria from proliferating so their population would eventually decrease to zero.

The only clue she had was the original name given the experimental preparation: EpAm848. She decided to start with the number. That was fairly clear-cut, and surely Google would help her run down its meaning. She had second thoughts when she saw that entering "848" yielded almost eighty million results. Then she tried "compound 848." Better—only three million. As she trolled through the answers, she discovered that Google put the most likely at the top of its list. Good.

After half an hour, Lillian was fairly certain that the number referred to R848, a compound associated with the immune response to harmful bacteria. Okay, immune response. That was a starting place. She jotted a note on the pad beside the computer monitor.

"Am" was more challenging. She dug deep, pounding the computer keys until her wrists were sore and her fingers stiff, but nothing seemed to click. Then she decided that maybe it wasn't "Am" at all. Maybe the designation had been "AM"—two words, each beginning with one of those letters. That led to a different search.

After an hour's digging into references, Lillian felt cross-eyed. She stretched, moved around in her chair, and wondered if it was worth it. She dug into her purse, found a couple of Tylenols, and journeyed to the water fountain to combat the headache she was developing.

Finally, she found an obscure reference in the *Journal of Ethnopharmacology*. It dealt with Chinese herbs, and stated that *Astragalus membranaceus* was thought to have "immuno-modulating and immunorestorative effects." In other words, it affected the immune system of the person receiving it, helping throw off infections. That had to be it. Two-thirds of the compound name, and both referred to the immune response to bacterial infection. She felt the flush of victory, but determined to make sure.

Instead of searching for words that began with "Ep," Lillian tried the same tack that yielded her last positive result. She looked for two words that started with the letters E and P. This wasn't easy, and she was about to give up when she encountered *Echinacea purpurea*. She was aware that a number of homeopathic and herbal remedies contained *Echinacea* for its alleged ability to help cold sufferers throw off their infection. Lillian plowed through reference after reference until, in one paper, she encountered the phrase: "*Echinacea purpurea* is known for its ability to kick-start the immune system." She also found that many people were highly allergic to this natural remedy, experiencing reactions ranging from rash and swollen tongue to anaphylaxis and death. Could this be the "unpleasant result" Ingersoll sloughed off during their discussion?

Lillian sat back and massaged her temples. This might be the clue she and her colleagues had sought. Jandramycin, in its final form, acted to kick-start the patient's immune system to make antibodies specific for the invader, *Staph luciferus*. Such a targeted response would undoubtedly assure that everyone capable of mounting a normal immune response would be rid of the bacteria within a few days. And the autoimmune responses? If these only occurred in patients with an allergic background, maybe the drug had an additional action on their immune system, generating antibodies to the patient's own tissue. Nervous system, bone marrow, thyroid, kidney, blood vessels—any of these could be the target of the process. That could explain the autoimmune complications seen in allergic patients who'd received Jandramycin.

It's all conjecture. And if it's true, what do we do to help those patients? She scooped her notebook into her backpack, stuffed her purse in after it, and hurried from the library. She had to call John.

John opened the refrigerator and peered in, not really seeing the contents. He wasn't particularly hungry, but knew that he needed to eat. "Keep up your strength." He was startled when he realized the voice in his head that delivered the words wasn't Beth's. Instead, he heard Lillian Goodman. Did that mean Lillian was taking Beth's place? Oh, please God, no.

John loved Beth. He'd always love her. Was her memory fading already? He prayed that wasn't the case. He'd worked hard not to build what one popular book on the loss of a spouse called a "shrine to grief." He'd donated Beth's clothes to a shelter for battered women. Her books went to their church library. He'd cried while doing it, but John finally erased Beth's voice from her cell phone message, although now he wondered if that had been wise. But he knew he had to move on. He just wasn't ready for anyone to replace Beth in his life.

The ringing phone startled John from his reverie. He closed the refrigerator door and hurried into the living room to catch the phone before the answering machine kicked in. He didn't bother with the caller ID. When loneliness had him in its grip, he was even glad to talk with telephone solicitors.

"Dr. Ramsey."

"John, this is Lillian. Did I catch you at a bad time?"

He dropped into a chair and wondered if through some mind-reading magic Lillian knew he was wrestling at that moment with her role in his life. More than that, he felt guilty at the pleasure he felt when he recognized her voice. "No, I'm fine. Just browsing in the refrigerator."

"Well, be sure to eat something. You have to keep up your strength."

No doubt about it. The woman was a mind reader. "I will," John said. "But surely you didn't call to remind me to eat dinner. What's up?"

"This may sound strange, but I need to ask you if you're allergic."

"I don't understand what you mean. To medicines? To foods? What?"

"Do you have hay fever? Asthma? Eczema? That kind of allergy."

"Oh, I see. Well, I was allergy tested several years ago. He said I was allergic to grasses, trees, and weeds. But I never got around to taking shots. I just treat the symptoms when they get bothersome." He frowned. "But why do you ask?"

"I think we need to talk," Lillian said. "Would it be okay if I came over?"

"Sure. Why don't I order a pizza, and we can eat together? What do you like on yours?"

"Just order what you usually get," she said. "I'm sure it will be fine. Besides, after I tell you what I've learned, neither of us may have much of an appetite."

21

THE CALL CAME THROUGH ON HIS CELL PHONE, NOT HIS LANDLINE, WHICH was the way he'd set things up with his informant. Either way, there would be a record of the call, but this way there was no possibility that anyone could be listening in. At least, not without some sophisticated electronics. As for his office, it was swept for bugs once a week by a man he paid in cash out of his own pocket. Absolute security was impossible, but this would do.

"So, who's still digging around looking for flaws in Jandramycin?" he asked.

"Still Sara Miles and Rip Pearson, but—" Traffic noise in the background intensified for a moment, and the caller waited for it to die down. "Sorry. I stepped outside to get some privacy. Anyway, Miles and Pearson are the main ones, but I'm pretty sure there are a couple of others involved."

"Give me the names, and we'll give them something to take their mind off that witch hunt."

"I've got to tell you. I'm not really comfortable with what you've done already. Dr. Miles could have been hurt or killed by a gunshot."

"Not if the person behind the trigger had better aim." He struggled to keep his voice level. "I said to scare her, put a couple of bullets through the car window behind her. Instead, the shots almost hit her. That wasn't my fault."

"And ramming Pearson's car—"

"Pure incompetence. There are teenagers off the street who'd be able to boost a car, follow someone, and sideswipe their vehicle just enough to run them off the road. And they'd know not to choose a location that would involve hitting a concrete wall. Again, not my fault." Idiots. The whole world was populated with idiots, and the worst ones were the ones he had to work with. "Now get those other names. Call me back and we'll arrange something to distract them."

"I really don't like—"

"It doesn't matter what you like. You're ours, bought and paid for. Don't ever forget it."

The informant was saying something, but he hung up, cutting him off in mid-sentence. *Stay focused. Remember what's at stake. I can't stop now. Not when success was so close.*

Morning rounds on the internal medicine floor of University Hospital found Sara frowning over Randall Moore's chart. Rip had started him on nafcillin yesterday, and he'd had four IV doses of two grams each since admission, but his fever remained high. True, it was early, but she'd be a lot happier if there was some evidence he was responding to treatment. If this were a run-of-the-mill *Staph* infection, even MRSA, she'd expect some improvement. Every hour that went by without that improvement made it more likely her patient was infected with The Killer, *Staph luciferus.*

"How's our guy?" Rip slid into the chair beside her and peered over her shoulder. "Still febrile?"

She handed over the chart. "I'd be a lot happier if his temp were a bit lower. Think it might be . . . " She let the words trail off, hesitant to give voice to her fears.

"I'm afraid so. We might have a preliminary culture report today, although tomorrow seems more likely. And once we know for sure, the fun begins. Should I give him Jandramycin, knowing there's a chance he might get a severe late complication?"

"Can't you simply inform the patient and let him make that decision?"

Rip shook his head. "It's not as simple as that. Ingersoll categorically denies that Jandramycin therapy carries any risk. And, based on what you've told me, the people at Jandra say the same thing. So if we tell Moore about the possible complications, there's no foundation to back up our story. Besides that, if Ingersoll finds out, I can kiss my fellowship good-bye."

"But if we don't tell Moore, and he's one of the unlucky ones—"

"Then there's another lawsuit against the medical center and a bunch of doctors, us included," Rip said. "Yeah, this is a tough call."

"Excuse me, do you both have a moment?" Lillian Goodman stopped several paces away, apparently not wanting to invade the space of the two doctors who sat with their heads together.

Sara motioned her to the chair on the other side of her. "Have a seat. We were just talking about Randall Moore's case. You really dodged a bullet when you asked me to see him yesterday."

Lillian made a dismissive gesture. "I'm really sorry I got you involved. In retrospect, I should have called Donald Schaeffer over to see him."

"Don't worry about it," Rip said. "Besides, I think we can agonize over his treatment plan as well as the department chair could. Maybe even better."

Lillian leaned across to address her remarks to both Sara and Rip. "You guys do know that—"

Sara stopped her with an upraised palm. "Yes, we know he's suing you and half the staff of the medical center. But that doesn't make any difference to me, and I believe Rip feels the same way."

"Suit? Has another lawsuit been filed?" John Ramsey slid into the chair beside Rip. "I'm seeing more of those since coming here than I ever saw in forty years of private practice."

"No, this is the same one you and I know about," Lillian said. "Sara, do you want to tell John what's going on?"

John sat quietly while Sara explained the situation. When she finished, he said, "Wow. I guess the best thing would be that the culture comes back as something other than *Staph luciferus*. Even MRSA would be better, I suppose."

"It would, but I'm not betting on it," Rip said.

Lillian held out her hand in silent request, and Rip passed her the chart. "What are you looking for?" he asked.

She thumbed through until she found the history sheet Moore had filled out when he first entered the clinic. "I'm looking for something in his history." Lillian frowned, flipped a page, frowned again. "Here it is. He has a history of hay fever and asthma, and both parents are allergic."

"What does that mean?" Rip asked.

"I'll give you my theory. Realize, this is all supposition," Lillian said, "but it makes sense to me, and it's all we have to work with right now. I began with your finding that about 15 percent of the people receiving Jandramycin ended up with late autoimmune complications. That's about the percentage of people in the U.S. with allergy."

"Yes," Rip said. "But so what?"

"I decided to look for a connection, and I think I found it. I took the original name of the experimental compound that became Jandramycin and searched for the components Ingersoll could have been working with to develop it. I started with 848 . . ."

John listened quietly as Lillian laid out what she'd found and knit together her hypothesis. Jandramycin stimulated a patient's immune system to form antibodies against *Staph luciferus*. Natural antibodies attacked the bacteria, destroying them and preventing them from multiplying. The action of this drug was different from that of other antibiotics, drugs that attacked bacterial cell walls or stopped their metabolism, but the end result was the same. The patient recovered.

Unfortunately, in patients with an underlying predisposition to allergy, the drug also did something to the immune system that turned it upon itself, making antibodies to the patient's own organs. For some reason, this was only seen in allergic patients. And he was allergic and had been treated with Jandramycin. The only question in his mind was which autoimmune disease he'd be stricken with, and how severe it would be.

"Assuming your hypothesis is correct," Rip said, "this still doesn't tell us how we can modify the process in vulnerable patients so they don't develop autoantibodies."

"Let's approach this logically," John said. "What do we use to treat autoimmune disorders?"

"Corticosteroids" came the reply from three mouths almost in unison.

"But that's a temporary measure at best. The patient with temporal arteritis may have to receive multiple courses of steroids as the symptoms recur. Steroid therapy doesn't cure rheumatoid arthritis. It only alleviates the symptoms," John said. "What else?"

"Antimetabolites," Sara suggested. "Methotrexate, for instance."

"Again, a temporary measure," John said. "What if there were something that, instead of cleaning up the symptoms they produce, could block those antibodies from attacking the person's own tissues in the first place?"

Rip shook his head. "That would be perfect, but unfortunately we don't have such a drug."

Lillian and John exchanged glances. Maybe being older did translate into being wiser and able to think outside the box. In response to a faint nod from Lillian, John spoke up again. "I have a suggestion. Omalizumab."

He told them what he had in mind. Perhaps this compound, developed specifically to block the antibodies responsible for hay fever and asthma, would neutralize the abnormal antibodies made by the patients who'd received Jandramycin.

John watched expressions in the group change as disbelief gradually gave way to the realization that it might actually work.

"It's an off-label usage for a preparation that might—I emphasize might—do what we want it to do. It's expensive, and we don't know how many doses it might take. Most important, there's risk in using it on patients whose immune system has probably already been modified by Jandramycin."

Rip frowned. "Wouldn't we have to get the approval of the IRB?"

"It would take weeks to get a proposal before the Investigational Review Board," Sara said, "and if we did, they might not approve it." She looked down at her clasped hands. "And I have a little girl who, despite large doses of steroids, is losing a fight with ascending paralysis with each day that passes."

"That's why I'm making this suggestion. And it can't go beyond the four of us in this room." He waited until he'd received nods of assent from the others. "I want to volunteer to test it on me."

"But you haven't developed any complications," Rip said.

"No, but I have a history of allergy, so I'm in line to do just that. I'll take it. If there are no adverse effects, if it doesn't appear that the Jandramycin has set me up to react adversely to the drug, that's a big step. Then if I don't develop an auto-immune complication, that tells us even more." He spread his hands. "Sure, it's not a double-blind, placebo-controlled study, but it's all we've got."

"How soon do you think we'd know something?" Sara asked.

"It generally takes effect within a few days. But if there are going to be complications from it, they'll show up within an hour or two," John said.

"And if it works, maybe I could give it to Chelsea?" Sara asked.

"Do you have something better?" John asked.

The silence in the room effectively answered the question.

Finally, Rip spoke. "Since I'm what passes for the second-in-command on this investigation, and none of us trust the principal investigator, I'll speak up. Go for it."

"I'm going to talk with Chelsea Ferguson's mother about giving it to her," Sara said. "I'm pretty sure she'll jump at the chance."

"Don't you want to wait—" Rip said.

"I don't think I can wait much longer. If John tolerates the test dose, Chelsea will be next," Sara said. "I just pray we're not already too late."

Sara wasted no time in going to Chelsea Ferguson's room. She told Mrs. Ferguson about omalizumab.

"What?"

"It's a long word," Sara said. "Just call it OMAL, like some of us do."

"Will it work?"

Sara decided to be blunt. "We don't know if it will work. But right now it's all we have."

Mrs. Ferguson grasped at the possibility like a drowning man reaching for a piece of driftwood. "Anything that might help Chelsea. Anything."

"You recognize that this is not only what we call off-label, but it's never been used in these circumstances. Frankly, it's a shot in the dark. It may not work, but—"

"But nothing else has. I know." Mrs. Ferguson cast a glance at Chelsea, who remained immobile, staring at the ceiling. For the past two days, she'd been virtually uncommunicative, withdrawn into her own private world. "I want you to use anything that might have a chance. And I know Chelsea does."

Sara nodded her understanding. She reached down to take Chelsea's hand and was pleasantly surprised to receive a weak squeeze in return. "Dr. Ramsey is getting his dose of the medication right now. If there are no ill effects, I'll plan on giving Chelsea hers. Of course, there'll be papers to sign—"

"Do you have them with you? I'll sign now. I just . . ." Mrs. Ferguson let the words trail off, but Sara knew what they were. The woman would do anything to make her daughter well.

Sara could identify with that. She'd feel that way about her child. She felt a tear form in her eye and turned away before

Chelsea could see it. "I have to get the papers ready. I'll see you soon." She hurried outside.

Sara was in the hallway when her cell phone vibrated in her pocket. She checked the caller ID and decided she was in no mood to talk with Mark Wilcox. He was a nice guy and obviously interested in her, but right now her total attention was focused on Chelsea. Besides, she was beginning to have her suspicions about Mark. Matter of fact, she was becoming positively paranoid about almost everyone with whom she came in contact, fearing they might be involved in the conspiracy to hide Jandramycin's side effects.

Time to focus on Chelsea. It was hard for Sara to imagine the teenager's growing fears as the weakness in her limbs progressed. She could no longer walk, and the strength in her arms diminished every day. It was harder and harder for Sara to present a smiling countenance when she entered Chelsea's room. She didn't know how Mrs. Ferguson managed it, but it was obvious that she was on the verge of exhaustion.

Sara hurried back to the clinic, where she found John Ramsey in a back room sitting on the edge of the treatment table. "Have you had the injection yet?" she asked.

John nodded toward the corner of the room, where Rip Pearson was withdrawing a clear, slightly thick solution from a vial into a syringe. Lillian Goodman stood beside him, holding several alcohol sponges and a couple of packaged injection needles.

"That's a full dose," Rip said. He went through the routine to eject residual air from the syringe, changed the needle, and stepped to John's side. "Ready?"

"Let's do it before I change my mind," John said.

Rip swabbed John's upper arm with one of the alcohol sponges, pinched the tissue between his left thumb and fingers, and plunged the needle into the soft tissue of the arm. "I have to inject this slowly because it's so thick. Hang with me."

John gritted his teeth, but said nothing. Sara began counting in her mind: one, two, three . . . She'd reached twenty-seven when Rip pulled the needle free and pressed a fresh alcohol sponge against the injection site. "Hold that for a moment, then I'll give you a Band-Aid."

Sara looked at her watch and did a quick calculation. The major risk with this drug was anaphylaxis—a massive allergic reaction that could cause the airway to close off, blood pressure to drop, resulting in death if not properly managed. In the rare instance this had happened after such an injection, the signs occurred within ninety minutes or less.

"I'll stay here with John for the next couple of hours," Rip said. "You guys go ahead to your clinics. I'll let you know if anything develops." He pointed to the emergency equipment on the table in the corner, and the message was clear. He was prepared to treat any allergic reaction that might develop. Expect the best, prepare for the worst.

"I don't think—" Lillian began.

"Please," John said. "Rip will be here with me. If you two both cancel your clinic this afternoon, someone's going to talk about it. Then word will get back to Ingersoll, and we don't know what might come of that."

Lillian squeezed John's hand. "I'll check on you as often as I can."

"No," John said. "We don't need a parade going in and out of this room. Rip told the nurses he needed the room this afternoon, but they don't know what's going on. So far as anyone knows, this is just another part of the Jandramycin study. Let's keep it low-key."

Sara looked at her watch. "It's a quarter to one now. We should know something in an hour and a half. Two hours at most. Why don't we meet in my office at three?"

There was grudging acceptance of the plan. Sara touched John's shoulder and whispered, "I'll be praying for you." As she slipped out of the door, butterflies gathered for a convention in her gut.

22

"Well, we've got some time to kill," John said. "Do you want to catch up on your journals? Do chart work? Go ahead. I'll just lie here quietly and wait for my throat to start closing up and my blood pressure to plummet."

"Don't even joke about it," Rip said. "I know that we believe Jandramycin may have affected your immune system, but in regular patients the risk of anaphylaxis is tiny—maybe one chance in a thousand."

"Ah, but there's the rub. What happens in someone after Jandramycin resets some of the switches in the immune system?" John didn't voice the rest of what he was thinking. In his case, did that risk go up to one in a hundred? One in ten? A hundred percent?

"Enough of that." Rip made one more note on the pad in his lap. If this went well, he'd add the material to John's chart. If it didn't, he might end up shredding it to avoid losing his medical license. "Tell me about Randall Moore."

John shifted on the exam table, trying in vain to find a comfortable spot. Finally, he gave up and swung into a sitting position with his feet dangling over the side. "All I know is what I've been told. He and his sister are the only children of a wealthy family. He inherited a good bit of that money when his father died and has been living off it ever since."

"Why is he suing?"

"His mother was headed for the internal medicine clinic to see someone for a second opinion when she had a fatal stroke. Apparently, in Randall's world, when something bad happens, filing a suit is a reflex action. So he filed one against the medical center and every doctor involved with her from the time she hit the floor. I started an IV while we waited for the EMT's." John spread his hands. "So they threw me in for good measure."

Rip lowered his head and massaged his temples. "That's just dandy. If his culture comes back *Staph luciferus*—and the odds are that it will—I can give him Jandramycin and probably save his life, but there's a chance that he'll get a life-changing and possibly fatal complication later." He looked up. "But if I don't, he'll probably die. And as a physician, I can't deny him treatment that would prevent that." *Even if it would put an end to his lawsuit against my friends.*

"There's another possibility, you know."

"What?"

"This drug may work. If I don't get a late complication, if Sara's teenage patient starts to recover, we may have stumbled onto the answer. Give this to every Jandramycin patient after their course of treatment, and they'll do fine."

"Sounds too good to be true, John." Rip shook his head. "Don't get me wrong. I don't want you to get a complication from your treatment. I hope and pray that Sara's patient pulls through. But something inside me keeps telling me not to get my hopes up."

"I guess I hear a different voice," John said. "Beth drummed it into me so often I can still hear her saying it. 'God's in control.' We may not see His hand, but it's there. And I think He's got this covered."

Rip looked at his watch. "Well, in about an hour we'll know what He's got up His sleeve for you . . . and the rest of us."

The afternoon dragged, and Sara found it difficult to focus on her patients. As she walked out of every patient's room, her eyes were drawn to the closed door at the end of the hall. How was John doing? Any problems after the injection? Fortunately, no big diagnostic challenges presented themselves, and she was able to care for her patients without too much trouble. By five minutes to three, she was caught up.

"Glenda, my next patient isn't due for twenty minutes. I'm going to run over to my academic office for a minute." Although she didn't actually run, Sara moved quickly through the halls. She nodded a brief greeting to a few of the people she met and prayed that none of them wanted to stop and chat.

Lillian was waiting in the hall outside Sara's office, looking at the notices on the bulletin board but obviously paying no attention to them.

"Heard anything?" Lillian said.

"Not a thing. Shall we go in and wait?"

Sara pointed down the hall. John and Rip were sauntering toward them, conversing in low tones. Neither seemed in a hurry to reach them. *Come on. I need to know if everything went okay.*

When they drew abreast of the two women, John spoke first. "Here I am, none the worse for wear."

"No problems?" Sara asked.

Rip answered with a smile. "None. Not even any itching or rash. Vital signs stable. He tolerated the drug with no problems."

His countenance turned somber. "Now we have to hope it has a protective action on patients who've had Jandramycin."

Sara ushered the group through the empty outer office. Her secretary's desk was vacant. She must be on a break.

"Come on in. I think we have enough chairs. I—"

As her foot touched the threshold of her office, Sara's scream was masked by the noise of the explosion.

Mark Wilcox scratched his head. He'd been calling Sara all day without success. No answer on her cell phone, no response to the messages he'd left with her secretary. He understood that she might be tied up, but he was hurt that she hadn't called back.

It was important to him to further his relationship with her. She had no idea how important it was, and maybe this was the time to let her know. He'd played his cards close to his vest up to this point, but he was about to change all that. Unfortunately, nothing was going to happen if she didn't respond to his calls.

Well, while he waited, maybe he could do a little legal work. He checked a number and dialed.

"Lewis Robinette, please," he told the perky female voice that answered the call.

"May I say who's calling?"

"Attorney Mark Wilcox. I'm lead counsel in an action Mr. Robinette is pursuing."

"One moment, please, Mr. Wilcox."

After almost a minute listening to saccharine strings playing an almost-familiar melody, Mark heard, "This is Lewis Robinette. Mr. Wilcox is it?"

"Matter of fact, it's Dr. Wilcox. I'm an MD and JD. But I didn't call to match credentials with you. I know your reputation in the legal community. Matter of fact, it's because of the respect you've earned that I'm calling."

"Nice words, but you need to explain them."

"You've been engaged by Randall Moore to pursue a malpractice action he's filed after the death of his mother. Along with Southwestern Medical Center and just about every doctor on its staff, he's included my client, Dr. John Ramsey." Mark transferred his phone to the other hand and wiped his moist palm on the bottom of his white coat. "If you don't remove him from the suit, you're going to end up with egg on your face."

The reply came without emotion—just a matter-of-fact question: "Exactly why do you say that?"

Mark began to explain, emphasizing John's limited activity in the event that preceded the death of Moore's mother. Then, after considering the pros and cons of his action, he told Robinette that John had no insurance company behind him, so there were no deep pockets there for the plaintiff to mine.

Robinette's voice was calm. "My client is interested in only one thing: justice. He believes that the medical center and its doctors should pay for their negligence that deprived his mother of her life."

"And do you have experts who've reviewed the case and are willing to testify that such negligence exists? Do they think the standard of care was breached at any point in the care of Mrs. Moore?" Mark decided to fire one more salvo. "Because I have some extremely qualified and persuasive witnesses who'll shoot yours out of the water. And after the judge throws out the suit, we could consider filing one against your client and your firm for frivolous litigation, among other things."

"Dr. Wilcox, I believe you mentioned my reputation. I didn't earn it by caving in when someone yelled 'boo' at me. I appreciate what you're doing on behalf of your client. Matter of fact, I'd do the same thing if I were in your shoes. But as soon as you file an answer to the suit, I'll review the situation. As of this time, I'm ready to proceed with discovery, and let the judicial process play out."

"I think—" Mark stopped when the click registered in his ear. Robinette was already gone, undoubtedly moving on to something else after making a note of the billable time he'd spent on the phone.

Mark shrugged and dialed a number that was becoming familiar to him. He'd better let John Ramsey know about this latest call. There was no answer on Ramsey's cell. The nurse in the general internal medicine clinic told Mark that Dr. Ramsey wasn't scheduled to see patients that day. When the answering machine picked up at Ramsey's home, Mark hung up.

Sara wasn't available. John wasn't available. He leaned back in his chair, put one foot on an opened bottom desk drawer, and wondered at the connection. Could this have something to do with their Jandramycin investigation? He'd need to find out.

Rip crouched protectively over Sara. "Don't move. Let me have a look."

She lay a few feet from the doorway of her office, huddled in the fetal position, sobbing quietly. Rip looked at her legs. A scorch mark ringed the hem of the right leg of her slacks. The bottom of her right shoe was burned, and a violet coloration marred the black finish. Rip eased the shoe off. The skin on the bottom of Sara's right foot was red, but there was no blood and no soft tissue damage. There'd been plenty of noise, but apparently the damage had been minimal.

"Can you sit up?" he asked.

Sara complied, scooting back further from the doorway in the process. "What . . . what happened?"

"You put your foot down and there was an explosion—a very limited one, but with plenty of flash and bang to it." Lillian leaned over Sara and spoke in a soft voice. "I don't know what it could have been."

"I'm pretty sure I do," John said. He knelt at the edge of the doorway and sniffed. "Smell that? Smell like iodine to you?"

At first no one seemed anxious to get close to the danger area, but eventually they crept forward and smelled the air there. There was a general murmur of assent.

"Maybe it's my misspent youth, filing away trivia about things that go 'boom,'" John said. "Perhaps it comes from working my way through pre-med as a clerk in the chemistry department stockroom." He pointed at a tiny area where dark brown crystals dotted the metal threshold that marked the junction of carpet in the outer and inner offices. "That's nitrogen triiodide."

"I remember that," Rip said. "My high school chemistry teacher did a demonstration with it. Man, that produced a bigger bang than anything I'd seen, even bigger than when we dropped a sliver of sodium metal into a bucket of water. But how did someone make this? And why put it here?"

"Nitrogen triiodide is the easiest thing in the world to make, if you don't care whether you lose a few fingers in the process," John said. "Mix a couple of common household chemicals, filter out the precipitate that forms, and as long as it's wet it's supposed to be stable. But when it dries, the slightest touch, sometimes even a drop of water landing on it or a strong breeze, can set it off. I've heard of snowflakes detonating nitrogen triiodide. Depending on the amount involved, you can do quite a bit of damage with it."

"Should we call the police?" Lillian asked.

"We can if you want to have the building evacuated while bomb-sniffing dogs go through it and the bomb squad detonates the rest of this stuff," John said. "If you just want to make the area safe, I suggest you call someone you trust in the biochem department. I seem to recall that you can deactivate this stuff with chemicals like sodium hydroxide or sodium thiosulfate."

By this time, Sara had risen from the floor and stood next to Rip, leaning on him to take weight off her right foot. "Let's get this cleaned up and move ahead with our plans. I'm not going to let a ruined pair of shoes stop me. We're too close."

Lillian looked at her watch. "I'm due back in clinic, and Sara, you are, too. We need to take care of that first."

Rip had his cell phone out already. "I've got a friend in biochem that I think will handle this for us. I'll call him."

"And I'll stay here to keep you company," John said.

"Meet back here at five?" Sara said. "And Lillian, walk back with me, would you? I've got to come up with a story to explain this burned right shoe."

By five o'clock, an instructor in the biochemistry department assured the group clustered around the secretary's desk that they could safely enter Sara's office. "I neutralized the nitrogen triiodide, then disposed of it. You're good to go." He fixed Rip with a serious gaze. "Don't you think this should be reported to the police?"

"We're trying to keep it quiet."

"Well, I'll tell you. I've done some work with nitrogen triiodide, and this guy meant business. If your lady friend had stepped a little more to one side or the other, she'd be walking on crutches for a while. This was no prank."

"I know." Rip didn't want this conversation to go on much longer. He moved toward the door and was grateful when the visitor followed. "Thanks again, Fred."

"No problem. Makes a change from grading freshmen medical students' mid-terms."

"And you'll keep this under your hat?"

"Sure thing. Dinner at Ruth's Chris Steak House will get you all the silence you want. I'll call you to set it up." Fred touched his finger to his forehead in a mock salute and sauntered away.

The group shuffled into the office, eyes down, watching for telltale brown specks on the carpet. Finding none, they settled into chairs. Sara took the chair behind her desk. She leaned back and closed her eyes.

Rip broke the silence. "Who could have done this? And when?"

"When my secretary got back, I asked her about that," Sara said. "She said she got a call to go to Shipping and Receiving to sign for a package. When she arrived, there was no package, but because that's two blocks away from this building, the trip took her out of the office for almost forty-five minutes."

"And anyone could have had access during that time," Rip said.

"Let's try to refocus on the problem at hand," Sara said. "John, are you still feeling okay?"

"Now that my pulse is back to normal, I'm doing fine. I tolerated the OMAL with no problem. Of course, we don't know if I was in line to get a late complication anyway, and if I were, it would occur several weeks down the line, so this doesn't prove anything except that patients who've had their immune system modulated by Jandramycin can tolerate a dose of that drug."

"That's good enough for me," Sara said. "I told Mrs. Ferguson I'd give Chelsea her dose tomorrow, but I don't want to wait. I'm going over to her room and administer the OMAL now. I don't have anything else to do, so I'll stay with her tonight until

I'm sure she's going to be okay. Then we just watch and wait, and pray for improvement."

"I'll stay with you," Rip said.

"Are you sure?"

"I don't have anything on the docket. Nobody is waiting for me at home either."

Lillian looked at John. "Actually, that goes for us, too. Want us to keep watch with you?"

Sara shook her head. "No, I don't think so. We can stay in touch by cell phone. You two go ahead home."

After John and Lillian departed, Rip said, "Okay, truth time. How are you feeling after all that?"

"Actually, other than a little soreness of my foot and being royally ticked at the damage to my favorite pair of shoes, I'm doing pretty well."

"Are you sure you don't want to go home and get some rest? Another day probably won't make that much difference in Chelsea's status."

Sara was on her feet before Rip finished speaking. "On the contrary, I don't think I can rest until I've given her the injection. But you don't have to hang around."

There's nothing I'd rather do than hang around. "Call it professional curiosity if you want to, but I'd like to see this thing through with you." Rip pushed back his chair and stood. "Let's get going."

23

An alarm bell intruded into Sara's consciousness, and she was on her feet before she realized where she was. A quick glance brought it all back. She was in a corner of Chelsea Ferguson's hospital room. Rip dozed in another chair next to her. Chelsea was in her hospital bed. Her mother stood watch at her side.

The bell stopped as quickly as it began. Rip roused long enough to say, "Somebody accidentally unplugged something. Nothing to worry about." He yawned and stretched. "How long has it been?"

Sara needed no explanation. He meant, "How long has it been since we gave Chelsea the dose of OMAL?" She did a rapid calculation in her head. "Ninety-seven minutes."

They shared a glance and a silent message passed between them. Most reactions to this drug occurred within the first ninety minutes, all within two hours. They were almost home free. "Let's wait another half hour or so to be sure," Sara said.

Mrs. Ferguson tiptoed over to where Sara stood and whispered, "Can we talk outside?"

Sara moved toward the door. Mrs. Ferguson said, "Chelsea, I'm going to step outside for a minute. Dr. Pearson is here, and I'll be right back. Okay?"

Chelsea didn't break the silence she'd maintained for the past hour. Instead, she made the smallest of hand gestures to signal she'd heard.

In the hall, Mrs. Ferguson leaned close to Sara and spoke in a low whisper. "It's been almost two hours. What do you think?"

Sara kept her voice low as well. "She hasn't shown any signs of a reaction from the OMAL. That's the first hurdle. Now we have to see if the drug does what we hope it'll do."

"How long will that take?"

"We don't know. I'd guess at least a couple of days, maybe a week," Sara said.

"Tell me again why you think this may work."

"The drug is sometimes called 'anti-IgE.' The substances that carry out the body's immune responses are called immunoglobulins. There are five of them, named with letters of the alphabet, and immunoglobulin E—IgE for short—is the one that's involved in what most people think of as allergy. This compound, anti-IgE, was developed to block that immunoglobulin in susceptible individuals. It keeps it from attaching to the cells where it would ordinarily do its dirty work."

"What does that have to do with Chelsea?" Mrs. Ferguson asked.

"We think the Jandramycin has not only stimulated her immune system to produce special substances that kill the *Staph luciferus*, but also some that attack her own cells. In Chelsea's case, it's the nerves, and it leads to weakness and eventual paralysis. We hope that in this particular scenario, the anti-IgE will block those other substances as well."

"Do you have any reason to think this will work?"

Sara had turned that question over in her mind again and again since John proposed using OMAL for this purpose. The answer she gave was what she'd come up with. "We think there's a good chance—and we have nothing else."

John and Rip were in the back treatment room of the clinic that had become John's unofficial home for his Jandramycin infusions. This time there was no IV setup in view, no syringes and vials on the treatment table. John perched on the end of the treatment table; Rip sat on a rolling stool. It seemed that each was waiting for the other to speak.

Rip took in a deep breath through his nose and let it out through pursed lips. He guessed it was up to him to talk about the elephant in the room. "John, you've had six IV doses of Jandramycin. How are you doing?"

John held up his hand and turned it back and forth in front of Rip. The needle puncture wound had long since healed. No redness, swelling, or any of the cardinal signs of inflammation. "I think it's pretty much back to normal. Don't you?"

"I do, but as you know, all our success with Jandramycin has been based on a protocol of ten days of treatment. Admittedly, that number was chosen empirically, but so far it's worked. Theoretically, you need four more doses." Rip waited to see if John saw the same thing that was bothering him.

Apparently, he did. "But since I've had the IM injection of OMAL," John said, "my immune system has been tweaked, hopefully to the point that the Jandramycin won't have any further effect. The good news is that my chances of getting a late autoimmune problem may have been reduced, maybe even down to zero. On the other hand . . . "

"Yeah, on the other hand, any more Jandramycin you receive would probably be ineffective against *Staph luciferus* if there are some still in your body."

"So I'm stuck at this point. Just wait and hope the bug's been killed out." John shook his head. "Guess I can add that to worrying about whether that needle-stick exposed me to HIV."

Rip reached out and gripped John's hand. "So far, your labs look clean from that standpoint. But remember, I'm in this with you. And we won't go down without a fight."

Rip entered Randall Moore's room ready for almost anything, but not for the sight that greeted him. Jack Ingersoll and Donald Schaeffer had their heads together at Moore's bedside. Each doctor wore a white lab coat. A stethoscope dangled from Ingersoll's neck, while Schaeffer held his at his side. Their demeanor suggested serious consultation, such as would befit two heads of state rather than two physicians at a medical center.

Rip turned his eyes from them to Moore. His previously pale skin was darker now, but not with a healthy tan. His lips had a bluish cast. The man wasn't getting enough oxygen into his blood, even with pure oxygen flowing into the mask that covered his face. His respirations were slow and shallow. Moore was dying before Rip's eyes.

"What's going on?" Rip asked, trying to keep his voice level.

"I was in the bacteriology lab and the chief technician showed me the final results from this patient's sputum culture. He has a *Staphylococcus luciferus* pneumonia, which is why the nafcillin you ordered has been ineffective."

"I suspected as much," Rip said. "I just phoned the lab and got the final culture report myself. I've already talked with Dr. Miles about it, and she's on her way to meet me here. We plan to discuss treatment alternatives with her patient." He pointed to the man in the bed. "But I don't think he's in any shape for a discussion. We'd better—"

Dr. Schaeffer turned to face Rip. "Dr. Pearson, the reason I'm here is that Dr. Ingersoll thought it best, given the high-profile status of this patient, that he take over the case. After reviewing the situation, I tend to agree." He frowned. "I don't want you to think this is a criticism of Dr. Miles's clinical ability or of yours. I just think it's more . . . expedient that the Chief of the Infectious Disease Service assume Mr. Moore's care."

Rip knew exactly what was going on. Moore was the plaintiff in a huge suit against the medical center. Currently his treatment was under the supervision of a junior faculty member and a fellow in training. Schaeffer wanted his high-profile professor treating Moore, in hopes that a good outcome, coupled with this display of the resources available at Southwestern, would convince the man to drop his suit.

"I can't speak for Dr. Miles. Personally, I don't care whose name is on the chart." Rip pointed to the small device on Moore's index finger. "But look at the pulse oximeter. His oxygen saturation has dropped to dangerous levels. We need to get him intubated and on a ventilator."

"I've already put in a call for someone to do that," Ingersoll said. "And I plan to write the orders to add Mr. . . . ." He consulted the chart in his hand. "Add Mr. Moore to the Jandramycin study. You will, of course, draw the necessary blood work, administer the drug, all the things you've been doing so well."

"What about permission?" Rip asked. "He's too far out of it to give informed consent. Let me contact his next of kin. Maybe they can sign."

"Not necessary," Ingersoll said. "Given Mr. Moore's inability to make that decision right now, Dr. Schaeffer and I will sign the permission, which, as you know, is possible in the case of a medical emergency where delay is unacceptable."

Rip's guts began to churn. This was wrong, all of it. There was no need to wait for an anesthesiologist or pulmonologist to do the intubation. Rip was perfectly capable of carrying out the procedure, but apparently, Ingersoll wanted it done by another specialist—under his direction, of course.

As for treatment with Jandramycin, Rip had come here with his mind made up. The only proper course was to lay out the risks and benefits of treatment with Jandramycin and let Moore decide. Unfortunately, Ingersoll was totally ignoring the risk that Rip felt the drug presented, a risk of late complications that would be life-changing in all cases and fatal in some. Since Moore was unable to make that decision, Ingersoll was taking the responsibility of deciding for the patient, and Schaeffer was going along with his division chief.

So be it, Rip thought. He turned on his heel and left to gather the material he'd need. He was back to drawing blood, giving medications IV, and charting vital signs. And if he was later asked why he didn't protest Ingersoll's actions, he guessed his response would be that he was just following orders. Wasn't that the excuse of the prison guards at Dachau?

Sara sat in her living room, slumped in her favorite chair, when the doorbell brought her up from a half-sleep. Was this Rip again? After he gave her the news about the decision of Ingersoll and Schaeffer to replace her as Randall Moore's primary physician, he'd asked if he could buy her dinner. She told him all she wanted to do was go home and relax with a hot bath and a pint of Cherry Garcia ice cream. Although she hadn't made it past the living room, she had a full-fledged pity party planned, and she resented this intrusion.

She tried to ignore the bell, but whoever was at her front door apparently had more persistence than a bill collector on commission. "I'm coming," she mumbled under her breath.

She eased out of her chair and padded to the door on stocking feet.

Halfway to the door, she heard the distinctive splash of rain dripping from her roof. When had it begun to rain? She put her eye to the peephole, only to discover that while she was napping, darkness had covered the world. Sara snapped on the porch light and saw a thoroughly soaked and bedraggled Mark Wilcox standing there.

She unlocked the door and said, "I'm so sorry. Come in." As soon as he was inside, she said, "Stay right there. Let me get you a bath towel or something."

Sara grabbed a couple of thick towels from the bathroom, hurried back, and handed one to Mark, who nodded his thanks. "You know, this wouldn't have happened if you answered your phone . . . or replied to my text messages . . . or my voicemails."

"I'm sorry, Mark. It's been a terrible day, and I didn't feel like talking with anyone." Sara took the sodden towel Mark handed her and gave him the second one. "When you've dried a bit, come on into the living room. I'll make some coffee."

"Hot coffee sounds good." Mark finger-combed his hair. "Here's your towel back. Shall I use it to mop up the puddle I've made?"

"Just drop it there. I'll deal with that later." She led him into the living room and pointed him to the couch. "Let me give you another towel to sit on, though."

"I can stand," Mark said. "I don't want to take all your towels."

"Don't be silly. I got lots of them as shower gifts when Jack and I . . ." Sara felt the words clog her throat. She tried again. "I have plenty of towels."

Sara brought coffee in thick white mugs, and when they were settled in the living room she said, "So what's so important that you'd risk drowning to come here and tell me in person?"

Mark blew across the top of his mug, then sipped. "What's going on? I thought there was some mutual attraction between us, but now it seems like you're keeping me at arm's length. Did I do something wrong?"

Sara shook her head. "It's not just you. Ever since Rip and I began trying to dig out the truth about Jandramycin, someone's been after us. I've been shot at. Rip was almost killed in a car accident. And you don't even know about the latest attack. Do you blame me for not enlarging my circle of friends at this point?"

"I thought I was already in that circle." Mark frowned. "And I hoped I was more than a friend."

Sara felt a tingle of apprehension within her chest. What now? She waited for Mark to go on.

"My wife and I were childhood sweethearts. We married when I was in law school, and I was happier than anyone has a right to be. Then one day, I got a call from the police. She was dead, killed in an auto accident. My world crumbled. I was resigned to life as a widower until I met you."

She didn't need to hear this. Not now. And not from Mark. She opened her mouth, then closed it. Let him talk.

"You and I had that one dinner, and I felt like everything clicked. I've wondered if somehow my finding that digital device in your attic made you feel ashamed to be around me, ashamed I'd find out the kind of marriage you had."

"No, I—"

"All that made me feel was angry, so angry at Jack Ingersoll that I wanted to shake him. How could anyone do that to you?" Mark leaned forward, his coffee forgotten. "Sara, I'm serious about this. If you want to hold me at arm's length until this Jandramycin thing is settled, I'll wait. But I'm not going away."

Sara's head was spinning. She had to admit, there was an attraction there, but there was also an element of doubt. It was hard to trust anyone she didn't know. And hadn't John told her Mark's practice was a blending of medicine and law, including some consulting for pharmaceutical companies? Was one of those Jandra? Could Mark—No, she couldn't think about this right now.

"Are you going to say something?" Mark asked. "I've spilled my guts, but I have no idea what you're thinking. Where do we stand, Sara?"

Sara held her mug in both hands and brought it to her lips. The coffee was cold by now, but she needed something to buy time. She finished the coffee and reluctantly set the mug aside. "Mark, I like you. I can see us possibly going forward in a relationship at some point, but not now."

"So you don't trust me?" The hurt in his voice was plain.

"I don't trust anyone! Especially someone who might have ties to the company that's quite likely behind efforts to kill me, the way they're willing to risk killing patients in the name of science." Sara bit her lip. "I'm sorry. That's not fair. But this is a terrible time for you to want to take our relationship to another level. Can't you understand? Can't you be patient?"

Mark stood and placed his mug on the table gently, as though it were made of fine china. "Can't I understand? No, frankly, I can't. I thought you trusted me. Less than a week ago I sat with you, Rip, John, and Lillian and talked about working together to solve the Jandramycin puzzle. Now you're freezing me out—out of that group and out of your life." His shoes made a soft squishing as he stalked toward the door. "Well, I can take a hint."

He closed the door softly behind him, leaving Sara alone. She padded to the front door and listened until his car pulled away. She wanted to call him back. Instead, she knelt with a towel and began to mop up the puddle of water where he'd stood, a puddle dotted with tiny circles from her tears. Not for the first time, Sara wished she could hit the rewind button on her life.

24

JOHN RAMSEY MATCHED LILLIAN'S SLOW, MEASURED PACE AS THEY WALKED together toward the medical center's parking garage. The rain of the past two days had left behind puddles to trap the unwary. It was fully dark now, and the security lights on the buildings he passed cast shadows that made John think of the childhood night terrors he experienced after reading a ghost story at bedtime. Only this time, the terrors were with him day and night, and had nothing to do with scary tales. No, they stemmed from the work of evil men—he had no idea how many—who were more interested in their own gain than the well-being of countless patients.

"John, you don't have to walk me to my car," Lillian said. "I can look out for myself. I'm a grown woman."

"With Mace in her purse, I'd wager."

"Matter of fact . . ."

He caught a glimpse of her grin in the reflected glow of headlights as cars began to stream out of the parking structure. John decided to risk it. "Would the unafraid, grown woman like to have a cup of coffee, or even dinner, with the courtly gentleman who insists on escorting her through the shadows?"

There was a hiatus in the parade of cars. Now darkness veiled Lillian's face. Was she frowning, smiling, what? Then John felt her hand take his. "I'd be pleased to, John. Remember, though—right now I'm just a friend."

"I know. And I appreciate your sensitivity. But a friend is what I most need."

Half an hour later, they were seated in a back booth at Amberjack, one of the nicer restaurants in town. Lillian looked at John over her menu and said, "I've always wanted to come here, but I could never bring myself to dine alone at one of these places."

"I know. I tried it once after Beth died. Since then, I don't think I've eaten out anywhere except fast-food restaurants. They sort of look at you funny, don't they?"

"You're exactly right," Lillian said. She returned her attention to the menu. "I think another reason I don't try to eat out alone is that there's no one to split an entrée with me. My late husband and I used to do that all the time. I guess I could take half my meal home and heat it up later, but it never tastes as good as when it's fresh."

John felt his eyes growing moist. "Beth and I split entrées all the time." He drank some water, then wiped his mouth and used the motion to touch his napkin to the tears on his cheeks. "I'll be happy to pay for whatever you want, but I have to ask. Would you like to split an entrée tonight?"

"I'd love it."

Their discussion went back and forth like an engaged couple picking out a silver pattern. John had been here before and knew that the side dishes were large. When the waiter returned, he said, "We'd like to split the Hawaiian snapper, with a side order of potatoes and vegetables. And please have them divide that in the kitchen."

"I'm sorry, sir, but our chef says that splitting an order disturbs the presentation of the dish."

John tried hard to maintain a stern expression. "You can ask the manager to come to the table, and I'll discuss your policy with him as well as anyone else within earshot. Or you can convey my compliments to your chef and tell him that we're more interested in the taste of the food than its appearance. And, by the way, the longer we sit here without something to eat, the more testy I tend to become."

"Very well, sir. I'll ask the chef to divide the order for you."

"Thank you . . . " John squinted at the nametag the man wore. "Thank you, Henry. I appreciate your doing that. I'll be certain to remember it when we've finished."

As Henry hurried off, undoubtedly to tell the chef about the demanding customer in booth twelve, Lillian giggled behind her hand. "John, you should be ashamed of yourself for coming down on that poor man that way."

"No," John said. "The restaurant should be ashamed of itself for such an obvious ploy to make people order more food than they should eat." He helped himself to a roll and buttered it. "Besides, what good is having a dinner companion if you can't show off for her a little bit?"

As they chatted, waiting for their meal, John realized that for the first time in several days he wasn't worried about his HIV tests, or his recovery from *Staph luciferus*, or the person or persons unknown who didn't want him and his colleagues to discover the truth about Jandramycin. He had a friend—someone to talk with, someone to encourage him, someone who might . . . No, that would be later, if at all. For now, a friend was more than enough.

The three men gathered in Dr. David Patel's office showed no outward evidence of the stress they bore. Patel presided from behind his desk, the coat of his gray pinstripe suit unbuttoned to show a pristine expanse of dress shirt on which a black and gold rep-stripe tie nested.

Dr. Bob Wolfe was seated across the desk from Patel. A white lab coat with his name embroidered over the breast pocket covered his blue oxford-cloth button-down shirt worn open-collared. His dress signified that, although he was a professional, he worked in the trenches with the lab techs and others he supervised.

Steve Lindberg had taken his usual seat at the edge of Patel's desk, halfway between the other two men—neutral in all respects, the Switzerland of Janus Pharmaceuticals. A Grateful Dead tie hung at half-mast on a wrinkled dress shirt. His jacket had been deposited on the back of his office door when he arrived this morning, and he wouldn't retrieve it until he left the building.

"Gentlemen, this meeting will be brief," Patel said. "Bob, what's the status of our NDA for Jandramycin?"

Wolfe cleared his throat. "Because of the unusual circumstances, the FDA appointed a special advisory committee to consider it. They've received clear marching orders from on high to fast-track it and recommend approval. They're working on it, and as I understand it, they're scattering exceptions and waivers along the way like beads from a Mardi Gras float. The wheels have been greased for approval." He rubbed his thumb and fingers together in a symbol everyone recognized. "It's costing—"

"I don't need to hear that," Patel said. "We'll approve the amount, whatever it is." He swiveled toward Lindberg. "And the marketing campaign?"

Lindberg beamed. "First rate, if I do say so myself. The ad agency came up with some great slogans and visuals. We have ad space reserved in every major medical journal, and until we have approval to market we're using it to 'tease' the forthcoming breakthrough that's the biggest antibacterial advance since penicillin. Our sales force has been trained. We've brought key docs and thought leaders to resorts for what we call 'advisory panels.' We make them sign a confidentiality agreement, then bombard them with information about Jandramycin so when it launches we have a ready-made set of lecturers. We'll send them out to national meetings and saturate the medical community with our message."

"Again, whatever you need to spend, I'll approve it," Patel said. "I've received word that the scientists at Darlington Pharmaceuticals are on track to develop a compound that is as effective as Jandramycin against *Staph luciferus*. Not only that, it has better activity against other bacteria than our drug, and although there is a risk of minor immediate reactions—rash, GI upset, and so forth—there's not a hint of severe or late problems." He waited for the import of those words to sink in. "We all know that the first drug on the market gets an almost unbeatable advantage on the ones that follow, even if they're better. So we cannot allow anything to slow the introduction of Jandramycin." He looked at Wolfe and Lindberg. "Clear?"

Wolfe squirmed in his chair. Lindberg tugged at his already open collar. Both nodded silently.

"That's all."

For all three men, the message was clear. The stakes, already high, had been raised. Winning was everything . . . whatever the cost.

"How's Chelsea Ferguson?" Rip asked.

"Maybe a little better," Sara said. "It's been almost two days now, and I hoped we'd see more improvement."

Rip stretched and yawned. "I was figuring forty-eight to seventy-two hours. Let's see how she's doing tomorrow."

They were sitting in Sara's office. She was on the computer, while he thumbed through a stack of journals, both desperately looking for the clue that would show them how Jandramycin could save lives, only to put them in jeopardy later. True, there was a chance that OMAL would stop or even reverse the process when complications arose, but that wasn't a sure thing. It was a shot in the dark, based on an educated guess.

Sara ran her fingers through her hair. "You can't believe how frustrated I am."

"All we can do is keep—" Rip stopped when Sara's cell phone rang.

She spoke for a few moments, but apparently whoever was on the other end of the conversation was in no mood to engage in dialogue. Sara returned the cell phone to her pocket. "That was strange."

"What?" Rip asked.

"That was Carter Resnick."

Rip closed the journal he was reading, marking the place with his finger. "Okay, I agree. It was strange that he'd call you, or anyone for that matter. Lately he's been sequestered in Ingersoll's 'secret' lab"—he set the word off with air quotes—"not talking with anyone."

"This is stranger still." Sara swiveled away from her computer to face Rip. "He wants to meet us in the lab tonight. He says he's tired of keeping secrets. He thinks we deserve to know."

"Know what?"

"He didn't say. But he wants us both there at midnight."

"Should I call John or Lillian?" Rip asked.

Sara thought for a moment. "I don't think so. Resnick said to come alone. He's just unstable enough that, if he gets word I've told anyone, he might back out. He's opened the door a bit, and I don't want to give him an excuse to close it."

They were engrossed in their searches when Sara's intercom buzzed. "Dr. Miles, there's a long-distance call for you on line one."

"Who is it?"

"He's got some kind of heavy accent. It sounded like he said 'Goober.'"

Sara shrugged and punched the blinking button on her phone. "Dr. Miles."

The man's accent was indeed thick, but Sara made out the words easily enough. "This is Dr. Heinz Gruber in Ulm, Germany. I believe you called me?"

Sara waved frantically to get Rip's attention. When he looked up, she motioned him toward the outer office and mouthed the words "Get on the phone." She waited until she heard a faint click before answering. "Doctor, thank you for calling back. I have a question for you."

There was silence on the line. "Did you hear me?" she asked.

"I was waiting for the question."

Fair enough. "I understand you and a colleague have been carrying out a clinical trial of the antibiotic Jandramycin. Is that correct?"

The answer sounded like "Yah." Was that the German word for "yes"? She assumed it was. "The same trial is going on at our medical center here. My question is—"

"So you are with Professor Ingersoll? Yes?"

"Yes. And some of our patients have had problems several weeks after they received Jandramycin. These are autoimmune

273

disorders. Do you understand autoimmune? I'm sorry, I don't know the German word."

"It is the same. And I have in turn a question for you. Why are you calling me when you have there Herr Professor Ingersoll?"

How much could she tell him? She decided to try to finesse the situation. "I've mentioned it to him, and he seems to think there's no such problem. But I thought that perhaps your experience might be different."

Gruber cleared his throat. When he spoke, the words were wooden and without inflection, as though he was reciting a prepared statement. "I know of no such problems with the drug."

"Then perhaps you can clarify for me the mechanism of action of Jandramycin. We think it might be an immunologic stimulus of the host to make antibodies against—"

"You must also ask that question of Professor Ingersoll. I have nothing to say."

There was a click, followed by the electronic hum of an empty line. Sara hung up and waited until Rip reappeared and settled into the chair opposite her. "What do you think?" she asked.

"I think he's been programmed to keep quiet. We're not going to get anything from him, and I doubt that we'll have any luck with his colleague, either."

"Nevertheless, I'm going to try it." Sara rummaged through the papers on her desk until she found a printed abstract of a paper. She jotted a note on a Post-It and centered it on her desk. "Maybe Dr. Rohde will be more forthcoming than his co-author, Dr. Gruber."

"Want me on the other line?"

"I don't think the department administrator would take too kindly to my making a transatlantic call from this phone," Sara said. "I guess I'll have to wait until I get home."

"No problem," Rip said. "Let's use my cell phone. We can put it on speaker and both hear."

"Won't that show up on the bill?"

"This is my private phone. I pay the bills, and it's nobody's business who I call."

"Even an international call?"

"I set it up a while back. Never know when I might need it, and sure enough, now I do. What's that number?"

"All I have is the internal medicine clinic number." She dug into her purse and pulled out a wrinkled slip of paper.

"Good enough. I just dial 011, then the country code—49—and the number." He held up a finger. "Okay, it's ringing. I'll put it on speaker and you can talk."

"*Klinik. Darf ich Ihnen helfen?*"

Sara gave a "here we go again" shrug. "Do you speak English?"

"*Bitte, Ich verstehe Sie nicht.*"

Sara was about to go into her raise-your-voice-to-be-understood act when Rip said, "*Wir wollen mit Herr Dr. Rohde sprechen.*"

"*Ja, ein minuten.*"

In the silence that followed, Sara looked at Rip in amazement. "When did you learn to speak German?"

"A product of my Ivy League education. Had two years of it in college. Spent a month in Germany between college and med school. Guess I still remember it."

"I wish I'd known that when I made my original call to Gruber," Sara said.

"*Ja, hier ist Rohde.*"

Sara felt her pulse quicken. Maybe she could convince this doctor to open up. "Doctor, do you speak English? This is Dr. Sara Miles in the U.S."

"Yes, I speak a little. What would you like?"

Sara went through the same speech that she'd given Gruber. This time the response was a full minute in coming, and she feared she'd lost the connection. She was about to hang up when Rohde said, "I have been warned not to discuss our research with anyone. And I would advise you to stop asking these questions."

This time there was a discernible click, and the cell phone screen showed the words, "Call Ended."

"I'm more convinced than ever that there's a cover-up in place," Sara said. "I guess we'll have to depend on Resnick. He's our last hope."

The voices captured his attention, so the man stopped in the hall and leaned closer to the closed door.

The first man spoke in a voice that was guttural and low, spitting sibilants like machine gun bullets as the words tumbled out. "How many times must I tell you? Only you and I know this. And the proof has already been destroyed. No one can resurrect a pile of ashes into a document."

The second voice also belonged to a man, but where the first was bold, this one was tentative, the words hesitant. "There are too many people asking questions about the matter, and I'm afraid what we did is going to come to light. Perhaps if we—"

"We will do nothing. We remain silent, let the scenario play out, and reap the rewards." The words rumbled like far-off artillery fire and carried the same hint of danger. "When you burned that paper, you ended the trail that could lead back to us. You *did* burn it, didn't you?"

The second voice was less timid now. "Of course . . . but how do you know I didn't keep a copy somewhere? If I came forward with the information now, perhaps I could escape any penalties. I can't stand the thought of being disgraced, of losing everything I've worked for. I couldn't live with that."

The first speaker's voice was full of menace. "Perhaps you won't have to live—with that or anything else."

"Don't think about it. If something happens to me, I have made arrangements for some very interesting documents to go to the right people." The second man's tone became placating. "You need me alive."

"I think you're bluffing."

"There's no reason for you to find out, is there? We can work this out."

A chair scraped back. "No, you've shown your true colors now. You'd throw me to the wolves to save your own worthless skin, wouldn't you?" The next words came out in a rush. "I guess there's only one thing to do to keep you muzzled."

The sounds of the argument were replaced by the thumps and groans of a struggle. The man in the hall tried the door, but it was locked. He pounded on it. "What's going on in there? Open up."

Glass shattered. The man's imagination supplied mental pictures as the noise intensified. A chair or perhaps even a desk was overturned.

When the first man spoke this time, it was as though he were reasoning with a recalcitrant child. "I didn't mean it. Put that away."

Now the second man's words were determined, as though he'd made up his mind to do something distasteful. "No. This is the best way . . ." The words trailed off.

Two shots rang out—the flat cracks of a handgun.

There was a long pause, then the second man's words came out in a rush. "God, forgive me."

Another shot, a muffled thump, then silence as the smell of gun powder drifted under the locked door.

25

MARK SAT BEHIND HIS DESK, HIS HEAD IN HIS HANDS. HIS STAFF HAD LEFT for the day. The office was dark except for one small lamp that burned on his desk. Only the tick of an antique clock in the corner broke the tomb-like silence.

He had one more call to make, one he'd dreaded since last night when the truth slapped him in the face. *Come on, there's no reason to be afraid. They can't climb through the phone lines and choke you. Just say what you have to say and hang up.* Easy to think it. Hard to do it.

Mark knew it had stared him in the face all along, but he refused to see. He'd been lied to from the beginning. He remembered the opening line of a John Grisham book, one that struck him as funny when he read it, but took on new meaning when he entered law practice: "Everybody lies." Maybe that was one of the reasons he'd chucked a thriving law practice and started over in medical school. He was tired of being lied to—by clients, witnesses, even other lawyers.

In law, there were always three sides—two attorneys and a judge—and the rules dictated an adversarial relationship between two of them. In medicine, the adversaries were disease and injuries. Mark took comfort in the knowledge that no one battled him to make sure the patient didn't recover. Everyone was on the same team. At least, that's what he'd thought. Now he knew better.

Mark swiveled to the bookshelf behind his desk and took down a thick volume. It had been there since the day he opened his office, and on days like today he reached for it like a drowning man for a life preserver. He opened the book and thumbed through the pages until he found the passage he wanted. "He has told you, O man, what is good. And what does the LORD require of you, but to do justice, to love kindness, and to walk humbly with your God?" *Do justice.* Even though he'd theoretically moved from law to medicine, the command was still in force. And he'd conveniently closed his eyes to it.

He closed the Bible, bowed his head, and tried to make his mind a complete blank. Sometimes this had worked—words that he was certain must have sprung from God came unbidden into his mind. Sometimes it didn't—his mind roiled with the emotions of the moment, and no guidance or comfort came to him. This was one of those times.

Finally, he looked up and said aloud, "Nothing for me today? Guess I have to go with what I just read." *Makes sense. Twenty-seven hundred years shouldn't make good advice turn bad.*

He scrolled through the memory of his cell phone and punched a button. The call rang five times before an android voice announced the numbers and invited the caller to leave a message. *Just as well. Makes it easier.* "This is Mark. I'm ending my relationship with Jandra Pharmaceuticals immediately, resigning from my position as adjunct counsel. I won't go into the reasons. I'm pretty sure you already know them."

He ended the call and tossed the phone onto his desk, where it skittered along and came to rest next to the Bible. Mark hit a key on his computer and the screen sprang to life. He opened a new Word document and began to type his letter of resignation. He already knew what it would say. Two or three sentences that would sever his relationship with the company, with no reference to his reasons. He'd fax it first thing in the morning, send a hard copy by express courier, and keep two copies in his safe. If things went as he thought they might, it would be helpful to show that he had distanced himself from the company.

He hoped it wasn't too late.

This part of Parkland Hospital was no longer a clinical ward. The hallway was dark and totally deserted. Nothing broke the silence. The patient rooms had been converted to various other uses: offices, storage, and in this case, Jack Ingersoll's ultra-secret research lab.

Sara consulted her watch. "Twelve oh five. Resnick's so compulsive, I can't believe he's late."

Rip shrugged. "Maybe he's already in the lab and expects us to meet him there."

Sara felt like hitting herself in the head, Three Stooges style. "I don't suppose you tried the door, did you?"

"Nope. He called you, not me. I figured I'd let you take the lead." His grin was almost lost in the shadows that covered his face. "I'm just the muscle."

"Okay, muscle. Stick close to me, would you?" She put her hand on the doorknob and twisted. It moved easily. "It's unlocked."

Sara took a deep breath and inched the door open. The lights were on in the room, but she couldn't see anyone in the area open to view.

"Want me to go in first?" Rip asked.

"No, he's expecting to see me. I can do it."

"I'll be right behind you."

She opened the door widely and entered on tiptoe. *Why am I trying to be quiet?* There was something weird and a bit scary about being here in Resnick and Ingersoll's inner sanctum after it had been declared off-limits for so long.

Sara took a full step inside and turned to scan the room. Lab counters contained a mixed array of equipment: computers, several machines she recognized as apparatus for doing blood analysis, and a profusion of glassware and bottles. Nothing here that wouldn't be found in a well-equipped hospital laboratory. No sinister machines labeled "Danger." No bottles marked with a skull and crossbones. None of the material in the room explained the feeling of unease she had. No, that came from the people who worked there.

A door at the far end of the room opened, and Carter Resnick walked in. "You're a few minutes late, but I'm glad you came." He had both hands in the pockets of a white lab coat. He removed the left one and pointed around the room. "I know you've both been anxious to see what's in here, and I can't fathom why that is. As you can see, there's nothing out of the ordinary in our setup."

"It's not the setup that worries us," Sara said. "It's what you do here. You have all the data about the Jandramycin study here, and that includes the actual mechanism by which it kills *Staph luciferus.*" She held up a hand. "And don't give me that 'destroys the cell wall' stuff. We know better than that."

Rip stepped forward to stand beside Sara. "It's an immuno-logic process, isn't it?"

Resnick used his free hand to rub his head. "Bingo. How did you find that out?"

Rip shook his head. "Never mind. What we really need to know is how we can prevent patients who receive the drug from getting a late complication."

"I'm interested," Resnick said. "Do you know what percent that would be?"

"Among the patients treated here, 15 percent, now approaching 20."

"Bravo," Resnick said. "Why do you suppose that is?"

"Let's not be coy, Carter," Sara said. "We know that the response is autoimmune, and we're pretty sure the patients who get it are those with underlying allergies like hay fever and asthma. The question remains, how do we counter that?"

"Truthfully, we don't know," Resnick said. "The drug alters the patient's immune system so it produces antibodies specific for *Staph luciferus*, essentially making the patient his own source of antibiotics. Unfortunately, when it's given to a patient with an allergic predisposition, that little late effect comes into play."

Rip took a step forward. "That little late effect, as you called it, is destroying lives. It's already killed one patient we know about, and there will probably be more. Don't you have any idea how to prevent it?"

"You may be surprised to know that my contact at Jandra and I are well aware of that problem. He's been sending me other compounds, modifications of the EpAm848 structure, and I've tried them, but so far they've all had a flaw. A fatal flaw in one instance."

"Tried them how?" Sara asked.

Resnick smiled. "Mainly I used mice and hamsters, although I had one very fortuitous opportunity to test a compound on a homeless man in the ER. Unfortunately, that one caused anaphylaxis and he died."

Sara noticed that Resnick's right hand never left the pocket of his lab coat. She eased her own right hand down and began to slowly unzip her bag that hung from her shoulder. *Keep him talking. Distract him.* "You said your 'contact at Jandra.' Who is that?"

"You don't really need to know." Resnick moved his hand slightly in his pocket. "And I'd appreciate it if you kept your hand out of your purse."

Sara let her hand rest lightly on top of the purse. "Did your contact at Jandra tell you to shoot at me?"

"And are you the one who tried to run my car into a concrete abutment?" Rip asked.

"Of course. And, before you ask, I'm the one who put the nitrogen triiodide on the floor of your office. It was all an effort to discourage you from prying. We've worked too hard keeping the side effects of Jandramycin hidden to let you spoil it for us. When the drug goes on the market, I'm going to share in the glory—and the profits."

"What about Jack?" Sara asked. "What was his role in all this?"

"No more questions. I have orders to put an end to your prying, no matter what it takes." He pulled a snub-nose revolver from the pocket of his lab coat and moved it back and forth between Sara and Rip. "So I'm going to shoot you."

"How are you going to explain this?" Sara asked. *As though it will matter to me, after I'm dead.* Her hand inched the zipper of her purse forward by millimeters. She had to keep Resnick talking.

"I've got it worked out. I have a gun locked in my desk drawer. I paid a hundred dollars for it one Saturday night at a bar in South Dallas, and it's untraceable. After I shoot you both, I'll put it in one of your hands."

"And what will you tell the police?" Sara's fingers moved with agonizing slowness. She felt the purse open. Just another inch or so.

"I came back here to work on some experiments, found that you two had broken in. You demanded information that Jandra deems proprietary. I refused. You pulled a gun on me, and I shot in self-defense." Resnick smirked. "It's perfect."

To her left, Sara sensed Rip shift his weight. *Don't do it Rip. Let me handle this.* "You didn't answer my question. What's Jack Ingersoll's role in all this?"

"Enough questions." Resnick leveled the gun at Rip, apparently thinking he represented the greater danger.

Sara plunged her hand into her purse and felt the welcome sensation of cold steel beneath her fingers. Her thumb flipped the safety. No time to draw the gun. Just point and shoot through the purse. Words from her gun safety class came back to her as though the instructor, an ex-policeman, were by her side. "Aim for the middle of the body mass. Don't try to wound."

At the moment Sara pulled the trigger, she saw flame spout from the end of Resnick's gun. Glass shattered behind her. Something struck her left side like the charge of a bull rhinoceros, and in an instant Rip's body covered her. "Stay down," he whispered.

When Sara finally raised her head, the first thing she saw was Resnick sprawled on the floor, his gun still in his hand. Blood oozed from his chest. Sightless eyes stared without blinking into the lights above him.

"Nice shooting, Sara. Wonder which one of us hit him." Jack Ingersoll stood in the doorway of the lab, an automatic pistol still pointed at Resnick's body. "I trust you remembered our instructor's words and aimed for his central mass."

Sara had read about it in books, but never thought she'd have the experience. She and Rip were placed in separate rooms at the police station. At first the questions were simple. Soon they became more pointed, the next thrown at her almost before she could answer the last. When the detective in charge read her a Miranda warning, she decided she'd said too much already. She wanted a lawyer. The detective tossed his cell phone on the table. "Be my guest."

Sara knew only one lawyer. And for some reason, she trusted him in this situation. He was groggy when he answered, but as soon as she began to explain, he said, "Don't say a word. I'm on my way."

The sun was up by the time Sara and Rip headed for the front door of the police station alongside Mark Wilcox. John Ramsey was sitting on a bench in the lobby, and he rose to join them as they walked out.

On the sidewalk, Sara stopped and stifled a yawn. "I'm going to call Gloria and have her cancel my patients this morning. I'm getting too old to miss a night's sleep."

"Already done," John said. "I called Verna last night when Mark phoned me from the police station. She and Gloria are going to block you and me out all day."

Rip stretched. "I guess I'd better make rounds this morning, since Ingersoll is still at the police station. But after that, I'm headed for the on-call room and some sleep."

"Why don't we get breakfast first? I'll buy," Mark said. He looked at Sara. "I have some explaining of my own to do, things I didn't say at the police station."

Half an hour later, they sat in a corner booth in the Renaissance Hotel's coffee shop, with steaming cups of coffee in front of them. Mark raised his cup in a silent toast.

Sara touched her cup to the others and drank deeply. She hadn't been this punch-drunk since pulling an all-nighter to study for the junior medicine final.

"Mark," John said, "since I wasn't in the rooms where the questioning was going on, can you fill me in? That is if it's okay with Sara and Rip."

"That would be fine with me," Rip said.

Sara nodded, too tired to speak.

Mark drained his cup and shoved it aside. "You already know that Resnick is dead. Two bullet wounds in his chest. The autopsy hasn't been done yet, but the medical examiner guessed that one of the shots severed the aorta. Resnick was dead by the time he hit the floor."

"I can't say I'm sorry," John said. The others yawned.

"Since Resnick was found with a gun still in his hand, and three witnesses agree that he was about to shoot Sara and Rip, there's no real question this was anything but self-defense." Mark waited while a waitress topped off their cups. "It just took a long time for the interviews. That's typical in a case like this—separate the witnesses, make sure their stories jibe. But I don't think my clients—" He looked from Sara to Rip. "I don't think they were ever in danger of being charged with anything. This may go to a grand jury, but if it does, it'll be a slam dunk to get a no-bill."

"I can't understand how Ingersoll knew to be there at the lab," Rip said. "Unless he was the one who had Resnick set up the meeting in the first place."

"As I understand it, he told the police he'd thought of a modification of Jandramycin that would 'make it more effective,' and he needed to see the journals and records Resnick kept under lock and key in the lab. He showed up, saw Resnick holding you all at gunpoint, and used the gun he was carrying." Mark shrugged. "The story's thin, but he's sticking with it, and I think they'll buy it."

"I still think Ingersoll set it all up as an opportunity to shoot Resnick. The lab assistant would be the only one who knew his boss had sanitized the Jandramycin data," Rip said. "And if Ingersoll was a little late shooting Resnick . . . well, that would get rid of two people who'd become a threat."

Sara shuddered at the thought. "I'm surprised he had the gun. I thought he'd stopped carrying it," she said.

Mark shrugged. "His story is that since he developed Jandramycin, he's received death threats from people who accuse him of 'tampering with nature.' So he strapped on his ankle holster, loaded his Glock 30, and started carrying it."

"Resnick mentioned his 'contact at Jandra.' But he'd never say who it was," Rip said. "So whoever was using Resnick as their pawn is still out there, still after Sara and me. What can we do about that?"

"I wish I knew," Mark said. He turned to Sara. "I don't have any contacts at Jandra any more. I used to be a consultant for that company, but I resigned the day after I was at your house."

"Did you—?"

"Did I ever give them any information about your hunt for their secrets? No. Never. But I couldn't work for a company that would lie, cover up, and even try to harm others. So I quit."

The waitress deposited a large tray beside their table, served their breakfasts, and replenished coffee. When she was gone, Rip said, "So Resnick was the conduit to Jandra? Then why did he feed me information about how two-faced Ingersoll was?"

John followed a forkful of eggs with a bite of toast, chewed, and swallowed. "I have a theory about that. Resnick was playing both ends against the middle. He was following orders from someone at Jandra, probably in return for money under the table and the promise of a position with them. But he was also engaged in a bit of back-stabbing, hoping that if he could make Ingersoll go down he'd be chosen to take over the Jandramycin study." John sipped coffee and wiped his lips with a napkin. "Since he was so deeply involved in the project, in his twisted logic he was the person who'd become the senior investigator, not Rip."

Sara pushed her plate away, unable to eat any more. She picked up her coffee cup and set it down without drinking. Her stomach felt queasy. Her head hurt. She wanted to awaken to find this was all a bad dream. "Do you think there's any chance the person behind this will be caught?" she asked of the table at large.

"What we've told the police should help point them in the right direction. And Resnick's phone records should lead them to Jandra." Mark made a writing-in-air gesture to call for the check. "There are a couple of people in the police department who might keep me posted on their investigation. If I can find out, I'll let everyone know."

"One question," Sara said. "I called you last night because you were the only lawyer I could think of. I expected you to say something like, 'I'll contact a criminal attorney to represent you.' Why did you come yourself?"

"Because two of my friends were in trouble, and I wanted to help." He pulled a dog-eared piece of cardboard from his breast pocket. "I brought the card of a criminal attorney with me." He smiled at Sara. "But I'm glad I didn't need to use it."

Sara eased into her seat, the last of the group to arrive. She had no idea why Rip asked them to gather, but she could guess. And she could hardly wait to hear the news.

"If this were an Agatha Christie novel, I'd say, 'I suppose you're wondering why I called you together.'" Rip looked around the room and relaxed when he saw a few smiles.

The meeting place was a conference room down the hall from the cubbyhole that served as Rip's office in the Internal

Medicine Department. Five people gathered at one end of a table that would seat thirty. John Ramsey and Lillian Goodman were seated across the table from Sara. Mark Wilcox sat beside her. Rip stood at the head of the table.

"Is this about Jandramycin?" Sara asked.

"Sort of. We can update everyone on the clinical developments first. Sara, tell them about Chelsea."

Sara cleared her throat. "Chelsea Ferguson, the little girl with progressive paralysis from Guillain-Barrè syndrome after receiving Jandramycin, is recovering nicely after she received a second dose of OMAL. She's getting some physical therapy to strengthen her muscles, and she'll be going home soon."

"Me next, I guess," John said. "It's been a month since I had my Jandramycin, followed by a dose of OMAL. I've had no recurrence of the *Staph luciferus* infection of my hand. There's been no sign of any autoimmune complication from the antibiotic."

"And John gave me permission to tell you his labs continue to be negative for HIV after the needle-stick that started all this," Rip added. "I think you can stop worrying now, John . . . for several reasons."

"What other reasons?" John asked.

"I'll get to that. First, Sara and I are once more caring for Randall Moore." Rip waited to be sure John recognized the name. Mark Wilcox obviously did, as he leaned forward in his chair. "He was treated with Jandramycin, and his S*taph luciferus* pneumonia cleared. Sara and I had a long talk with him about the risks of the drug, and he elected to receive OMAL. Thus far, he's doing well. He's pleased enough with the care he's received at the medical center that he's dropping his lawsuit."

Sara kept her eyes on John, and when the import of the news hit him, he relaxed and let out a deep breath. She knew the feeling.

"Why are you and Sara back on that case?" Lillian asked. "I thought the department chair asked Ingersoll to take over."

"He did," Rip said, "but after the shooting, Dr. Schaeffer decided that perhaps it was best for Ingersoll to keep a low profile for a while."

"He must be doing that, all right," John said. "I usually pass him in the hall at least once a day, but haven't seen him recently."

"It gets better," Rip said. "On Monday, Ingersoll didn't show up at his office. His secretary was worried when he didn't respond to a page or phone messages. She let the chairman know, but he elected to sit on the news. This morning, the dean received a faxed letter of resignation. Ingersoll apparently packed up and left, and no one has any idea where he is."

Sara opened her purse and pulled out a wrinkled envelope bearing a strange-looking postage stamp. "I guess it's my turn now. This came to my home yesterday. It's from Jack."

She pulled a single page from the envelope. "Once he realized his professional reputation was down the tubes, he packed his bags, grabbed his passport, and caught a flight to Belize. He says he's got four million dollars in an offshore account 'thanks to Jandramycin's flaws,' whatever that means. Apparently, he's gone for good."

She handed the letter to Rip.

"So what happens now?" John asked.

"I just came from a meeting with the department chair. Dr. Schaeffer asked me to take over all of Ingersoll's patients and to complete the Jandramycin study. He will act as division head for now. In a month, when my fellowship is over, he'll solicit applications for a new head of the division. He assures me I have the inside track for that appointment."

There were murmurs of approval. When the noise died down, Mark spoke up. "I doubt that my news can trump this, but I'll try." He waited until everyone was turned toward him. "I have a friend who's a criminal attorney, and I asked him to keep his ears open around police headquarters. This morning he called to tell me that agents of the FBI and representatives of the local police went to the offices of Jandra Pharmaceuticals and arrested . . ." He pulled a wrinkled piece of paper from his pocket and read from it. "Arrested Jandra's Chief Operating Officer, Dr. David Patel. They're certain he was behind the attacks on Sara and Rip."

"How did they get him?" Sara asked.

"The FBI received a packet of information from one of the doctors in Germany who were doing a parallel study of Jandramycin. It confirmed that Patel ordered them to hide the data that showed late complications from the drug. According to the letter that came with the packet, one of them apparently got an attack of conscience, fought with the other, and ended up killing him, then shooting himself." Mark folded the paper and returned it to his pocket. "But he left behind some 'in case of my death' instructions with his attorney. In this instance, the instructions were to mail the packets, containing information that incriminated Patel. It's only a matter of time before phone records tie him to Resnick. I predict his associates will rush to save their skins by testifying against him, and . . . you can guess the rest."

Sara looked around the room and saw the expressions of relief on every face. Across the table, John and Lillian allowed their hands to touch as they exchanged smiles. It was good to see John with someone who could help him through his loss. And Sara had no doubt that relationship would blossom after an appropriate time.

She looked from Rip to Mark and back again. Both men had stood by her through this trying time. Since she'd first met Rip, she'd been fond of him, but more like a brother than anything else. After Jack had swept her off her feet, Rip had melted into the background, always there to talk to, never showing his true feelings. But those feelings had become clearer as they'd worked side by side to solve the Jandramycin problem. There was affection there, and she had to admit that she felt the same thing.

Mark had only been in Sara's life a short time, but he'd let her know clearly he wanted to be more than just a friend. She was no psychologist, but Sara recognized the likelihood that Mark's attraction to her was a reaction to his own loss in the death of his first wife. She hoped he'd find another woman to love, but she was certain it wouldn't be her. On the other hand, the possibility of a great friendship—with her and with Rip—was certainly there.

She'd have to deal with her feelings for both men in the days ahead, but that would come later. For now, she was overcome with relief that this ordeal was over.

Sara was no longer experiencing nighttime terrors. No one was trying to harm her anymore. And out of this terrible scenario had come the cure for a disease that would rival the pestilence and plague of the Old Testament.

Her mind went back to the words she'd read in her mother's Bible. "You will not fear the terror of night, nor the arrow that flies by day, nor the pestilence that stalks in the darkness, nor the plague that destroys at midday."

Thank you, God, for that promise, and for fulfilling it in my life.

Author's Note

In my thirty-six years of medical practice I was privileged to serve as a consultant to a number of pharmaceutical companies, and I never encountered even a hint of actions such as those portrayed here. Jandra Pharmaceuticals and the characters in this book are products of my imagination, and have no basis in fact. The novel contains instances in which I exercise literary license and in those areas I ask my readers to extend the traditional "suspension of disbelief" that is a hallmark of some fiction. But this is not to suggest that the events described here could not take place. Given enough power, money, and self-centered greed, I have no doubt that men and corporations could act in this way. We are fortunate that they do not.

I'd like to express my appreciation to the clinicians and researchers who work to develop and make available the medications we have come to take for granted. We've come a long way since Fleming accidentally discovered penicillin almost a century ago. Who can predict what frontiers medical research will conquer next? I can hardly wait.

Discussion Questions

1. One of the reasons for the increasing emergence of antibiotic-resistant bacteria is the use of antibiotics when they are not indicated. Has this ever affected your doctor's treatment decision? How did you react?

2. Do you believe that most researchers are ethical? Why or why not? Does this affect your confidence in medications your doctor prescribes?

3. Were you able to form a mental picture of John Ramsey's late wife, Beth? How would you characterize her? Do you think her advice to him was good?

4. Picture yourself as Sara Miles, forced to work closely with a man who has hurt you deeply. Could you maintain a professional relationship, or would your history color your actions? What if he held the only key to your patient's survival?

5. Did your concept of Rip Pearson change as the story progressed? Was there a point when you didn't trust him? What about Mark Wilcox?

6. What qualities did you find in Jack Ingersoll? What about Carter Resnick? What did you think their driving force was?

7. Contrast Sara's feelings toward Chelsea Ferguson and Randall Moore. What factors influenced her attitude?

8. Rip was faced with suggesting a treatment that would save a patient's life but might have late consequences that would be life changing and possibly fatal. Assume the patient was unable to make a decision and no family was available. What would you do?

9. Do you believe God should have punished Jack for his deeds? What do you think is the basis for bad things happening to people?

10. What did you take away from this novel? How will it affect the way you live your own life?

Want to learn more about author
Richard L. Mabry, M.D., and check out other great fiction
from Abingdon Press?

Sign up for our fiction newsletter at
www.AbingdonPress.com/fiction
to read interviews with your favorite authors, find tips
for starting a reading group, and stay posted on what
new titles are on the horizon. It's a place to connect
with other fiction readers or post a
comment about this book.

Be sure to visit Richard Mabry online for
"Medical suspense with heart."

www.rmabry.com
www.rmabry.blogspot.com

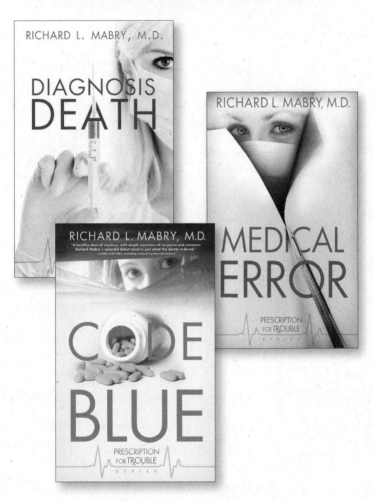

What They're Saying About...

The Glory of Green, by Judy Christie
"Once again, Christie draws her readers into the town, the life, the humor and the drama in Green. *The Glory of Green* is a wonderful narrative of small-town America, pulling together in tragedy. A great read!"
—Ane Mulligan, editor of *Novel Journey*

Always the Baker, Never the Bride, by Sandra Bricker
"[It] had just the right touch of humor, and I loved the characters. Emma Rae is a character who will stay with me. Highly recommended!"
—Colleen Coble, author of *The Lightkeeper's Daughter* and the *Rock Harbor* series

Diagnosis Death, by Richard Mabry
"Realistic medical flavor graces a story rich with characters I loved and with enough twists and turns to keep the sleuth in me off-center. Keep 'em coming!"—**Dr. Harry Krauss, author of *Salty Like Blood* and *The Six-Liter Club***

Sweet Baklava, by Debby Mayne
"A sweet romance, a feel-good ending, and a surprise cache of yummy Greek recipes at the book's end? I'm sold!"—**Trish Perry, author of *Unforgettable* and *Tea for Two***

The Dead Saint, by Marilyn Brown Oden
"An intriguing story of international espionage with just the right amount of inspirational seasoning."—*Fresh Fiction*

Shrouded in Silence, by Robert L. Wise
"It's a story fraught with death, danger, and deception—of never knowing whom to trust, and with a twist of an ending I didn't see coming. Great read!"—Sharon Sala, author of *The Searcher's Trilogy: Blood Stains, Blood Ties,* and *Blood Trails.*

Delivered with Love, by Sherry Kyle
"Sherry Kyle has created an engaging story of forgiveness, sweet romance, and faith reawakened—and I looked forward to every page. A fun and charming debut!"—Julie Carobini, author of *A Shore Thing* and *Fade to Blue.*

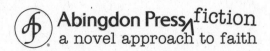

Abingdon Press fiction
a novel approach to faith

AbingdonPress.com | 800.251.3320